FALLEN FOR YOU

Jules Dee

A NineStar Press Publication

Published by NineStar Press
P.O. Box 91792,
Albuquerque, New Mexico, 87199 USA.
www.ninestarpress.com

Fallen for You

Printed in the USA
First Edition
July, 2018

Print ISBN: 978-1-949340-14-3

Also available in eBook, ISBN: 978-1-949340-11-2

When you work with someone for years, you *think* you know them pretty well.

Casey Wicker and Martin Bishop are a British Secret Service team with a reputation for ignoring rules but delivering results. They've also built a tight friendship, with more than a spark of unspoken attraction.

While on assignment to Scotland Yard, Martin rescues Casey and exposes him to a life-changing secret. Martin is not what he seems, and now that Casey is aware of that, the knowledge most likely comes with a death sentence.

When a way to avoid the tragic ending is suggested, it may very well take more cooperation than anyone is willing to expend.

For Ian, who gave me my wings

Chapter One

"YOU'RE UTTER RUBBISH at this, you know that, right?" Casey shouted as Martin's long legs ate up the distance ahead of them, arms and shoulders bunching and rolling in graceful synchronicity.

"In what particular way—" Martin ducked around a corner and took off down the next street, shouting back over his shoulder "—am I rubbish?"

"You, Martin Christopher Bishop—" Casey suddenly grabbed his arm roughly and pulled him into a shadowed doorway. "—are rubbish at the whole *secret* part of secret agent."

They stood close together, heads almost level, breathing hard and grinning in spite of the danger as the sounds of angry shouting faded in the distance.

"We got the document we were after, didn't we? I don't see the problem." Martin's eyes sparkled bright blue even in the dimly lit recess as he ran a hand quickly through his short dark hair. Casey smiled at the familiar habit that tended to appear when in risky situations.

"You don't see—" Casey took a moment to bend, putting his hands on his knees, and gasped great lungfuls of air as his shaggy blonde hair fell over his eyes. "You don't see the problem? We can never come back to Liberec, you idiot. You might as well have signed into the hotel as James Bond if you intended to grab the papers in broad daylight."

Martin leant against the rough bricks, chuckling as he tucked the documents in question away inside his jacket. "Don't make such a fuss. What're the chances we'll ever need to come back to this area of Prague anyway?"

Casey straightened and tried for his most withering stare, his brown gaze meeting Martin's, before giving in and laughing along with his partner. "Hopeless. You're hopeless. Why do I work with you?"

"My rakish charm, my scintillating conversation? C'mon, admit it, you love me." He ducked his head out, casting a quick glance both ways. "The coast is clear. Ready for another sprint?"

"Always." He took one last breath and broke into a run. "And I don't love you, for the record. You're a complete tit."

Chapter Two

"GENTLEMEN." THE SINGLE word held a weary tolerance as Director Lockhart opened the file sitting on the desk in front of her. "Welcome home."

Martin and Casey both knew better than to respond to that particular tone; it didn't bode well.

"Well—" The director licked her lips. "—let's take a look, shall we?"

Casey suppressed the instinct to wince.

"Intel retrieved." She looked up, a false smile plastered on her face. "That's just lovely, isn't it, boys? Always nice to see a big tick at the bottom of the page. Well done." Her tone indicated it was anything but.

"Loss of life? Well, that's an excellent result too. No messy cleanup to deal with. That makes a nice change for you, doesn't it, Casey?"

Casey studiously kept his head down, his long fringe obscuring his eyes from the director's cutting look. From the corner of his eye, Martin opened his mouth, perhaps to defend him. He kicked his partner's ankle hard, and Martin's teeth clicked shut again.

"Hmm." With unhappy pursed lips, the director turned the page. "Not so good on this page, is it, boys? Damage to property, nearly two million pounds, including three cars and an ice-cream stand, fifteen innocent bystanders injured." She frowned up at them both. "Two of them seriously, and...what's this? Oh, a formal complaint lodged by the Prague government with Her Majesty. We haven't had one of those for over a decade."

The director closed the file and linked her fingers together on the desk in front of her, holding the two men in her steely gaze. "Which brings us to the question of what to do with the two of you."

Both raised their heads to hear their sentence like naughty schoolboys caught smoking behind the shed.

She sighed and continued more gently. "Look, lads, it's not that we don't appreciate your success rate. And I'm the first to concede that it's often your unorthodox approach that delivers it. But I can't overlook the political consequences. The order's come from above to make an example of you, so—"

Martin heaved a noisy sigh, and Casey shot him a warning glance.

"You'll be spending some time on home soil. That way, we can inform the Prague government that we're taking this seriously, but we can still give you boys the headroom you need. God help us if we tried to confine either of you to a desk." She lifted a second file from a drawer beneath her desk. "We've had a request from Scotland Yard for assistance with a rather high-level jewellery theft."

"You want us to waste our time retrieving some lost earrings?" Martin spluttered in disbelief.

"Yes, *Agent* Bishop, we want you to assist, and you'll be damned happy to do it." The steel was back in her voice.

"Yes, ma'am," Martin corrected himself as Casey held his tongue, lips tight.

"In fact, the request came from—let me just check— Detective Inspector Carrington. When I spoke to him about the case earlier today, he suggested he has dealt with you in the past, Agent Bishop."

At the name, something behind Martin's eyes lit, and with a short nod, there was a subtle change in his demeanour. Casey wondered if perhaps Martin saw something in the case beyond the obvious.

"Very well, gentlemen, we're done, then. Tomorrow morning, you'll report to DI Jared Carrington, and I don't expect to see you back until the case is resolved to his satisfaction."

The two men rose to leave until her voice drew their attention back.

"Oh, and boys? Try not to blow anything up, please."

THEY FINISHED THE evening over scotches in front of the fire at their local club. The Retreat was less of a bar and more of a lounge, providing a quiet haven for many of the British Secret Service. Known for its discretion and exceptional liquid refreshments, the owner kept a careful eye on the clientele, allowing the patrons precious hours to let their guard down and recharge their emotional batteries.

"So—" Casey rolled the oversized ice cube around within the crystal tumbler as the firelight shone through the rich amber of the twenty-year-old Glenlivet. "You know this Carrington bloke?"

"My brother, Leon, knows him." Martin avoided Casey's eyes, turning his own glass this way and that on the small side table. "I think I've only met the DI twice."

Casey ran fingers through his fringe, pushing it out of his eyes. "Your brother's a lawyer, yeah?" Martin rarely mentioned his family, and when he did talk about Leon, it was usually with a note of derision.

Martin hummed a vaguely affirmative noise, his deep voice rumbling. "A QC, Queen's Council. The whole robe-and-wig bit. He looks like an idiot in them."

Casey laughed, the ice in his glass rattling as his hand shook with mirth. "I can imagine."

"Hey, look." A voice came from the shadows to their right. "It's Agents Destruction and Mayhem. We hear you destroyed Prague. A round of applause, folks."

The slow clap was taken up sporadically by a couple of others in the dim room, and Casey sighed, trying to sink farther back into the cushions of his chair. It wasn't unusual for the two of them to become the butt of jokes. Their reputations were well known, and the pointed jibes were often as much from jealousy at their record as the mess they tended to leave behind.

"It bothers you." Martin had leant forward in his chair, dropping his already deep voice to whisper only for their ears. When Casey lifted his gaze, there was a clear concern in his partner's. Martin might be reckless and headstrong, but there was never any doubt where his loyalty lay. They'd die for each other. In fact, they almost had on several occasions, and with a tight-lipped nod, Casey conceded it was true.

"We're bloody good agents, Martin, and we get fuck-all respect from these tossers." He gestured minutely into the darkness of the pub. "I know you come from money, but I had to work to get where I am. So, yes, it pisses me off that they treat us like the Service's joke."

Martin nodded thoughtfully, anger rising behind his eyes. "Right...stay here." He was up and out of the chair before Casey could even consider stopping him. He could only watch as his partner strode across the room, cocky swagger and attitude in every muscle, looking the tiniest bit like a jaguar stalking its prey.

"Agent McKenzie," Martin's baritone carried clearly through the room as he approached the man. "How pleasant to see you. Have you finished for the day? I imagine it must be rather challenging, keeping up with...what was it you're doing today, evidence cataloguing, isn't it?"

Casey didn't see who threw the first punch, but he assumed it was McKenzie since he saw Martin throw the second. From that point, things became a bit complicated and ended shortly afterwards with someone's fist flying toward Martin and his partner twisting awkwardly as he tried to dodge. As Casey watched, Martin seemed to fall in slow motion, cracking his head against the bar on the way to the floor.

Casey was up out of his seat and moving across the room before he'd even had time to consider whether it was the wisest move. He pulled Martin away from the angry shouting. Martin's arms were loose and uncoordinated as he tried to wipe the welling blood from his eyes. Casey dragged him toward the back of the bar. He shoved at the back door with one arm, the other firmly wedged beneath Martin's arm, then dragged the semiconscious man out into the night.

"OH, FOR GOD'S sake, Martin!" The small brown-haired woman could put a surprising amount of disapproval behind her usually gentle tone when stretched.

Casey hauled Martin through Dr. Alissa Satterfield's apartment door.

"Again?" she queried as Casey lowered his messy burden into the kitchen chair with a sigh of resignation.

"Again" came the reply as she bustled off to retrieve her first-aid kit from the bathroom. "Bar fight, but to be fair, he was defending my honour."

"As if your *honour* needs defending by him," she called from down the hall.

In truth, she knew they were fortunate to have a colleague like her. She kept to businesslike efficiency and protocol during the day, but this wasn't the first time she'd surreptitiously tended to after-hours injuries. She and Martin had an odd relationship. While she took every opportunity to berate him, she'd never—absolutely *never*—turn him away, and there was a familiar fondness in the jibes they exchanged. Both she and Martin had already been with the Service when Casey had joined, and their shared history made them close.

Alissa reentered the room and, with a frustrated growl, snatched the cloth away from Martin's forehead. "Don't use that, it's filthy. What are you, twelve?" she hissed, tossing it toward the bench.

"Sorry S-s-s-s-Alissa," Martin slurred, blinking in the bright light of the kitchen.

Her tight lips softened at his tone, and she bent closer, nudging Casey out of the way as she did so. "Okay, Martin, let's take a look at you."

Familiar with the routine, Casey put the kettle on as the doctor worked silently, cleaning, stitching, and checking Martin's pupillary responsiveness.

"Any vomiting, headache?" she asked when she was done, and sipped at a bright-red mug that said *I found this humerus* together with a picture of a bone below it.

Martin shook his head, before moaning and mumbling, "A little."

As she cleared her things away, she delivered her verdict. "Mild concussion. You know the drill, Casey. He can spend the night on my couch, and you can watch him until the morning, waking him every hour. I'll be damned if I'm staying up."

Casey nodded. It wouldn't be the first—or likely the last—time he spent a sleepless night standing vigil over his reckless partner.

"You know where the blankets are." Alissa grabbed the kit and made her way down the hall in the direction of her bedroom. "I think eggs would be lovely for breakfast; scrambled if you don't mind."

As she paused in the doorway, she threw back a playful smile. "A pleasure as always, boys. Sleep well."

By the time Alissa had showered and dressed the following morning, the kitchen was full of the smells of bacon, eggs, and toast. The indestructible Martin, seemingly no worse for his run-in was at the stove, deftly mixing herbs into a pile of creamy eggs. He'd retrieved one of the spare shirts he had squirrelled away in her hall closet and apparently taken the time to iron his rumpled suit if the crisp pleats that showed under the edge of a ridiculously flowery apron were any indication. Casey, meanwhile, was still half-dressed in her lounge, ludicrous superhero boxers hiding his modesty as he did the best he could with her ironing board.

"Boys," she greeted them brightly, taking a seat at the kitchen table, then sniffed appreciatively. "No ill effects?"

"Once again, I've had the assistance of a truly excellent doctor." Martin tipped an invisible hat to her expertise and then proceeded to shovel eggs onto the waiting plate.

"Rumour has it that we're loaning you two to Scotland Yard?"

"Rumours would be correct." Having pulled on his trousers and shirt, Casey joined them in the kitchen. "We're to see DI Carrington this morning."

"Jared?" She looked up to Martin, and there was the barest hint of a shake of his head as their eyes met.

"Yeah," Martin confirmed after the smallest of pauses. "The guy my brother knows. I think I told you about him once or twice."

"Of course," she replied with a light laugh, "that's where I heard the name. What will you be doing?"

Martin took the opportunity to move the topic from the man to the case. "Something about some missing jewellery. Complete waste of our time, but, of course, we go where our government demands."

"Yes." The sarcastic tone wasn't lost on them. "Because you two are such proper little rule followers."

Twenty minutes later, dishes tucked away in the dishwasher, both men stooped slightly to place matching kisses on the short woman's cheek. She bid them both farewell and sent them on their way to what she had no doubt would be yet another case containing more than its fair share of drama.

Chapter Three

TWO WEEKS LATER, Casey and Martin were hot on the trail of the missing jewellery and had narrowed the search to a small town in Surrey. In search of more information, they'd managed to break into the barn belonging to one of their prime suspects. And that's when things all went wrong.

They'd climbed to the upper floor of a rustic barn, hoping for some clue that either the thieves or their bounty had been there. Martin was hunting among boxes and sacks in the corner, leaving Casey to check in the loose hay covering the floor near the edge.

The third to last thought after Casey snagged his foot on something and tumbled over the edge with a shout was that he hoped the landing would be hard enough to kill him immediately. He'd seen the effects of long agonizing months of paralysis and injury on other agents. If it were all right with the universe, he'd much rather skip all that and head straight to the pearly gates.

The second to last thought was a momentary confusion as to how Martin had somehow managed to materialize between him and the ground and was falling with him, his body a physical barrier between him and the no-doubt punishing floor below.

The very last thought, barely a flicker in the final moments before the wind was knocked out of him and he lost consciousness was that their descent was slowing... and that was fundamentally impossible.

"TURN AWAY, CASEY." Martin's deep voice, cracking with pain, reached him as he struggled back from oblivion.

Casey, for the moment, could neither turn toward or away from the voice, his every rational thought taken up with dragging air into his lungs, mercifully still working after his fall from the landing two stories above. He looked at the distant floorboards far overhead and wondered again how he was alive and awake.

"Martin?"

"Just don't move, Casey. Don't sit up, don't roll over, and for the love of God, don't look in my direction."

Snippets of memories tripped over each other in Casey's head. Falling, Martin's strong arms cradling him from below as they tumbled, hitting the ground, Martin beneath him, shielding him from the worst of it. Panic rose like a wave in response to the sound of pain and fear in Martin's voice, and the possibility that his partner was critically injured hit him like a bullet.

In spite of Martin's desperate pleas to remain still, Casey slowly stretched one arm and then the other. Having reassured himself that they worked normally, he repeated the gentle flexing with his legs and then an agonizingly slow twist of his spine this way and that. He again marvelled at the lack of damage, and his thoughts circled back to concern for Martin, who must surely have fared worse in their joined fall.

"Martin, hang on. I'm coming over to you."

The alarm in Martin's voice rose to new heights. "NO! Stay over there, Casey."

Casey assumed Martin had attempted to move from the clipped gasp of pain that followed the outburst.

Ignoring his pleas, Casey rolled over. First bracing himself on his hands, he lifted himself onto all fours and then sat up. He paused as his head swam at the motion. His turn for a mild concussion probably. Drawing a deep breath, he turned toward his colleague, fearing the worst. Martin sat, leaning against one of the wide beams that supported the high, arching roof.

There was a new smear of blood on his head, running down his forehead and into his eye. More worrying was the odd angle he was holding his left arm. Broken, or at least dislocated. But most alarming of all was the panicked look in his eyes as he avoided Casey's gaze. There was something of the trapped animal in their dark depths as if, given a chance, Martin would bolt from the barn and into the night if only his legs would support him. He held up his one functional hand in warning and tried to angle his bad shoulder away from Casey, farther into the shadows.

"Please, Casey, no."

"You're hurt."

"I know," Martin answered simply. "Nevertheless, you should leave."

"I don't understand." Casey edged towards him as if approaching a skittish colt.

"I know you don't, and it needs to stay that way." Martin hissed in pain as he moved his injured shoulder again. "Please, I'm begging you."

"That decides it. You never beg." Casey pushed himself to his feet and pulled his shoulders back, adopting his most officious stance and took two determined steps towards his flatmate.

"It'll be okay, Martin. Trust me. It will all...be..." Casey caught sight of what Martin had been trying desperately to conceal. Visible behind his dislocated shoulder, hanging limply behind the fabric of his sleeve was something impossible. Something that couldn't possibly be what it appeared to be. And yet there was no doubt in Casey's mind that what he was seeing wasn't a hallucination brought on by a concussion.

Emerging from Martin's back, covered in thick black feathers, shot through with iridescent green and indigo, and hanging at an awkward, unnatural angle, was the edge of an enormous wing.

Martin moaned in a sick mix of pain and despair as Casey's eyes widened and then narrowed in an attempt to process what he was seeing. Martin closed his eyes and leant his head back against the wood of the beam as if just ignoring it could somehow change reality.

"Martin? That's a..."

"Please, don't say it out loud. It's bad enough that you know. Saying it aloud only makes it more real." Martin's eyes remained resolutely shut.

Casey came and knelt next to his friend, reaching a gentle hand to rest on his uninjured arm. "Okay...okay...I'll skip the obvious." Trying to keep his tone level, Casey cleared his throat before starting again. "Martin...that's a nasty break you have in your...the thing you have sticking out of your shoulder."

The pale eyes opened, his gaze turned and connected with Casey's. There was still pain, but there was a flicker of humour and an underlying trust that Casey would somehow make things right.

Casey continued. "May I...touch it?"

Mutely, Martin nodded, easing away from the wall and wincing.

With the delicate touch, using all his training in field medicine, Casey assessed first with his eyes before laying gentle fingers on both Martin's injured shoulder and then, even more gingerly, the broad length of feathered skin and bone jutting improbably from Martin's shoulder blade. Shaking his head in wonder and disbelief, he sighed and settled back on his heels.

"Well, your shoulder's dislocated rather than broken. Normally, we could get that back in its socket, but... obviously...there's a bit of a complication."

Martin rolled his eyes.

"The...ummm...wing"—Casey finally gave voice to the word—"is broken. But I suspect you already know that, and honestly, Martin, I have no idea where even to start. I want to help you, but I don't know how."

Martin muttered, "Do you think you can immobilize it? Strap it until we get home?"

Casey tipped his head to the side thoughtfully. "Maybe. I'll need some guidance so I don't cause more damage, but..." He continued more assuredly after a moment, "Yeah...I think I could."

"Then let's do that. I don't want to be here when our quarry gets back. We've already been here longer than we planned and I'm a sitting duck like this."

Casey snorted briefly, and Martin threw him a filthy look.

"I'd appreciate you saving the feathers jokes for the moment, Casey."

"Sorry." Casey looked contrite before stripping off his jumper and shirt and tearing the latter into long, broad strips. "This will hurt."

Martin's mouth drew into a tight line. "I know."

THIRTY MINUTES LATER, the adrenaline ebbed away from Casey as their rented four-wheel drive entered the highway. Martin was stretched face down on the back seat. When Casey looked in the rear-view mirror, the glossy top edges of the wings were visible as they caught the afternoon sunlight.

He'd managed to immobilize them by using the uninjured wing as a brace and then wrapping them together against his back as if he were binding a broken rib. Martin had sworn more in the past hour than Casey had heard in all their years together, and by the end of it, they were both drenched with sweat and Martin was faint from shock and pain. He'd taken the opportunity, while Martin was mercifully unconscious for several minutes, to manipulate his shoulder back into its socket and tie it in a sling.

Having to manoeuvre the fabric so it avoided the broad bulge of a pair of wrapped wings had been a puzzle Casey had never expected to face. However, by the time Martin regained consciousness, the job was done and it was just a matter of a short stumble to the car, and they were on their way as Martin fainted again.

A weak groan from the back seat alerted Casey that his patient had regained consciousness. He'd vaguely hoped he might spare Martin the bouncing and jostling of the trip home, but perhaps the quiet of the car might provide an opportunity to gain some much needed information.

"Martin, how are you doing?"

"I'll live," came the terse reply, muffled by the back seat. "Pain's better than it was. I must say, you're taking all of this remarkably well."

Casey smiled to himself. "Thanks, I think so too. Not every day your partner sprouts a set of wings. I can count the number of times on the fingers of one hand that I've thought, 'You know, I wonder if Martin's hiding a set of wings under that beautifully tailored suit.'"

There was a brief laugh, quickly stifled by a gasp. "Don't make me laugh, you sadist. But, fair enough, this is a lot to take in."

"A lot?" Casey immediately regretted the touch of anger in the words and softened his next question.

"Where did they come from? Have you always been... this?"

After a moment's silence, Martin began slowly, "Obviously, they're usually not visible. No, wait. Visible isn't the right word... Corporeal is closer. When they're whole and undamaged, I can summon or dismiss them at will. Does that help?"

"Sure." Casey nodded. "Invisible, magical wings... perfectly reasonable. But why?"

"Why what?"

"Why do you have them? Does everybody get a set and just... I don't know... not get the instruction manual?"

"No. They're an evolutionary glitch. We estimate less than one in ten thousand are born to the Avian species. That's the name for it, by the way; Avian. Tends to run in families, mostly."

"So...Leon?"

"Yes."

"Are they...can you..."

"Can I fly?"

"Yeah."

"Yes, Casey, I'm capable of flying," he explained, a touch of pride to his words. "Not everyone is and keeping my bodyweight down and my fitness up helps. Leon hasn't flown for years. Too much desk work." He huffed a little laugh, taking care to breathe shallowly.

Casey stilled for a moment before murmuring with something like awe. "God, I'd love to see you fly. It must be amazing."

Martin sighed. "Perhaps one day. I may never fly again, after this."

"You will, Martin. If I have any influence on the outcome, I swear it. Why didn't you tell me?"

There was a yawn from the back seat. Casey had found some painkillers in the glove compartment before Martin had fainted the second time, and from the slurring of Martin's words, they were beginning to take effect.

"To keep you...safe...Casey. Not...safe...anymore. Will tell...you...later."

CASEY PULLED THEIR rented four-wheel drive outside the safe house a little after 10:00 p.m. He was exhausted, and the splitting headache that had been dogging him since leaving the farm continued to thrum incessantly. But at least they could rest there.

He'd considered his options during the long drive back. The precious little information he had gave him the impression that the fewer people who knew about what had happened, the better. Both their apartments were in busy areas, and neither had a garage. He'd finally decided to take advantage of one of the Service's safe houses on the northern fringes of London. They'd used this one before, and its underground garage seemed the best bet for getting his injured partner inside unseen.

Once he got Martin upstairs, he could accurately assess the situation, call Leon, and maybe greet the new day feeling a little less like he'd lost his grip on reality.

In the back seat, Martin tossed restlessly, on the edge of waking. There were streaks of blood from the knock on his head smeared on the seats. *There goes our deposit.* But the strapping around his chest looked secure, and his arm was still snugly tucked in the makeshift sling.

"Martin...we're home. How're you doing?"

"Home, good." He struggled to sit up far enough to glance out the window, then thought better of it and lay back down with a groan. "We're at the Camden safe house? Smart move, Casey. You need to go and check if anyone's there. If they are...tell them to get out. Don't ask, *tell them.* Casey, it's important."

Casey briefly considered asking why but thought better of it. He was well out of his depth, and until he knew more, following Martin's cryptic instructions was the fastest way to get things sorted out. He continued to turn over the odd, slurred warning Martin had managed on the way home. *Not safe anymore.* Why?

In the end, the flat was empty, which made the task of getting Martin up the stairs and through the door a little easier. Even with nobody home, Casey worried that the swearing and thumps as they negotiated the stairs and walls might have attracted attention from the neighbours, but things remained blissfully quiet.

"Bed?" Casey panted; Martin was tall and slight, but the long day and pain made him near to a dead weight, and if he didn't find somewhere to lay Martin down soon, his increasingly sweaty grip was bound to fail.

"Please," Martin grunted between gritted teeth. "That way, I won't have to move again for a while."

It was a short stumble before Casey tipped Martin onto soft, clean sheets, face down to allow access to his back. Martin gasped as his injured shoulder took more pressure than he'd ideally like, but given the alternatives, it was the lesser of two evils. Martin dragged a pillow from the other side with his good hand and tucked it under his head and shoulder as Casey grabbed the first-aid kit, always kept fully stocked in the kitchen.

"I'll start with your head. May as well sort out the bits I have some chance at making sense of."

Martin reached fingers to his scalp and toyed with the matted hair, gingerly poking amongst the short strands until Casey brushed them away for a closer look.

"Okay, that's at least one thing we don't have to worry about. It's messy but just a nick. I'll disinfect it and check how it's looking tomorrow. How's the shoulder?"

"Sore," he replied. "Although I appreciate you dealing with when I blacked out," Martin paused, and with uncharacteristic vulnerability, continued, "Casey, you got a better look than I did. How's it look, honestly?"

He laid a hand on the smooth feathers of the exposed top edge. "Well," he huffed, struggling with the fact that all this was real, "the skin's not broken, so it's a simple fracture, thank God. I know nothing about bird anatomy, so I can't tell you what's going on inside without an X-ray—"

Martin tensed. "No hospitals, Casey. We can't involve them."

"No... You've already said that. What I was going to say was that I'd read up online and see what I can work out. There's codeine in the kit, so I'll dose you for the pain first, and you can get some sleep."

"Can you bring your laptop in here? I'd be grateful for the company." Martin reached up an unsteady hand, and Casey clasped it tightly. Being virtually immobilized was evidently wearing on Martin's nerves, leaving him feeling trapped and edgy, and for a man who rarely showed vulnerability, Casey saw the request as the desperate grasp for comfort that it was.

"Sure, of course. I'd like to get some food into you with the painkillers. Think you could manage a sandwich?"

"Only if there's roast beef in the fridge," Martin blurted.

Casey laughed. "And there's the imperiousness I miss. I thought I'd lost the old Martin for a second."

"I have a broken wing, Casey. I'm not dead."

Casey shook his head as he rose from the bed and walked to the door. "And we're back to the surreal statements again."

An hour later, Martin was fed, watered, and more comfortable. Casey was tucked up next to him with his laptop on his knees and sipping contentedly at his third cup of tea in a row.

"Does this look right to you?" He pointed, and Martin turned his head to look. The diagram on the screen showed an outstretched hawk wing, the bones clearly marked in colour and labelled.

"From what my parents taught me, yes."

Casey glanced down at Martin's back and back at the screen. "I'll need to check again, but I think you've broken your radius." Casey held out his forearm and pointed at the corresponding bone. "There was enough rigidity left when I was strapping it for me to be confident that you haven't broken your ulna too."

"Do you think you'll be able to set it here?" Martin asked worriedly.

"Maybe, if you can take the pain. It looks pretty much like splinting any other bone. But Martin...?"

"Mmmmm?"

"I still don't understand why we can't call Leon," Casey asked carefully.

Martin sighed and looked into Casey's eyes. "Yes, I suppose at this point, you deserve to know all of it. Make yourself comfortable. This will take a while."

"Then let me get what I need to set your wing. Having to explain it to me slowly and in small words—" Casey smiled sympathetically at his injured friend. "—will take your mind off the pain."

It was odd how quickly one adapted to unexpected situations. Once he'd accepted the fact that his friend *had* wings, Casey's natural instincts to approach the situation logically kicked in, and it became a simple matter of field triage; deciding how to pad, support, and protect the injured wing while dealing with the damage. When setting a standard arm, he'd have probably co-opted someone nearby to stabilize the limb while Casey dealt with the wrapping.

So, instead, Casey retrieved virtually every pillow and cushion from the flat and gradually surrounded the enormous wing, leaving it extended and gently supported as best he could while Martin was tucked warmly under the blankets, lying shirtless on his side of the bed. The remaining, undamaged wing rested, tucked under the extended wing, padded by more cushions.

"How does it look?" Martin asked, comfortably numb after a solid dose of painkillers and a large scotch.

Casey took a moment to appraise the situation. Not for the first time, he quietly marvelled at the way Martin seemed to hide his generously muscled shoulders beneath his high-end Italian shirts, his true physique only obvious in private moments like this. Idly, Casey wondered if there was a link between the solid strength and the wings that now sat in place high on his back.

"It's beautiful," Casey muttered reflexively, looking at the glossy feathers spread across the white sheets. The wing, overall, was verging on black, but the feathers were shot through with rich iridescent greens and purples, gemlike colours catching the dim light of the bedroom. Contrasting against the dark, a shock of white feathers ran along the middle, which thanks to the internet, Casey now knew were secondary coverts. The contrast brought the wing to life, startling with their vivid brightness.

Martin chuckled. "The description is flattering, but not really what I was after."

Casey blushed and cleared his throat. "Sorry. Just, they're amazing." Casey reached out to smooth fingers down the elongated flight feathers against the trailing edge.

"Casey..." Martin whispered restlessly as the wing shivered and goose bumps rose on Martin's bare shoulder.

Casey slowed his delicate path through the oversized primaries, sifting between the individual feathers to the skin beneath. "You okay?"

"Yes...they're very sensitive. As you can imagine, there haven't been many people in my life who have seen them, much less touched them. It's...considered rather intimate."

"Oh." Casey's hand stilled, but he didn't lift it away. "Should I stop?" The question was laden with more than the mere words, and Casey waited, not entirely sure which answer he wanted.

Martin went silent for a long moment, and the room fell into an awkward hush before he finally murmured more roughly than his usual smooth tone. "Just until it heals."

That was as close as they'd ever come to admitting to each other a desire to push their working relationship beyond friendship. Over nearly a decade together, the two men had shared more than most, and the on-again off-again undercurrent of potential had simmered for years. Perhaps it was the bizarreness of the situation, Martin's injuries, or maybe it was just time. Whatever the case, Casey's heart did an odd dip and rise before he quietly removed his fingers and bent to splint the long edge of the beautiful wing as gently as possible, feeling entirely out of his depth.

With a voice he hoped sounded more dispassionate than he felt, he asked, "So tell me about Leon, and why we can't call him."

Letting the unspoken drop, for now, Martin continued with a tone closer to normal. "Avians are rare, Casey, incredibly rare. There was a time we were treasured too; our wings, our feathers were the prizes of the obscenely wealthy, and old habits and the instinct to protect ourselves die hard. There are hard rules, savage, brutal rules for dealing with anyone who knows our secret and any Avian who exposes us. You finding out about me is a death sentence to us both, and if Leon is informed, he becomes complicit. Any punishment would probably be extended to him."

"So, let me get this straight." Casey continued to work on the dressings as the full consequences of Martin's actions became clear, because apparently... "You dove off that edge to catch me, and you already knew that doing it would probably end up with us both dead?"

Martin's reply was hushed and full of something complicated. "I wasn't thinking that far ahead."

"I see. So, basically we're alone in this."

"I'm afraid so." Martin turned to look over his shoulder. "Us against the world."

"When has it been any different?" He chuckled low in his chest and paused to lay a hand on Martin's bare back. "We'll get through this."

It took Casey over an hour to splint and strap the wing in a way that he was comfortable Martin would have the ability to draw it in towards his body and yet protect the limb from further harm while it healed. Casey helped Martin to stand, and they tested out the rig of bandage and bracing, finally pronouncing it sound if a little clumsy. As Casey helped support the weight of the damaged right, Martin tentatively stretched both wings out in the confines of the room and ruffled them gently. Casey's mouth fell open as the tips of the enormous span brushed opposite walls. Now, Martin took a moment to look smug.

"Casey, you're the first non-Avian to see my wings. It's easy to become complacent about how astonishing they can be, but the look on your face...it says a lot. Thank you."

Casey whispered, struggling with emotion at the majesty of them as he pictured Martin soaring and swooping in graceful arcs. "I still can't believe they're real. I keep expecting to wake up."

Martin carefully brought the wings back to rest against his back and turned to Casey. "Speaking of which, it's been a very long day. We should get some sleep."

"Yes...I'll just..." Casey eyed the door, thinking how cold and lonely the sofa in the lounge looked.

"Wash up? If it's all right with you, I'd prefer to have you close. That's if you don't mind?"

Casey jumped at the offer. "Yes, of course. I'll just pop to the bathroom, back in a tick."

By the time Casey returned, Martin had gotten back into bed and shrugged his trousers off, leaving them in a pile on the floor. He'd managed to arrange himself in bed, turned to face the centre, wings down the outside edge.

"Sorry, might be a bit cramped."

"We'll manage. How's the pain?" Casey climbed in the other side, stripped down to his boxers.

"The strapping helps, as did the scotch you found in the cupboard."

"Probably shouldn't have given you that on top of the pills, but…I'll keep an eye on you."

"You always do." Martin yawned, and Casey smiled at the sound of feathers rustling as he settled for the night.

"Sleep well, Martin. Wake me if you need anything."

"What else could I possibly need?" he mumbled as exhaustion finally took him. "You're already here."

Chapter Four

HOT...SO HOT. Casey lay on a sandy beach under the baking sun, sweat dripping down his neck.

The tendrils of sleep released their hold, and Casey shifted as a bead of sweat rolled across his back. *I'm still hot... Why am I so hot?*

The answer came to him as he tried to roll over and found himself effectively encapsulated on all sides by sheets, blankets, Martin's long arm, and a broad feathered wing protectively wrapped around him. He was held snug against Martin's chest and was, it appeared, in danger of melting from the abundance of heat sources near his skin.

Casey was by no means a prude. Flat-shares during university and more bills than income often saw friends piled two and three to a bed. So accidental bedfellows wrapping themselves around him was nothing new. And if sometimes casual hands lingered and friends became temporarily something more, well, it was human nature to seek comfort, and no harm was done. In many cases, what happened in dark, secluded corners was rarely spoken of and often never repeated.

Casey was loath to disturb Martin, but the situation was becoming urgent as Casey felt another bead of sweat pool unpleasantly in the notch between his spine and Martin's flat stomach. Casey might have, more than occasionally, fantasized about getting sweaty with Martin, but this in no way lived up to his expectations.

Levering up with his top arm, Casey tried to wriggle out from under the combined weight with limited success. Although the bedclothes and wing lifted begrudgingly, the arm wrapped possessively around his chest tightened as Martin attempted to gather him closer into his curled body with an irritated huff.

"Martin...let me up." Casey butted his head gently back against Martin's chest. "I need to pee."

"Mmmm, then come back." There was a vague relaxation of the arm, allowing Casey to shift it to one side and slip out of bed.

The short trip to the bathroom allowed Casey to cool down, and he gulped down several glasses before bringing back another to the bedroom.

"Martin...wake up. You need to keep your fluids up."

"Hnnffmmm... Don't want to," came the mumbled reply.

Casey noted the thin sheen of sweat on his patient's forehead and laid the back of his hand on it.

"Martin...come on. Wake up a bit for me. You're too warm. I want to check your temperature."

Martin flailed with his free arm, the wing swinging up to mimic the gesture, but Casey had enough battle training to duck under and grab the errant wrist. The wing, however, was more of a challenge, and Casey eventually found himself kneeling on the bed, wrist clamped in one hand and the undamaged wing tucked under an arm. Thus incapacitated, Martin's eyes finally cracked open, squinting in the morning light.

"What are you doing? I was asleep." Martin frowned and grumbled, "And I'd appreciate you taking my wing out of your armpit; it doesn't belong there."

Casey lifted his arm and released his feathery captive. It folded back behind Martin's naked torso, and its owner settled back under the sheets.

"You're running a fever, I'm worried."

Martin huffed, "I am not running a fever. My metabolism runs hot, and I'm healing a broken bone. Relax and come back to bed."

Casey remained crouched on the bed. "Well, how am I supposed to know what's normal? Yesterday, you were my idiot partner, and today, you're impersonating the angel Gabriel after a run-in with a lorry."

Martin smiled up at Casey.

"What?" Casey asked, confused.

"Angel." Martin snorted behind the grin.

"So...you're not..."

Martin snorted again. "Certainly not, Casey. Angels don't exist."

"Says the man with the wings."

Martin smiled. "You make a fair point, I grant you. Nevertheless, not an angel. Now, are you going to perch there, pardon the Avian reference, or come back to bed?"

Morning light streamed through the window, breaking the fragile intimacy of the previous evening. While it had seemed the most normal thing in the world to crawl between the crisp sheets the night before, he was now painfully aware that he'd woken comfortably nestled against his flatmate's chest and would be euphoric to be back there again. His discomfort had apparently shown on his face because Martin huffed in frustration before he drew a long breath to dispel Casey's doubts.

"Do you want me to list a dozen boring, mundane reasons you should already be back in this bed? I could begin with the fact that we'll probably be stuck here for the remainder of the day and I'll be bored witless without you here. I could argue that, as my partner, you have a duty of care to oversee my recuperation and that is more easily done from within the room. Or…" Martin quirked up the corner of his mouth. "I could bribe you with answers to what must be a veritable avalanche of questions." With the last, he lifted the edge of the sheets and nodded to the gap, waiting for Casey to capitulate.

This is how Martin won arguments. Rattle off a seemingly sensible list of reasons to justify some truly insane schemes. Knowing in his head that he'd already surrendered, he tried to hold onto just a sliver of control.

"I'll go and make us some breakfast, get you some more painkillers, and *then* I'll come back to bed. But you'd better be prepared to tell me all of it this time. If we're going to have to face this together, no more secrets."

"Agreed." Martin nodded.

WHILE CASEY WAS gone, Martin lay back as best he could, given the strapping and splints at his back. The pain was certainly more bearable this morning. His shoulder, bruised and strained from the dislocation, was actually the more unpleasant of the injuries, and he knew there was a long road of remedial therapy ahead of him to recover the full strength. His wing could take weeks or potentially months to heal, depending on the break, and until he was up and around, there was no way to accurately assess it. While Casey had done an exceptional job at triage, the reality was that he needed specialist treatment if he was to stand a chance of ever flying again. If there was any way of getting the care he needed without making their situation worse, he'd take it. The idea of being stripped of the power of flight was almost beyond bearing.

Of equal concern was Casey's fate. Although Martin had no doubt whatsoever at Casey's commitment to keeping his knowledge of the Avian society a secret, the Avian law was clear, and he doubted the hierarchy would be as willing to entrust their future to even a member of Her Majesty's Secret Service. They needed help, and from people they could trust with their lives. But first, Casey should know what he'd unwittingly stumbled into, and all of it. Martin owed him that.

Deep in thought, Martin only looked up when Casey returned with a tray laden with toast, coffee, and a nondescript pill bottle.

"You look like you've come to some conclusions. Care to share?" Casey queried.

"Mmmm, just thinking about next steps."

"And...?" Casey balanced the tray on the bedside table.

"And... I'm going to need to make a call."

"I thought you said we couldn't call Leon."

"Not Leon." Martin shook his head.

"Then who?"

Martin tapped a message and hit send before looking back up to meet Casey's eyes. "I'm calling Alissa."

Chapter Five

"I'M SORRY... DID you say *Alissa*? You wave your hands around and say, 'nobody must know,' and then you say you're ringing Alissa."

"Casey...calm down."

"Telling a human about the wings is a death sentence," Casey mimed Martin's dramatic announcement from the previous night.

"Casey...I need proper medical help if I'm to retain the ability to fly."

"We'll both be—" Casey stalked back and forth in the dim light of the bedroom and then added in a whisper fit for a film villain, "put to death."

"She's one of us," Martin interjected quietly.

"Can't call Leon...can't go to A&E."

"Casey, Alissa's an Avian."

"Us against the world...what?"

"Alissa... She's Avian."

"She's not," Casey said quite definitively.

"She is," he assured Casey.

"Seriously?" Casey's tone said it all. He was saved from further ridicule by Martin's phone chiming in response to Alissa's text.

Glancing down, Martin assessed the reply before putting the phone aside. "She'll need a couple of hours to collect what she needs and slip away."

"Right, then..." Casey turned back to the forgotten tray of breakfast staples. "You promised me answers."

"And you promised to come back to bed."

"SO..." THE LAST piece of toast paused in transit to Casey's mouth. "Let me see if I have this straight, you... Avians."

Martin nodded.

Casey continued, "Have been around all the time, happily flapping around in secret, right under our noses."

Martin sipped at his tea. "Humans can be remarkably adept at ignoring perfectly obvious things if they don't fit with their world view. Meanwhile, the conspiracy theorists continue to complicate the world with ludicrous tales of secret societies and monsters in Scottish lochs. It's a bit of a win-win arrangement, really. On the odd occasion that something is seen, we just..."

There was the rattle of a key in the front door followed by a shout of "Restock!" as the door swung open.

"Shit!" Casey vaulted from the bed and through the bedroom door as the singsong voice continued to make progress in the flat.

"Oh, it's Agent Wicker, isn't it? I'm not disturbing anything, I hope?"

The restock team was known for their discretion. They had to be, given some of the stories regarding what went on at some of the safe houses. He thought this woman's name was Bethany or Barbara or something like that. She was blonde and pretty in a vacuous, superficial way. She also had a hopeless crush on Martin, which Casey never ceased to ridicule him about.

Casey swung the bedroom door shut behind him, stepping into the breach with nothing but his boxers and courage. Martin listened as his partner's voice carried through the timber barrier, "No. No, of course not. We just had a little run-in with some trouble and needed a bolt hole."

Leaving Casey to soothe and redirect her attention, Martin closed his eyes, his brow furrowing as he tried to concentrate through the fog of painkillers and pain.

The focus would be essential for what he needed to do.

"Martin got a bit banged up, but he'll be okay. I was just taking him a spot of breakfast."

"Oh! Should I pop in and give my regards? I'm sure he'd like…"

"No…no…he'll be—"

"Stand down, Agent!"

Their voices were noticeably closer, and through the fog of Martin's intense concentration, he heard the alarm in Casey's voice.

"I'll just see if he needs anything and then I'll be off… leave you two alone," she insisted.

The door handle rattled. It crossed his mind that for such an administrative role, she was remarkably nimble. The door swung open just as Martin released a long cleansing breath.

"Agent…Martin really isn't…" Casey stuttered to a halt with whatever he was about to say as he tried in vain to get between the petite blonde and her view of the bed. Where Martin's wings should have been, loose wrappings draped his bare torso, and the splints lay on the bed like discarded kindling.

Shifting his injured shoulder in the sling, Martin faked a weak smile at their insistent guest. "How nice to see you,

Bethany. As you can see, I'm in Casey's capable hands. What I need now"—he gave her a pointed look—"is some sleep, if you don't mind."

"Oh, yes, of course. I can see you're fine. I'll leave you two alone, then." She looked abashed at Casey. "Let me know if you need anything extra, milk, bread."

Casey smiled back kindly as he guided her back toward the door of the flat. Martin heard it open, "We'll be all right. He never eats much, and I'll pop out later for essentials."

"Well, if you're sure..."

"Yes, thank you." The sound of the door closing again signalled an end to the conversation and Martin suspected Casey had probably closed the door in her face. He made a mental note to apologise at some point in the future, but there were larger matters to attend to and often the only way to combat her tenaciousness was with bluntness.

He heard Casey lock the door, and this time, there was the sound of a security chain being drawn. Casey's relieved sigh carried through the flat before he reappeared at the bedroom doorway. Martin looked up at him from his nest of pillows and discarded bandages.

"So..." Casey began, "feel like telling me how you've hidden your bloody great big pair of wings, given you haven't been able to since the barn? I assume it's not some sleight-of-hand magic trick."

He settled on patting the bed where he'd turned down the blankets again. "It was on my list of things to explain before we got interrupted. I promise."

Casey checked his watch. They still had over an hour before Alissa was due to arrive, and in his haste to waylay Bethany he had rushed barefoot through the cold flat in nothing but his boxers. When he crawled back under the blankets, Martin's excess heat was gratefully received as he sidled up to him, careful not to jostle his shoulder. Martin's good arm reached to draw him closer, and as his chilled feet warmed again, he sighed and waited for Martin to continue.

"You want to know where my wings went. The truth is, Casey, we don't know. We don't know where they come from when we summon them, and we don't know where they go. What we do know is that they are dispelled dirty, and they come back clean, leaving the dirt behind, but if they go away injured, they come back the same way, regardless of how long we dismiss them.

"That's why I've kept them visible; they won't heal unless they're here, with me."

"So why didn't you—" Casey waved a hand. "—dismiss them at the barn? Hide them from me and worry about caring for them later? Surely, that would have been safer?"

"If it had been an option, then I would have, believe me. But bringing them forth and sending them away takes concentration, and when we're in pain, we can't focus. It's a blessing and a curse. It means they won't appear without our intent if we're hurt, or worse, under torture. We can't be forced to summon them, not with pain, at least."

"So, why not bring them back now? I assume I'll need to redress them, given that the bandages didn't go with them."

"I thought you deserved my long overdue explanation first," Martin began a little hesitantly. "And then you can stay and watch them come back... If you'd like to, that is."

"You've left something out. Come on, Martin, no secrets," Casey prompted gently.

Martin nodded, stronger in his resolve. "You know me too well, Casey." He drew in a breath. "All right, then, all of it. You've earned the truth. We usually don't like summoning and dismissing our wings with an audience. I've talked about the concentration required?"

Casey nodded.

"It's not insignificant, the concentration... There's no time during which we're more vulnerable, more exposed. We're virtually helpless as our wings appear. I've told you about the value of our wings to some people? Can you imagine the power we place in the hands of a human if we change in front of them? It's—" Martin locked his gaze with Casey's. "Well, let's just say, you should never underestimate my trust in you or my regard, that I've suggested this."

A subtle flush rose in Martin's cheeks.

"There's one more thing you need to prepare yourself for, Casey. Avians know that seeing this has a powerful effect on humans. In fact, we think this is where the stories of angels probably originate. The words people use include rapture, sacrament, bliss. It can be intense, or so I've been told. There have been...incidents."

Casey looked slightly alarmed, and Martin huffed a frustrated breath and tried again. "Not of violence, of desire. I'm not sure how you'll react, given our working relationship and your..." After a moment, Martin quietly added, "interest."

"Ahh...I see." Casey smiled. "I thought I'd been subtle?"

"You have been, don't get me wrong. But I know you, and I know when you're interested in someone."

"You've never mentioned it. In fact, I've never seen you make a move on anyone at all."

Martin smiled. "What can I say, I'm picky. I thought it might make things awkward with us working together and all. But this, what I'm about to do... I just thought you should know that I'm aware."

"I'm sure it'll be fine." Casey shrugged off the warning uneasily.

Martin smirked. "Don't say I didn't warn you. I'll just leave you with this to consider. You're the best partner I've ever had, Casey. And by a partner, I'm open to all senses of that word. So it's fine, Casey, whatever happens. Whether I've said it or not, the door has always been open to you."

Without pausing to let Casey respond, Martin swivelled his legs off the bed and stood, straightening his shoulders as best he could, giving Casey one last openly fond look, and took three steadying breaths. An odd, deep silence enfolded the room and the temperature seemed to rise slightly. Martin became unnaturally still, and he knew Casey's gaze was being drawn unerringly to his.

Casey's eyes watered as the air around them shimmered, a thin, glowing halo surrounding them both. Martin's rich brown eyes glowed in the dim light and the air seemed to ripple and bend around him. If pressed, he knew Casey would have been unable to say at what point the wings appeared. The line before and after would be blurred in his memory. What he could pinpoint was the moment at which an overwhelming rush of lust flooded Casey, and he watched as his partner staggered as his knees threatened to give way.

Martin could see Casey struggling to catch his breath, struggling with the wash of arousal, and merely smiled at him as the change continued. The light around him pulsed and shimmered as it ebbed and flowed around his limbs and the now clearly visible wings. Casey whimpered a broken noise that rose and fell in time with the movement.

He extended a hand, his body acting independent of conscious thought, and Martin took it in his own to draw him closer.

Casey approached willingly, irresistibly, one step and then another until he was close enough to lean against Martin's softly glowing skin, clinging with his arms around Martin's waist and finding a resting place for his hand between the two furled wings. Casey's erection was obvious, pressed hard against Martin's hip, as his partner was lost in sensation and the need to be close.

Martin looked down as the last of the light receded, his voice quiet and warm. "Casey?"

"Martin... You have no idea how much I want to fuck you right now," Casey managed to murmur between gritted teeth.

Martin chuckled, deep and rich. "I did warn you... And I did say I'd welcome the idea, but Alissa's just rung the doorbell, so we might have to put a pin in it for now."

Casey buried his head in Martin's shoulder and groaned, "You'll have to give me a minute or two, just to..." Casey made a valiant effort to move away as his hips, seemingly with a mind of their own, threatened to grind against Martin's offered hip.

Martin laughed again and placed a gentle kiss against Casey's temple. "Take your time and have a shower. I'll text her and tell her to get us some coffee." Martin gently moved away and then chuckled again as Casey's hips sought to follow his movement before he managed to detach himself and turn to the bathroom.

As Martin's fingers tapped out a message, Casey's voice floated through the rising steam. "And don't tell her you changed in front of me; I don't need her to have that image stuck in her head."

Martin gave a quiet, smug smile and hit send.

Chapter Six

CASEY LEANT HIS head against the shower tiles as the water ran over him, taking the last traces of his hasty wank down the drain with it. Lingering twitches of the bizarre, almost ecstatic bliss still fizzed in his veins, and although the worst of his arousal had now abated, it left him unsatisfied and oddly hollow, with a strange desire to stride back into the bedroom and curl around Martin under the covers.

Casey couldn't discern how much of this new, aching loneliness was a result of what he'd seen and how much was simply a growing awareness of the increasing attraction between them. The confusion clung to him even as he towelled himself dry.

Fortunately, the safe houses were stocked with a decent selection of casual clothes, so jeans and a warm jumper left him feeling more able to greet the day. He'd just finished running a comb through his damp hair when the doorbell rang again, followed by a cheerful greeting from the other side of the door.

When he opened it, he found Alissa, a sizable backpack slung over her shoulder and a travel tray of coffees in her right hand.

"Hi, Casey," she said brightly, closing the door behind her.

"Thanks for coming, Alissa. We appreciate it." Casey assessed the woman with new eyes. Knowing that, under her quiet, shy façade, Alissa had the same unusual genetic makeup as his flatmate answered a lot of questions. In hindsight, the hints of Alissa and Martin's shared history made sense.

Dropping her backpack to the floor, she approached and quickly embraced Casey before pulling back, the smile dropping from her face as she whispered, "Martin told me...you saw his wings."

Casey nodded.

"This isn't good, Casey. It's not good at all," she said.

"It couldn't be helped; he did it to save my life, Alissa. Whatever happens now, at least we'll face it together."

"As you always would, I suppose. Where is he?"

"In the bedroom." Casey led the way. "I don't mind saying I'm a bit out of my depth. I strapped and splinted it, and we've got the pain sorted, but then, well...you can see for yourself."

For ease of access, Martin had once again arranged himself face down, wings spread across the width of the bed. He'd managed to arrange the pillows in such a way as to give support to his shoulder but leaving his remaining hand free to tap determinedly on the keyboard of Casey's laptop.

"How is it"—Alissa stood beside the bed, arms crossed—"that you can make even the most awkward position look elegant?"

Martin craned his neck to look over his shoulder and grinned broadly. "It's a gift. Thanks for coming, Sparrow."

Casey noted the comfortable warmth between them in light of what he now knew. Alissa had always been more than just a work colleague to them, and watching her with Martin, it all made sense.

"Sparrow?" Casey queried.

Martin chuckled. "I've been calling her that since we were kids. If you saw her wings, you'd know why."

Alissa countered but without real malice. "At least mine are in one piece, Martin Bishop!"

Score one to Alissa Satterfield.

She huffed a frustrated breath that Casey found rather familiar before sitting carefully on the edge of the bed to inspect Martin's wing.

"Well, Casey's done a good job." She looked over to him where he stood in the doorway. "It looks like it was a clean break. It'll set well, and all but one of your flight feathers are in place." She put a gentle hand on Martin's injured shoulder, now a riot of blues and purple from the dislocation and leant in. "What I'm trying to say, Martin, is that...you'll likely fly again."

Martin and Casey released a tense breath in unison. Casey hadn't realized the responsibility he'd felt for Martin's initial care, and Alissa's reassurance acted as a surprising relief valve.

She continued, "But it has to stay splinted. You know what that means?"

Martin replied taciturnly, "It means I'm about to be stuck in this flat for two weeks."

She swatted Martin's arse, hidden under the bunched bedclothes. "At least two weeks. No mucking around, Martin. If you want to fly again, you'll get one shot at it healing properly. It's up to you; if you want to be stuck on the ground for the rest of your life, feel free to pop them in and out and go running off to crime scenes."

Martin paled as the meaning behind her spirited tone hit home. While he might appear brash and arrogant, it was evident to Casey that the thought of being tethered to the ground for the remainder of his life bordered on unbearable.

"Come closer, Casey." Alissa motioned to him. "I want to show you how to strap a wing properly. At least that way, you can change the dressings more quickly."

Alissa dispensed avian care instructions to Casey, reinforced reasonable excuses for dismissing Martin's wings and the things Martin would just need to put up with.

They agreed that sleeping with them corporeal was preferable, but that it made sense to dismiss them while showering. Martin could roam the flat freely as long as the curtains remained drawn, and the door was locked at all times. Together, the three of them estimated that he could begin gentle rehabilitation of the muscles in a week and that Alissa would return in a fortnight if all went to plan.

Tying off the last of the bandages, the three of them sat in a cosy cluster on the bed and Alissa looked at them both.

"I'll take care of reporting your leave of absence, and I'll square things away with Scotland Yard. I have a few favours I can pull. What do you want me to do about the Avian Council? You know I'm obligated to notify them?" she said sadly.

Glancing first to Casey, Martin nodded sombrely. "They were bound to find out one way or another. They always do. I don't want you putting yourself at risk trying to hide this. At least this way, Casey isn't dead on the floor of a barn, and I won't be crippled. We'll deal with the council when we have to."

She looked to Casey thoughtfully. "Casey, would you be willing to commit to staying in the flat until Martin's healed? I might be able to get you an exemption as his primary carer until he's fit for trial."

"Trial?" Casey asked, alarmed.

"I've broken Avian law, and there'll be a price to be paid. But our people aren't barbarians." Martin smiled wryly. "They'll probably wait until I'm fit before they sentence us to death."

Alissa looked at the two men, clearly distressed. "I'm so sorry, Martin. You know I'd hide this if I thought we'd get away with it."

Casey stood and paced the room, frustrated. "This is insane. You risk your life to save me, we spend two weeks getting you well, and then...*then* they get to kill you." He turned to meet Martin's eyes. "It's not right, Martin... It's not *fair*."

"It's the law." Martin sounded wretched.

Casey's voice dropped low and bitter. "Then your laws are wrong."

Chapter Seven

"THREE DAYS, MARTIN. It's been *three days!*" Casey's patience finally snapped as Martin made yet another circuit of the tiny flat, prowling like a caged animal. Casey had known it would be bad, but he'd failed to anticipate exactly how bad it was going to be. Martin's boundless energy rarely tolerated him staying in one spot for too long.

"This is *intolerable*, Casey. I need space; I need air. I need"—he looked hungrily towards the curtained window—"*out*... I need out!"

"You don't need out; you need to stay in here and heal. Should I repeat...*again*...what Alissa told you?"

Martin wasn't the only one visibly on edge. Usually, Casey would be perfectly content to hang around in one location for days on end, reading up on the local culture and trying to make inroads into his endless book list, but the knowledge that he was forbidden from going out made the incarceration stifling. With the added burden of a restless, injured partner, the situation was fast becoming untenable.

"*Yes*," Martin shouted at him, "because that will help. Repeating the same thing over and *over* again. What a *brilliant* idea, Casey. Repetition is an *inspired* way to divert my attention from how unbearably *boring* this is." Martin theatrically threw himself face down into the pile of cushions and blankets they'd arranged in front of the fireplace when it became apparent the sofa wouldn't accommodate his strapped wings.

Casey put the coffee mug down more gently than he thought possible and drew in a long, steadying breath before walking over and crouching next to his friend. "Look, Martin," he began softly. "I know you're bored, and I know it's hard being stuck inside, but it's only for a couple of weeks. Whatever happens next, you need to be fit to face it."

Martin mumbled something incomprehensible into the cushions, the anger seemingly having burnt itself out and been replaced by despair.

Casey absently laid a hand on the ridge of Martin's wing, feeling the warmth under the feathers. Over the intervening days, he seemed to have developed an irresistible urge to touch them casually, and in spite of the initial warning about the intimacy of the act, Martin not only permitted but seemed to encourage the contact. His face, with the tired circles under his eyes making him look despondent, turned on the pillows to look up at where Casey knelt beside him.

"Wretched," he murmured.

"I know...I know," Casey comforted. "Look, why don't you take a shower? Freshen up a bit. Always makes me feel better and maybe get you into some fresh pyjamas." Casey's nose wrinkled slightly. "You're getting a bit whiffy, to be honest."

Martin looked appalled before lifting an arm and conceding with a nod that Casey was right. Rising gracefully from the floor, he silently padded towards the bathroom, leaving Casey still kneeling by the abandoned nest of blankets.

Casey had expected the next he'd see would be Martin, clean and dry. However, he reappeared at Casey's elbow several minutes later and placed a warm hand on his shoulder.

"I hate to ask, but I'm going to need help," he asked.

Casey turned and looked at Martin's slumping shoulders and the hint of vulnerable defeat in the usually bright eyes. For all his bluster and arrogance, Casey knew Martin rarely found himself truly beaten, either by physical incapacity or circumstance. There was a significant difference between allowing Casey to play nursemaid to him in the frantic aftermath of a case and this more intimate submission; the admission that he needed help to achieve simple cleanliness and personal care.

Casey smiled in a way he hoped would be interpreted as camaraderie rather than pity. "Of course. Of course, I'll help. Obviously, I should have realized." Without another word, Casey followed him to the bathroom, trying to dismiss the sense of unease that was rising with each step.

I can do this. It's just a shower. I can do this. Casey pulled towels from the linen cupboard. *Martin is injured. Just stay objective, focus on the job, get through it.*

Every step towards the bathroom had ratcheted up his nervousness. Images of Martin, surrounded by a flickering halo of light, his blood thrumming through his veins sprang unbidden to his mind.

He needs me now; he doesn't need...this, Casey berated himself, pushing the errant thoughts away. Pulling his shoulders back and tightening his mouth, he turned to where Martin was standing isolated under the fluorescent light of the bathroom. The sweet smells of vanilla shampoo and coconut soap drifted in the enclosed space.

"All right..." Casey began dispassionately. "Let's get you clean."

Martin's brow furrowed and his soft lips turned hard. Taking a step away, Martin's posture stiffened, and Casey felt another angry outburst coming before Martin opened his mouth.

"No, stop. Just...stop."

Frustration? Anger? Casey grasped at possible reasons as he rolled up the sleeves of his shirt with clinical efficiency.

If anything, Martin's face hardened further, and he balled his hands into fists. "Stop it, Casey... just...stop it." The anger was clearer to see now.

"It's all right, Martin. I'll be careful of your shoulder. I've done this before. First-aid training."

"Damn it!" Martin strode forward the short two steps it took to bring them face-to-face and bore down into Casey's personal space.

"Martin?"

"I don't want Agent Wicker. I don't want first aid fucking Wicker of Her Majesty's Secret Service." Martin's voice had dropped low and harsh as he was clearly working hard to keep his frustrated anger in hand, but it softened and broke as he added finally, "I just want...Casey Wicker. Can you do that, Casey? Can you leave all the others outside the door and, for a little while, just be Casey?"

Casey blinked up at Martin's haggard face, at the dark eyes so open and plaintive and wondered why it had taken him so long to see it. Martin's manic cycling between anger and despair, being emotionally thrown against the constraints of his injury over and over again. He didn't need aloof; he didn't need distant or professional. He needed a lifeline, and as always, the lifeline's name was Casey Wicker.

Casey slid his arms easily around Martin, finding an increasingly natural-feeling home amongst the wrappings and exposed feathers. He tipped forward to better slot their bodies together as Martin sighed and gratefully rested his head on Casey's shoulder, the tension slipping from his muscles.

"My Casey..." Martin murmured against the fabric.

"I'm here."

Things moved more slowly after that. Gone was the efficient stripping and disposal of clothes. Gone was the impersonal banter. Instead, Casey touched gently and lingered, communicating with contact that they were in this together, both in body and spirit. He rambled quietly about scars he uncovered, reminiscing about cases they'd shared and stitching him up afterwards. He often stopped to look into Martin's eyes, reforming the connection between them over and over again and hiding nothing of the feelings they were finally admitting they shared.

It was just another form of caring for a patient, Casey supposed, giving Martin what he needed to heal. But it was light-years away from professional, and Casey was under no illusions that every textbook would have this behaviour under "inappropriate." This had become simply about Casey and Martin, and Casey was getting as much from this as his damaged Avian.

At some point, they'd slipped gently to the floor, Casey leaning up against the wall, protected from its chill by the pile of towels they'd dragged over. Martin was slumped against him, pliant and boneless as Casey smoothed hands over exposed skin and feathers time and time again. Curled against his chest, Martin had somehow wedged himself below Casey's chin, short black hair brushing against his neck whenever he moved.

"We still need to get you clean," Casey whispered against the hair, "but there's no rush."

Martin nodded lazily, and a murmur of agreement rumbled through him. "Mmmm, don't move yet. I'll dismiss my wings so we can shower."

Casey tensed slightly, and Martin chuckled. "Don't worry. It's not as dramatic as when they appear; you might get a bit...warm, but nothing like the other day."

The intimacy of the room gave Casey the courage he needed to say the words out loud, and when Martin finished talking, he murmured, "I wouldn't have minded... if it had been like the other day." He paused before adding, "Now that I know you want it as much as I do."

Now, it was Martin's turn to tense, and he shifted so he could lift his head to look at Casey. "You do...want it?"

"Yes. Oh, yes." Casey smiled and ran a thumb over Martin's plump lips. "Wings or not, I want it."

Martin grinned, relaxed and more open than Casey had seen in a long time before he scrubbed a hand over his face and sighed. "Well, I hope you're proud of yourself, Casey."

Casey quirked an eyebrow.

"I can't focus enough to banish my wings now. Seems my mind is on...other things."

Casey leant in to bring their lips together for the very first time as he asked quietly, "Problem?"

Martin smiled, and his breath ghosted warmly over Casey's as he replied, "It seems not."

"SO..." CASEY PULLED back slightly, noting with satisfaction the way Martin's already plush lips were swollen from kisses. Somewhere in the past half hour,

Casey's shirt had been peeled away, followed by his increasingly restrictive jeans and pants. They still, however, nestled together on the bathroom floor, both naked, advancing this newly discovered aspect of their relationship slowly, savouring each step down this new intimate path.

Martin smiled, lids heavy, and pupils dilated. "Shower?"

"Shower," Casey said more definitively. No less affected than Martin, he was, however, more motivated to get the man under the spray and lathered in the rich vanilla and coconut body wash that was standard in all the flats.

Martin discarded his sling and rolled to his knees, where he arched his back. The lines of his torso stretched, and his abdominal muscles sprung into stark relief When Martin looked back down, Casey sat staring.

"What?"

Martin ran a hand through his hair. "You have that look you sometimes get."

"What look?"

"The *you're gonna get us both killed* look."

Casey grinned as the heat rose in his cheeks. "Probably because every time you do something idiotically reckless, I've wanted to do what I'm about to do to you."

"I don't follow." Martin frowned.

"Drag you into a corner and push you up against the wall."

"Oh."

"Just...hold still." Casey stood behind Martin in the cramped shower stall. While brilliant in principle, in practice, there was limited room for Casey, Martin, *and* the wings.

"Sorry...I'll just—" Martin shifted in place, further squeezing Casey against the cold tiles.

Casey giggled with the absurdity. What had started out as a vague plan for some sort of sexual encounter under the warm water was fast becoming one of the crazier escapades they'd shared.

"Just...*wait!*" he shouted as cold tiles pressed against his arse, stilling Martin's movement with hands on his strapped wings.

Martin ceased his attempts to shift around and opted instead for turning on the taps, and Casey was grateful that at least he'd aimed the spray away from him while he waited for the water to heat.

"If I take these bandages off, will you be all right?" Casey fingered the edges of the strapping. "It'll be easier without all this material."

Martin's voice echoed in the enclosed space. "Alissa said it should be. In any case, I want them off."

Casey smiled and set to unwinding the bandages, letting them drop to the floor of the shower where they formed a small, but steadily growing, sodden pile. As Martin adjusted the showerhead to cascade across his shoulders and down his back, Casey stood, fascinated, as the water beaded and rolled down the exposed wings. Martin tipped his head back so the water slicked his hair down and sighed hedonistically.

Casey smiled, confined in a pocket of dry space between Martin's wings and the wall as he continued to unwrap. "Better?"

"You have no idea." Martin sighed, rolling his neck gently back and forth.

"The water's beading on your wings. I assume that's normal?"

Martin nodded. "Mmmm, they're water repellent. Much like a swan or a cormorant. Again, we don't know why, but they're all the same, regardless of the colouring."

As the last of the wrapping slipped away, Casey knelt awkwardly to gather the sopping pile to press the worst of the water out before tossing them toward the sink, out of the way.

Casey's breath caught as he turned and looked up at Martin, facing away and towering above. The long inky wings with their rivulets of water streaming down them gave tantalizing glimpses of pale skin between them, leading a path to his arse and down to legs below the trailing wingtips, water dripping from the lowest feathers.

"Amazing," Casey muttered, reaching out to capture a falling droplet with his fingertip as some of the earlier heat returned to warm his desire.

Martin responded by turning his head to look down, and Casey was suddenly confronted with a face full of wet feathers as they moved against Martin's shoulders.

As the intimate moment was broken yet again, Casey took the opportunity to dodge under the advancing wing and climb to his feet in front of his friend.

He huffed in frustration, but there was no anger in it. "This isn't working."

"What isn't?" Martin brushed a wet lock of hair from Casey's temple.

"You, me, and them"—Casey tilted his head over Martin's shoulder—"in the shower. I'll admit it; the reality has turned out to be less appealing than the image in my head."

Martin snorted. "It *is* a little crowded in here."

"Any chance you could, you know, put them away? Alissa said there was no need to shower with them." Casey ran both hands up Martin's chest, brushing thumbs over Martin's pebbled nipples. "It might give us a bit more room. Then, I'll rewrap them...after."

Martin huffed in amusement again and arched into the touch. "Not if you keep doing that. I thought I explained that earlier."

Casey lifted his hands away with a grin. "Yes, right. Sorry, my mistake. I'll just stand here quietly..." He made a space between them as best he could, but couldn't resist adding, "Naked. And wet."

Martin rolled his eyes before closing them, then took three slow breaths. Martin had been right, the blazing rush of lust Casey had been half expecting didn't flash through him. Nevertheless, as Martin's face took on a preternatural stillness, something deeper and more consuming unfurled. As the wings faded and Martin's eyes reopened, Casey stepped up, cupped Martin's cheeks in his hands, and fixed him with a serious gaze.

"I'm going to push you up against the wall now, Martin. And then, unless I'm very much mistaken, I'm going to ask if I can touch your cock."

The distance in Martin's eyes vanished and a hungry fire replaced it as Martin groaned and pulled Casey into his arms, crushing their mouths together. Clearly, the time for gentleness had passed, and Casey was thankful for it.

A firm hand on the small of Martin's back made it clear that Casey wanted their bodies as close together as possible in the confined space, and Martin obliged with a lazy roll of his hips. He ground against Casey's crotch, then reached to clasp and knead Casey's arse to keep Casey pressed against him.

Casey slid his hand up Martin's back, running across smooth shoulder blades now free of their feathered burden. He took hold of Martin's hips and swung him around so he could pepper wet kisses across the now pristine skin on either side of his spine.

"Casey...yes."

"Fucking gorgeous. You're a miracle, Martin." Casey leant in, his full weight pushing him against the tiles as he trailed kisses across shoulders and down. Moving his hands to Martin's hips, he knelt on the hard tiles and continued his exploration down each defined rib and bone in Martin's back as he lowered himself. Stopping at the top of Martin's arse, he lavished attention on the concave dimples on either side before placing a final kiss where the skin began its division into two firm globes.

"Gorgeous," he murmured, resting his forehead against the smooth skin for a moment.

Martin's only response was a muffled groan of desire and a press of his hips back towards Casey.

With a hand on each hip, Casey turned Martin in place, admiring the new view of Martin from the front before pushing himself quickly to his feet and crowding against his partner where he was still pressed to the tiles.

"God, Casey..." he moaned brokenly. "Will you fucking touch me already?"

"If you insist." Casey smiled against Martin's neck, where his face was buried. He slipped his hand down Martin's slick chest and ran fingers across the defined abdominal muscles until he touched the top of his partner's cock. He circled teasingly when Martin bucked upward, greedy for more contact. At another begging moan, Casey took pity and finally circled his fingers around the thick velvet skin, his knuckles pressed into the neat thatch of hair behind it.

"Oh, God," came the muffled cry as Martin leant his head back, propped against the shower wall. "Please."

"I've got you, love. I'm here. Feels good, doesn't it? I'm going to make you feel so good, I promise."

Martin shifted his feet farther apart, a silent appeal for more and Casey didn't disappoint, settling in and working at a steady rhythm as Martin's needy whimpers gained in pitch and volume.

Casey's own neglected cock twitched, begging for attention and just as he was considering the logistics of perhaps using his nondominant hand to give himself a couple of quick strokes, Martin was there instead, his larger hand wrapped around his length, matching the pattern Casey was using on him.

Casey fumbled blindly to the side until he managed to grab the bottle of conditioner, wordlessly asked the question, and grinned at Martin's enthusiastic nod. Some awkward one-handed effort had the cap flipped open and a puddle of creamy liquid in his palm.

After discarding the bottle to the floor of the shower, the contents dribbled out to run ignored down the drain. Martin released his hold on Casey long enough to scoop some onto his fingers before catching his eyes and tugging them closer together with a questioning look.

"Brilliant," Casey murmured as he moved within reach, and Martin's large hand closed around the both of them, holding their lengths together and starting a leisurely stroke. Covering it with his own, Casey couldn't hold in the whimper as he felt the tightness beginning to build low in his balls.

Martin's hips twitched. "Yeah, that's it. C'mon."

"Martin..."

Martin moaned brokenly, his thighs trembling and hips shifting restlessly, stuttering forward and back. "God, please."

"I'm... God, Martin..." Casey's rhythm faltered as he teetered on the brink. He was fighting a losing battle. The push-pull of Martin's hips drove them together over and over again, and Casey mumbled filthy endearments that mingled with the slick sounds of their bodies moving together.

Martin shifted his feet again and gasped as the new angle brought Casey's cock into perfect alignment. Martin's hand stuttered once, twice, and then he arched and spasmed under their joined hands, groaning and covering the space between them with his release, his stomach muscles clenching reflexively. With a cry, Casey stilled and pushed one last time, shuddering against Martin.

Casey moved his hand back to Martin's hip as they shakily struggled to maintain their footing. Casey pulled back gently, moving his arms to encircle Martin's torso as they caught their breath together.

"Good... that was—" Martin grasped for words. "—that was...good."

"Only good?" Casey chuckled, leaning against his chest, his cheek resting on Martin's shoulder.

"I'll find a better word later," he huffed. "I'm concentrating on not falling down."

"Mmmmm," Casey murmured happily. "Fair enough. But I expect a proper review later."

"And if I give you a low score?" Martin asked hopefully.

"Then I suppose I'll have to try again." Casey placed one last kiss at the top of Martin's neck, just below his ear. "And I'll keep trying until we get it right."

Chapter Eight

RECURRENT NIGHTMARES WEREN'T uncommon for agents, and Casey was no exception. Less common were the gentle, comforting dreams of warmth and love and peace.

"You are safe, Casey Wicker... you are home," the voice came from within and without, with a genderless depth as if it were coming from the land itself. Perhaps it was.

Casey lay on soft green grass, the delicate blades providing a cushion beneath him, their smell like freshly mown springtime in his nostrils.

"Rest here a while. Let us gather you to us and keep you whole."

Curling tendrils of ivy erupted from the ground, poking inquisitively at him. There was no sense of threat in their movements, just a kindly, childlike brush and twitch. With wordless affirmation, Casey granted them permission to explore.

"Let us share our life with you, hold you tight in the planet's embrace."

The ivy twined around his limbs in partnership and welcome; there's no sense of alarm.

He could rise whenever he wanted, but there was no desire to do so.

"Let us stay with you."

Arms pinned to his side, the gathering vines exerted a gentle pressure on his chest and hips. He'd never felt as secure, so treasured, so loved.

"Casey..."

Casey opened his eyes to find himself staring directly into Martin's gaze, barely a hand's length away. The weight on his chest and hips resulting from Martin's warm body rather than the living vines of ivy.

They'd achieved little more than drying themselves off before crawling into bed, sated and lethargic. They curled around each other in unspoken agreement, shutting out worries about the future and just luxuriating in the feel of their bodies pressed together and the knowledge they'd wake together at some undefined point in the future.

"Good morning. Sleep well?" Casey smiled fondly, then leaned up to kiss the offered lips gently.

Martin rumbled an agreement to Casey's question with a satisfied nod. "Better than I have for some time, but I fear I'm paying the price for our earlier neglect. My shoulder was verging on unbearable when I woke up."

"I'll get you something." Casey made an unsuccessful attempt to roll Martin off him before it became evident his lover had no intention of letting him move.

"I took something a while ago and came back." Martin nuzzled his nose against Casey's jaw. "It's warmer here."

Tightening his hands around Martin's waist, Casey arched into the sinuous, increasingly rhythmic movements. "Mmmm." He paused and added, "We should get your wings strapped again."

"In a little while. There's something I've always wanted to try." Martin's tone was distracted as he gently rubbed against Casey, aligning their cocks and rutting gently together.

"If you're going to start kinky experiments in the bedroom—" Casey began to object before he rethought and chuckled lazily. "What am I saying? I'm in; I'm up for anything."

Martin lifted his head from where he was diligently sucking a bruise on Casey's collarbone and grinned, clearly delighted at Casey's capitulation. "Excellent."

"So, what do you have planned?" Casey managed to ask as Martin returned to his worship of Casey's shoulders.

"All in good time; just lie back and relax." Martin's hips maintained their steady yet maddening motion as Martin shifted his attention to one of Casey's nipples.

"I'm in your hands," Casey murmured.

"Yes...you are." Martin eased a hand down and spread some of their shared pre-come over them both, reducing the friction.

Martin took his time, showing patience at odds with his usual frenetic activity. Every gasp and whimper brought a flash of insight in his bright eyes. Repetition brought either variation or confirmation. Each thrust of Casey's hips and a shiver of muscles elicited its delightful response as Martin encouraged and built on experience. Soon, Casey was moaning against Martin's relentless attention, rolling and thrusting toward his ecstatic destination.

"I think you're ready. Casey? Can I try something?" Martin whispered against his neck.

"That wasn't the experiment?" he asked roughly.

"No...I want to see what happens if I do this...when you're close."

Martin's eyes closed, and the familiar stillness rolled through the room as Martin sought to focus and summoned his wings.

Casey could swear the ripples were penetrating the outer layers of his skin, the warmth and glow rippling wherever he touched Martin. And then the rise of bliss, engulfing as it rolled across him in a drowning wave. He cried out as it crested, arching as his muscles locked and he spilt helplessly between their bodies. A broken sob slipped from his lips, carrying Martin's name with it, and Casey wasn't entirely sure if it was pleasure or pain.

He gulped lungfuls of air, still shuddering as his thighs threatened to cramp and his fingers clawed harshly at Martin's arse, clenched tight as Martin's orgasm ripped through him as well.

With agonizing slowness, his muscles relaxed and he slumped under Martin's body, his breathing calming as the snowy sparkles dissipated from his eyes and his vision returned.

Martin smiled smugly down at him with hooded eyes. "Too much?"

"You arse!" Casey panted. "I thought I was dying!" Then he broke into giggles and pulled Martin down into a forgiving hug. "You could have warned me."

Pressing his lips to Casey's shoulder, Martin's response was somewhat muffled as he smiled against the skin. "Where's the fun in that?"

They chuckled together helplessly as endorphins and dopamine washed through their systems until Casey prodded gently at Martin. "I'll get us a flannel and we can clean up."

"Mmmmm, and then splint my wings?" As the endorphins of sex dissipated, there was a new hint of pain in his patient's voice.

Casey edged out from under Martin and left him sprawled across the bed. "Yes, Martin, and then I'll splint your wings."

OVER AN HOUR later, when his phone pinged with a message, Casey had Martin reinstated on his pile of cushions and blankets in the living room, contentedly perusing articles and books related to the jewellery case they'd been working on before Casey's unfortunate fall from the loft.

His wings were splinted and strapped, and his arm was back in its supportive sling. He glanced at his phone and then up toward Casey, tucked in an armchair and tapping out notes on his laptop, a cup of tea cooling at his elbow.

"We're about to have a visit from my brother. Alissa's notified the council, as we knew she was obligated to do. As much as it pains me to admit it, for once, he might be of some use in this."

He looked down at the invalid. "You're voluntarily letting Leon get involved?"

"His legal experience will come in handy, and he knows our laws. I received notification from the Avian Council this morning that he's volunteered to act as their intermediary until the trial and then represent us when the time comes."

"Right, then. I'll put an extra cup out."

True to plan, slightly more than two minutes later, Leon was perched on an uncomfortable kitchen chair, his usual officious stare directed at Casey and Martin.

"It's good to see you both looking so well—" Leon paused for effect "—rested."

Casey saw Martin's badly hidden eye roll. "Don't be obtuse, Leon. My sex life is not, and never has been, any of your business. Can we get on with this?"

A brief but pertinent staring contest, excluding Casey entirely, took place before Leon sighed and looked away.

"Very well, Martin. As you know, I have been counselling you for some time on the dangers of your chosen profession and the risks of exposure inherent in it."

Martin didn't respond, his silence carrying all the response his brother would expect.

"And I have long suspected that Agent Wicker discovering this was inevitable. I want you to know I'm not celebrating being right."

"I doubt that, Leon."

The volume of Leon's voice rose in a rare display of frustrated anger. "It's a *death sentence,* Martin. Do you *honestly* believe I wish you—or Agent Wicker, for that matter—dead?"

Martin conceded Leon's point, briefly averting his gaze.

"Our options are limited. However, I have negotiated what may be your only chance to salvage this disaster," Leon continued. "Martin, I am authorized to notify you that—" Leon drew a long slow breath, then read with precision from a page in front of him. "—should you be able to resecure the stake that Hedwig lost to Pooh, the council would look favourably, possibly very favourably on it."

As Martin's eyes narrowed, Casey looked between the two of them. "I have *no* idea what the hell you just said."

Leon spared Casey no more than a brief glance before smoothly rising to his feet and striding to the door. "I'll leave you to explain it to your...mascot. Solve the case, Martin. It may be the only chance you have."

"Leon—" Martin murmured dangerously before Casey stopped him with a shake of his head.

"Let it go, Martin. We've got more important issues." Casey hurried to overtake Leon, opened the door, and escorted him back down the stairs.

By the time he returned to the flat, Martin was sitting cross-legged amongst his pillows, doing his best to cross his arms in spite of the fact that one was in a sling.

"So…" Casey said. "Pooh… Hedwig… stakes… Is this some weird literary crossover?"

Martin's eyes opened, and he gestured for Casey to join him on the cushions. "Oh, no, Casey. It's far more interesting than that."

"LET ME GET this straight." Casey ran fingers through his hair as he processed the information.

Martin nodded encouragingly. Now that Casey had the information, it was just a matter of him confronting another set of highly unlikely facts in a week that had already passed its quota several days before.

"So, Pooh is"—Casey shook his head in disbelief—"code for Theodore Roosevelt."

Another nod from Martin. "Yes…Teddy Roosevelt, teddy bear, Pooh bear."

"And Hedwig is code for King…?"

"Edward. Yes."

"Because?" he asked blankly.

"Come on, Casey. Work it through. I'll help you if you get bogged down." Martin smiled as if he were teaching a small child to tie his laces.

"Well…" Casey began slowly. "Hedwig is a *Harry Potter* character, right?"

"Yes. Go on."

"In fact, Hedwig is the owl…" Casey's eyes widened, and he exclaimed, words running together in a rush. "Oh, my God, are the royal family Avian?"

Martin leaned across the pillows and clamped his good hand over Casey's mouth, grunting in pain at the need for sudden movement. "I rather think they'd prefer to keep that a secret, Casey, if you don't mind."

Casey's muffled voice continued under Martin's silencing hand until he moved it away. "Seriously?" Casey whispered. "Owls?"

"Not all owls, but King Edward was. A rather glorious, snowy owl, as a matter of fact," he said proudly. "Quite rare."

Casey shook his head, blinking as he scratched his cheek. "Right...right. Shit, an owl. Okay, all right...good."

Martin gave him the time he needed to internalize the information, sitting back and watching Casey for impending signs of more shouting.

"Okay, I've got that," Casey said thoughtfully. "So, what was that bit about a stake? Was the prime minister a vampire?" He smiled weakly.

Martin chuckled. "No, and Pooh isn't an *actual* bear, for the sake of clarity. But the stake that Edward lost to Theodore was the culmination of a rather unfortunate card game at which, well, let's just say, bids were made at a rather exceptional level."

"And we lost?" Casey sat spellbound, hanging on each word.

"Yes. Now, a *gentleman* would have allowed His Majesty to step away from the table, but we're talking about Americans here, and a rather competitive American, at that so..." Martin looked vaguely ashamed on behalf of the British nation.

"So..." Casey prompted.

"So." Martin looked terribly discomforted. "We lost the damned Crown jewels, Casey! We lost the jewels to the

United States of America." Martin spat it out as if the entire sentence was made of something bitter.

A silence fell on the room. Thick, unrelenting silence as if the country had fainted for a moment at Martin's words and only slowly came around to fan itself weakly.

Martin turned finally, meeting Casey's eyes and expecting to see the face of an Englishman whose very soul had been torn asunder. Instead, Casey had pressed his fist to his mouth and was stifling a giggle, the corners of his mouth curving up at each side of his fingers.

Giving it up as a lost cause, Casey began with a short laugh, quickly descending into helpless mirth. He wiped tears from his face as he struggled for air, holding a hand up to still Martin as his flatmate tried to interject some decorum.

"We...lost the... Oh, my God, Martin..." Casey collapsed into laughter again.

Casey's hysteria was infectious, and however inappropriate, Martin found himself first tentatively, and then more wholehearted, joining in.

"Well..." he added between uncontrolled chuckles, "stakes were proposed, as stakes are. And being who they were, things became a little ridiculous. When the president tables the Statue of Liberty, His Majesty was bound to raise the ante."

Casey was gripped by a new round of rolling giggles. "Well, who wouldn't?" he managed breathlessly. "That statue would have looked good in the forecourt of the palace."

Martin snorted through another round of laughter as he used his one good hand to hold himself up off the cushions and he did a passable impersonation of a clipped authoritative voice.

"Look, Alexandra, I can see our house from here."

"Stop," Casey wheezed. "Stop...I can't..." He gasped for breath. "It shouldn't be funny. They're our Crown jewels, for God's sake."

Martin's laughter stilled before he solemnly added, "*Were* our Crown jewels," which set another round of improper giggles again.

A calm, restorative cup of tea later and they had gathered themselves enough to discuss the situation more rationally.

"In all seriousness, Martin. I don't see how we're supposed to get them back from the States. Surely, they're—I don't know—locked up."

"And if we were recovering the originals, I'd agree. But haven't you wondered if the Americans have the Crown jewels, what do we have on display in the Tower all these years?"

Casey's eyes narrowed in thought. "Sorry, you've lost me. If the Americans have the jewels, and our replicas are in the Tower, what is Leon asking us to do?"

Martin was shaking his head slowly. "The fakes aren't in the Tower at the moment."

Understanding lit up Casey's face. "That advertisement in the Times last month that the display is 'closed for routine cleaning' is a fake!"

Martin was grinning broadly, proud as Casey logically laid the pieces out and came to conclusions. "Quite right. The forgeries were stolen over a month ago. We hope the thieves are still unaware that what they have are little more than sideshow props. It's imperative that we recover them before they discover the ruse."

Casey nodded. "Wait." Casey leant forward as a thought struck him. "That case we were working on for

Scotland Yard, were we really looking for diamond thieves?"

"Well," Martin answered cagily, "to be strictly correct, they *look* like diamonds. And the government does want them back *quite* badly."

Casey put his mug down rather roughly before he huffed an angry breath and pushed out of his chair. "So, we've been on this case all along, and you just didn't see fit to share it with me. Thanks, Martin, thanks a *lot*."

"Need-to-know basis, Casey," Martin explained quietly.

"Damn it, Martin, *I needed to know*! Fat lot of use I can be to you when you hide things from me." Casey was building up a good head of steam as he paced the flat. "You do this *all* the *time*." He looked back with a mix of anger and sadness. "Sometimes...honestly, Martin, I wonder if I know you at all."

Martin looked up agape, lost for an excuse as Casey stormed down the corridor to the bedroom. Martin winced at the sound of the heavy door slamming after him.

Chapter Nine

SOMETIMES I WONDER if I know you at all... the words repeated in Martin's head.

What rubbish. Of all the people in his life, Casey knew him best of all. Surely, Casey could see that. Only with Casey did he drop the artificial mantle of bravado and admit that sometimes he was scared. Casey shared his private moments of insecurity, sadness, tiredness, and frustration. Not even Leon knew Martin well enough to recognize when his reckless abandon needed to be tempered by the need for sleep, but Casey knew, Casey saw, and it was Casey that would order him to bed. And Martin listened, because Casey knew him best of all. He would go without question and without much complaint.

It couldn't be a matter of trust, could it? *Trust issues* both their personnel files said, not that he'd *seen* the data of course. Martin conceded that perhaps the scales were a little unevenly weighted in the trust stakes. There'd been an unfortunate string of undercover operations in which Casey might have been excluded from, both physically and mentally. And although they'd saved each other's life what seemed like countless times, if Martin looked at the matter objectively, most of the situations were ones Martin was responsible for in the first place, and often without prior warning that they would be walking into danger.

To be fair, Martin admitted to himself, he sometimes lied to Casey. All right, *often* lied to him. Or perhaps not lied…more, he rather…omitted facts. But he only did it for Casey's benefit. Should he apologize for that? There was any number of details and facts that weren't immediately pertinent to the situation or could put Casey at risk or would simply take too long to explain when Martin had already planned for contingencies. Casey couldn't expect Martin to waste valuable time sharing those with him…could he? Still enthroned in his pile of pillows, Martin tapped his fingers on the floor in frustration. At what point did informing his partner of unnecessary details impact the efficiency of getting the job done?

Glancing at the time, Martin was unexpectedly dismayed to note that it was over an hour since Casey had stormed off in a huff. Usually, there would be a notable increase in the noise level signalling Casey's irritated pacing and occasional launch of projectiles from within his room, followed by a period of silence during which Casey would no doubt be taking a series of deep, calming breaths. This would then be followed by his partner's return to the room, an extended and excruciating conversation when Martin would commit to changes he never intended to make, and life would then resume its regular cadence.

Well, if the mountain won't come to Muhammad… He pushed himself up from the cushions and headed down the hall.

"Casey…" Martin knocked gently and waited. The silence in response spoke volumes, and he tapped again. "Casey, please."

"Not ready to talk yet. Go away," came the brief reply.

This was unprecedented. Not only was Casey clearly still furious, but he was also obviously in no mood to negotiate, much less capitulate.

"I'll just sit here...in the cold...with my arm in a sling...where *anyone* could walk in." Martin sighed dramatically, loud enough to be heard through the door, the description of his injuries purposefully excluding the obvious.

In fact, there was little risk sitting on the floor in the locked apartment in the middle of the night. Nevertheless, Martin made what he hoped was an audibly dramatic show of settling in on the floorboards at the foot of Casey's door.

"Perhaps, if you're lucky, my weakened condition may make me susceptible to a life-threatening chill, and all your problems will be solved." All right, that might have been overdoing it, but desperate times were beginning to demand desperate measures, and Martin gave a pathetic cough to seal the deal.

After only a moment, Casey's frustrated voice came clearly, even muffled as it was by the wood of the door. "Oh, for *God's* sake."

The door abruptly opened, and Martin found himself being manhandled up onto his feet and through the door by his good arm before it slammed again behind him.

"Could you *be* any more dramatic?" Casey let go of his arm and returned to sitting on the bed. "No. Don't answer that. I'm afraid you'll take it as a challenge."

Martin smiled carefully and then adopted a more neutral expression when it became apparent Casey wasn't joking. He stood uneasily, crowded against the doorway and unwilling to further invade Casey's space without permission.

Silence settled between them. Not the comfortable, post-chase, crossword-finishing, tea-drinking silence of camaraderie; but the uncomfortable, I-don't-know-what-to-do, I'm-not-good at-talking-about-this-stuff silence that Martin had hoped the revelations of the past week might have banished once and for all. He realised the rising unpleasant feeling, the slow, churning unease was fear. He sensed a line had been crossed somewhere in the past days, probably several, and he was suddenly, desperately afraid that he might be on the other side of that line alone. He grasped for the right thing to say, anything to pull Casey over the line with him. Together, they could face it. They'd faced so much together.

"I can't do it without you," Martin whispered, wincing at how weak and vulnerable the words sounded.

"What can't you do? Change your bandages, make the tea, find your passport?" Casey spat back.

Even more softly, Martin admitted, "Any of it. I can't do any of it without you. Be an agent, take care of myself—" He lifted his head to ensure he caught Casey's eyes. "—be Martin Bishop."

"I don't even know who that is...apparently." Casey stood but remained unmoved next to the bed.

"But you do, Casey. You know what it means to be Martin Bishop. You show me how to do it. I can't do it." He shook his head and corrected himself. "I don't *want* to do it without you."

Surely, that will be enough, Martin thought, *tell Casey how much he's needed. Reassure him that he's essential and he'll come around, and things can get back to normal. Please, let it be enough.*

Except that it wasn't. Casey sighed and dropped his head, shaking it slowly. When he looked back up, there was a distance in Casey's eyes that Martin didn't like at all. He wanted the warmth and spirit that usually greeted him, the affectionate sparkle that had been greeting him over the breakfast table more recently, and the hooded look of desire that he'd glimpsed the past few days. Any trace of that had been replaced by a rigid stare more suited to an emergency room or a train station.

Casey shook his head again, lines furrowed between his brows, and dealt a swift, savage verbal blow. "I can't."

Martin stared at him, confused and adrift. "Can't what?"

"I can't do this. It's too much, too fast, Martin, so—" Casey's eyes hardened even as they held a hint of tears. "I'm saying no."

Martin blinked. Whatever Casey was saying refused to be parsed by his brain. "I don't understand. No to what?" He was afraid of the answer.

Casey sat heavily on his bed. "This...you...all of it. I thought I could deal with it, that it was worth it, that you, us, could be worth it, but I don't believe it is. I want it to be. God, I desperately want it. I have done, for so long. But I can't do it, not like this. You've always been like this, hiding stuff, but now..." Casey's voice broke. "It hurts, Martin, and if I'm going to stop before it breaks me, it needs to be now. I need to be able to trust you, to believe that you'll be there to catch me if I fall, and every time, *every* time, there's another bloody lie, and I end up hurt again."

Martin smiled bitterly at the irony of Casey's words. In the most literal sense of the phrase, he did catch him when he fell, and Martin ended up being the one who was hurt. But that wasn't what Casey meant. Martin found he had no words in response. His mouth opened and then closed again while Casey continued to look at him steadily with cold, detached eyes.

"I'll stay until all this shit is sorted out and then..." Casey paused as if the words were killing him. "I'll ask for a transfer, a new partner, if we survive this at all."

Martin felt the first sting of angry, impotent tears prick at the corner of his eyes and couldn't bear the thought of Casey seeing them. His steadfast, unshakable partner was declaring the situation so hopeless that he was running, and Martin's heart shattered into jagged, painful pieces that threatened to rob his lungs of air.

"You won't even try?" Martin managed brokenly.

"Damn it, Martin. I *have* been trying. Can you not see that? You can't expect me to..." Casey turned his back to Martin, and he could see his hands clenched at his sides even as the rigid shoulders slumped in defeat.

Without another word, Martin left the room and clicked the door closed behind him before returning to the too-quiet lounge.

He stared blankly at the roof for over an hour, listening for any sound that Casey might have changed his mind and was coming to talk, but the silence remained. Either Casey had fallen asleep, or he was similarly mired in shock. Finally, Martin picked up his phone and made a call.

"Alissa, it's Martin. Yes... I need a place to stay..." His voice threatened to break as he stumbled over the next words. "No, just me. Sparrow, please help me."

CASEY FINALLY MADE his way back to the lounge room over three hours later. He fully expected to find Martin in the single lounge chair, probably asleep, eyes closed and a familiar scowl on his face.

Although still firm in his resolve that a few things needed to change and, assuming they could find a way to get themselves out of the mess they'd dug themselves into this time, he hoped they could approach the situation like rational adults and preserve their professional relationship. Even if the fragile love they'd been building was irreparably damaged, perhaps they could salvage at least that.

He was prepared to admit he might have overreacted and that probably anger and exhaustion had made his message seem harsher than he intended. It wasn't that he didn't admire Martin or respect the work he did or the way he did it, and those wings were amazing...but the fact was, Martin kept shutting him out, and it just couldn't continue. Not if Casey was to stand some chance at retaining his sanity.

"Martin, look I know you're probably upset but..." Casey entered the room and found not Martin sitting in his chair but a stony-faced Leon Bishop.

"Take a seat, Agent Wicker."

"Leon, what... where's Martin?" The size of the apartment made it clear that wherever Martin was, he wasn't here.

"Sit...down...Agent Wicker," Leon repeated.

Sparing one last glance at the door of the flat, Casey nonetheless sat on the hard kitchen chair Leon had dragged over for the purpose, feeling somewhat like an eight-year-old boy caught drawing a vulgar picture on the back of the school office building.

"Thank you." Never one for joyful exuberance, Leon's flat and monotonic voice made it clear that this was far from a social visit. "In answer to your question, my brother is no longer in the apartment."

It became apparent that Leon had no intention of supplying anything but direct answers, forcing Casey to ask, "Where is he?"

"He's left. Given your last interaction, that can hardly be a surprise to you."

Casey's eyes widened momentarily. Leon continued, "And yet...it is." He added, almost as an afterthought to himself. "Dear God, please preserve us from sentiment and the ruin it rains down on otherwise intelligent men."

"Why would he leave?" Casey asked, bewildered.

Leon leant forward, his eyes narrowed. "For God's sake, Casey, what would make you think he would stay? You made your feelings quite clear. My brother may be many things, but a masochist isn't one of them."

Casey winced at the implication. "But his injuries, he needs care."

"Care?" The word came with a laugh, and it wasn't a happy one. "Yes, and he's getting it, Casey. There are others who will care for him, that *do* care for him."

Leon's not pulling any punches. "But the case?" He reached for other reasons Martin should have stayed, and then it hit him; he was expecting from Martin exactly what Martin had asked of him, the words echoed back to him, *You aren't even going to try?*

"I have other people assigned to it. They'll continue with Martin's assistance when he's well enough. Don't concern yourself; I will, of course, carry on as your advocate before the council." Leon paused for effect. "Martin would want that."

Casey realized that he'd effectively been dismissed from the investigation and a flash of anger rose. "No, I can help."

Leon got up from Martin's chair and stepped into Casey's personal space, his extra two inches giving him higher ground. "No, I rather think you can't. If you've indeed decided to distance yourself from my brother, I think you'd best start the process as soon as possible...for all concerned."

Casey pulled his shoulders back, refusing to be dismissed like an employee who'd outlived their usefulness. "So, your brother can run off and work without me?"

Leon's reaction was swift and vicious. Placing a hand on Casey's shoulder, he shoved hard until he'd pushed him up against a wall. "Don't be an idiot, Wicker. If you honestly think my brother is currently out gallivanting around London, let me disabuse you of that fantasy."

Leon pushed a USB stick into Casey's hand roughly before releasing him and storming out the door, down the stairs, and through the front door.

Casey stared down at the unassuming data-key before moving to his laptop and plugging it in.

Minutes later, he was stifling a sob with the back of his hand as tears pricked at his eyes and bile rose in his throat.

Oh, my God. What have I done?

Chapter Ten

TWO HOURS EARLIER

Alissa didn't have time to ring the doorbell, as Martin opened the door to the street and stepped through it.

He stood, immaculately dressed...*armored*, she thought, in trousers, pressed shirt, and suit jacket, his battle raiment. He carried nothing in his hands but his mobile phone and a toothbrush, both of which he tucked into a pocket before closing the door behind him.

As he flagged down a cab, Alissa approached and asked quietly, "What happened?"

The only response was a firm shake of the head and silence. She hadn't missed the lost and vulnerable look as he passed her coming through the door and didn't press further.

The trip to Alissa's flat was quiet. She was long used to Martin's silent periods. As a child, he'd never quite fitted in and had been singled out and teased as "the strange one" by the other kids. Always more opinionated, more adventurous, and more likely to get into trouble, he'd made few friends, and most of them hadn't lasted long. Alissa had found herself drawn to this insightful and solitary boy, and when all others had faded away, she and Martin became known as something of an indivisible unit.

They grew and flew together, and reaching their teenage years, it became apparent that both Martin and Alissa were finding themselves attracted to boys. After a few disappointed and hormonal tears by Alissa, they swore a lifelong friendship. One that remained sometimes bent, but never broken.

She reached over the seat of the cab and laid a supportive hand on Martin's thigh, and in a moment, it was covered by Martin's own. With a heavy sigh, he slumped in the chair, and his head fell to rest on her shoulder as if he'd simply run out of energy to hold it up any longer. They spent the remainder of the trip like that.

SHRUGGING OFF HIS jacket, he gravitated to the sofa and settled into the corner, drawing his knees up to his chest, making himself as small as possible. Alissa made a couple of quick cups of tea and came to join him.

"Want to talk yet?" she asked gently, mirroring his position at the other end of the couch.

"Soon. Promise." He held the cup with hands that shook slightly. Without warning, the words tumbled from his lips. "I can't believe I've just...left. I'm not sure why I've done that." He looked up as if hoping Alissa would have the answer.

Instead, she lowered her legs along the length of the sofa and patted her lap. Like a small boy rather than a full-grown man, Martin unfolded himself from the corner and crawled up to curl around her, his head resting on her chest, arms bending to drape loosely.

This was the Martin that nobody else saw; the ten-year-old who had been told he was being sent to boarding school, the Martin who struggled through his parents' divorce, and the grown man who had sobbed brokenly after the funeral of his first partner, as the irrational feelings of guilt consumed him. After all those moments,

Martin had crawled into Alissa's lap and let himself be held. They never talked about it, and there was never a price to be paid.

Alissa stroked Martin's hair tenderly. "Tell me all about it, Raven. Tell me what happened." Alissa kissed the skin of his forehead and smoothed soothing circles on his back.

"Casey..." Martin choked on the first word and took a shuddering breath before trying again. "He...he's had enough."

"Enough of what, Raven?" Alissa pressed gently, knowing that until he got the words out, he wouldn't be able to begin healing.

Martin buried his face in her shirt as the tears started to fall. "Enough of me, Sparrow. Like all the rest...he said I'm not worth it."

She tightened her arms around him as if she could somehow hold his heart together with her bare hands.

The gulping sobs broke her heart as he managed between breaths. "I don't know what to do. I thought maybe, this time. I thought finally... But, I never deserved him...and now...he's realized it too."

As sympathetic tears ran unheeded down Alissa's cheeks, she looked up to where she knew Leon's tiny webcam sat on the top shelf and mouthed, *"Help him!"*

CASEY SHOULD HAVE expected the shiny black town car waiting outside the safe house, and yet his head was so full of the need to get to Martin's side, its presence still came as a shock.

The electric window lowered with a mechanical hum to reveal Leon Bishop. "Get in the car, Agent Wicker."

For once, Casey didn't argue. If Leon were willing to take him to Alissa's, and therefore Martin, then he wouldn't complain. After admitting Casey to its darkened interior, the car pulled away from the footpath and into the busy London streets.

"Thanks, Leon."

"Don't thank me just yet, Casey. I rather fear you've come to the wrong conclusion regarding our destination." The door locks snicked as Leon turned in his seat to face Casey.

"I don't understand. I thought you were taking me to Martin."

Leon smiled grimly. "Yes, I know you did. Unfortunately, that's not the case."

The reality of the situation came in a rush. He was locked in a car with Leon Bishop, being taken...God knows where and for God knows what purpose. He resisted the urge to try the door handle and look any more like the small trapped animal he knew himself to be. Instead, he contented himself with a belligerent glare and crossed his arms over his chest.

"You see, Casey," Leon began slowly and deliberately. "I believe we'd made it quite clear. You were to remain at the safe house until the trial. Alissa went to some pains to ensure you understood that, I believe?" He paused and then continued. "In any case, the change in your... disposition toward my brother and your exit from the flat has necessitated something of a review of our plans."

Fighting down the urge to lash out, Casey managed between gritted teeth, "Meaning?"

"A decision has been taken by the council that you shall be accommodated until we are ready to hear Martin's case." At Casey's look of alarm, he added, "Don't be concerned, Agent. We don't believe it will take Martin more than a fortnight to overcome his injuries and recover the missing jewels."

"He won't stand for this, you know that. Martin won't help if you have me in custody."

Casey's certainty was absolute. Whatever the situation between them, Martin wouldn't abandon him.

"You're assuming he'll be informed." Leon's expression was cold and immovable. "I'm afraid you've given Martin good reason to expect that you may not want any contact with him for some time. I have to apologize for taking advantage of that."

Casey's tactical mind was working hard, sifting through options and outcomes, before he tried a different approach. "You can't just lock me up. People don't *do* that, Leon. There are laws."

"Quite correct. People don't. Avian, however..." He left it at that, and Casey came to his own conclusions.

Despairing, Casey turned away and stared out the window as the streets of London fell away behind them and the lower buildings of the outskirts began appearing through the windows.

Chapter Eleven

FOUR DAYS LATER

"Get your hands off me." Martin swatted at the doctor ineffectually. "It hurts."

She stretched the wing out again. "I know. It's supposed to hurt." *No, that's not right.* But she was out of patience with her endlessly grumbling patient.

Martin flinched away again as she stretched his recovering muscles out again and shouted, "Ow! Enough. You're a sadistic butcher."

"Oh, grow *up*, you pathetic child!" she shouted back.

They stood facing each other, both breathing hard and staring fearlessly at each other with feathers bristling at their backs. Then, in a blink, the tension broke, and they laughed hard, shaking their heads in joint defeat.

"All right." Martin straightened his shoulders and nodded. "Let's go again."

"No. Let's take a break. Tea?" Alissa threw him a towel and headed for her kitchen. "I think we might nearly be ready for you to try getting off the ground later today; maybe after dark on the roof?"

Martin grunted in agreement. He stood leaning against the doorjamb and asked more hesitantly, "Any news from Casey? He's still not answering my messages."

Alissa hated lying to him, but she had strict instructions, and Leon wasn't a person to be crossed lightly. "Give him time, Martin. Time to think might do you both good."

"Hmm. I don't see how," he replied sadly. "I'm the same irritating, thoughtless man he met five years ago. Time hasn't changed me. Now that he's worked that out, why would he come back?"

They'd had variants of this conversation several times over the past four days. Whatever Alissa said, it seemed that Martin's self-esteem had taken a battering, and with Casey "incommunicado," there was no way to resolve it. Whilst Alissa might be firmly on Martin's side, she understood. Casey had no way of knowing how fragile Martin's self-image was and how the particular words he'd chosen in haste had been thrown at Martin by others throughout his formative years in a deliberate attempt to hurt and belittle.

Additionally, although Martin might have given him a vague idea, Casey really had no way to understand just how vulnerable Avians felt exposing their wings to a human, much less entering into a sexual relationship with one. Add to that Martin's limited romantic interactions in the past, and it was a perfect storm for her injured friend.

Ultimately, the resolution would be up to them both, but Leon was right. First...they needed to save their lives.

"DAMN IT, I feel like a bloody fledgling." Martin stood and dusted off his knees again, having tripped in yet another attempt to get airborne.

"Then you know it's all normal. Come on, up you get and try again," Alissa encouraged as she touched down next to him.

"I will *never* take this for granted again. If I can only..." Martin grunted and pushed off again, the broad wings flexing strongly but unevenly, resulting in another dangerous lurch to the right. "Damn it to hell!"

"It's the price you pay for such dramatic plumage," she offered, fighting frustration with flattery. "You know that the larger the wings, the stronger the downstroke. You wouldn't be having these issues with ones like mine. Come on, Raven... adapt!" she challenged. With several strong beats of her own wings, she lifted in the air and hovered near him.

Martin growled and dropped his head for a moment, concentrating. He extended his wings and beat down once, then twice testing the push of air against them and tilting his shoulders to compensate for the weakness on one side. With a look of grim determination, he sidestepped Alissa, took three certain steps, and pushed up hard off the balls of his feet, matching the move with a downstroke of his wings, gaining enough height to allow him to build some momentum in the beats.

The grin was joyous, if somewhat short-lived as the muscles soon cramped, forcing him back to the rooftop, but he'd proven that all that was needed was time and strength and his wings could hold him again.

He grabbed Alissa and swung her around, and they laughed in shared relief.

The real work could begin now. Restore proper flight, find those damned fake jewels, and deal with the council. Then...perhaps he and Casey might have a chance to make a fresh start, or at least return to speaking terms. At least now, it was clear he felt a little less like a broken bird and a bit more like a real man again.

THE CASE, WHEN Martin was well enough to assist Leon's men, was straightforward, only the consequences to himself and Casey that gave it any sort of imperative.

Throughout the search, Martin's mood had been somewhere between headstrong and brooding. Every time he suggested something overly risky, at the moment where he'd usually expect Casey to grin at him and nod in boyish enthusiasm, he instead got a terse, disapproving glare from the operations leader. Martin's scowl had become a little deeper, a bit more withdrawn until Leon was called and requested to intervene for the team's well-being.

They'd returned to the barn Martin and Casey had been investigating, and then followed the trail to the local village. The breakthrough was made when Martin pointed out that newcomers were always...always noticed. Sure enough, three rounds of drinks at the pub and a substantial lead had directed them down a convoluted path finally culminating in a brutal fight, three dead thieves, and the "jewels" safely stashed away in a padded box in the boot of Leon's car. In all, it was very anticlimactic.

Shortly afterwards, Martin had disappeared during the laborious debriefing, and a call to Alissa quickly ascertained that he hadn't returned home.

Chapter Twelve

MARTIN TOOK THE stairs three at a time, scaling all seventeen in a few hyperactive bounds. Bursting through the door of the safe house, he called, "Casey...CASEY!" *No coat on the hook. Casey's out. Dishes put away, no plate draining on the rack. Wasn't home for breakfast. Laptop missing, curtains are drawn, a slight layer of dust on the furniture; he's been gone for over a week.*

Confirming his supposition with a quick glance in the bedroom, he pulled out his mobile and tried Casey's flat. His calls had remained unanswered despite several attempts on the way there, and now his landline was similarly unresponsive.

Information...I need information...data... Martin paced the tiny space. *Need to contact the Service, DI Carrington, friends.*

A half-dozen strides took him out of the flat, back down the stairs to the front door. He pulled it open, still making plans.

But first, I'll try his flat. Perhaps he's just sulking. Perhaps he's just...

The large black sedan sat idling at the curb, the window lowered enough for Martin to see his brother's profile through the gap. Martin pulled the door open hard enough that the handle creaked alarmingly before throwing himself in and closing it behind him.

"Drive," he snarled.

Leon nodded to the driver, eyes meeting in the rear-view mirror and they pulled into the traffic as Martin lunged at his brother, fingers encircling his throat and face inches away.

"Where. Is. He?"

CASEY FLIPPED IDLY through the stack of magazines for what seemed like the hundredth time. After the first few days of shouting and attempts to escape, he'd resigned himself to the fact that where he was being held was well-secured and guarded. With no outside contact and restricted internet access, there'd been a dwindling supply of activities to keep him amused. He'd contented himself with demanding exercise equipment and thrown himself into a slightly zealous regime of physical therapy that at least left him physically able to sleep.

But it was the mental tedium that was wearing him down. Day after endless day with nothing to challenge him. He hadn't realized how much Martin pushed him to reach beyond his own expectations. Before Martin was part of his life, the embers of his natural inquisitiveness had been banked, glowing deep inside, but now they roared and licked at his mind, threatening to consume him if he didn't find a new fuel to feed them.

He could feel the prickling of nervous anxiety picking at the edges, the sure knowledge that it was only a matter of time before the enforced idleness brought out the worst in him. He wasn't proud of his temper, and this environment was systematically robbing him of all his coping mechanisms to keep it in check. At some point, all the pent-up mental and physical energy was going to come out. The question was becoming when and towards whom.

A distant echo of shouting from far beyond his locked door brought him to his feet. The sound of distant things breaking and dull thuds of objects striking walls and floors, drew him to the barrier between himself and what was obviously something more interesting than which celebrity was cheating on their partner. He reflexively licked his lips with the desire to be on the other side of the door and knee-deep in action. The rise in his pulse rate matched the approach of the sounds, nearer and then nearer still. A pair of shouts and dull thuds matched what Casey knew to be two guards stationed at his door before a frantic rattling of the door handle motivated him to take a step back. The sound of a body forcibly striking the door accompanied a shudder of its hinges before an alarming crack signalled its swing open.

In the doorway, like an out-of-breath avenging angel, stood Martin Bishop. A bloody knick on his cheek and clearly scuffed knuckles, the only signs that he was more human than luminary being. His wings were arched aggressively behind his shoulders, and he wore a scowl that brooked no arguments.

He cast a quick, distracted glance at Casey. "You okay?"

Casey nodded dumbly as Martin strode into the room, pale eyes flashing with unsuppressed fury.

Martin stalked to the window and glanced out of it. "Unbelievable. As if they thought abducting you was ever going to end in anything but this. Totally unacceptable."

As Martin surveyed the courtyard, Leon Bishop stepped delicately over the bodies of Casey's unconscious guards, pushing some of the wreckage of Casey's door aside with the toe of a polished shoe, and stepped into the room.

"Really, Martin. You don't think this is something of an overreaction?"

Martin turned and glared at his brother. "You tell me, Leon. If the council had kidnapped, let's say...Jared..."

Leon's eyes narrowed dangerously, and he opened his mouth to speak before Martin interrupted him to continue.

"Would your retribution have been any less?" Martin crossed the room and into Leon's personal space. "What would you have done if they'd taken Jared?"

"Enough, Martin. You've made your point." Leon's sneer didn't quite hide the twitch in his cheek. "Well, gentlemen, now that I've been fortunate enough to witness this happy reunion, I'll leave you to settle your differences. I expect you have a great deal to discuss." He took a step backwards, conceding ground to his brother. "The trial is scheduled for 9:00 a.m., please be prompt. Martin, your usual room is available. Given the state of Casey's room, you may want to talk there. It would offer more...privacy."

And with that final barb, Leon turned and left them alone.

The two men stared at each other across the seemingly insurmountable distance of three feet. Neither could meet the eyes of the other for more than a few moments, and both fidgeted uneasily in the quiet of the room.

"Oh, this is unbearable!" Martin snapped before crossing the space and engulfing Casey in his arms, wings bending forward to complete the impression of surrounding him. After a brief, startled moment, Casey relaxed against him with a sigh, and they stood in silence for a few moments.

"Martin..." Casey began.

"Just a few moments, Casey," Martin asked, his voice thick. "That's all... Just give me a few minutes to pretend, before you leave me. Please."

"But…"

"Please!" Martin pleaded. "I know, nothing has changed. I came to ensure your release. I owed you that… just…please. Just let me have one last memory of you in my arms."

"I was coming to find you," Casey whispered softly against Martin's shirt.

Martin stilled, and Casey gave him time to sort through the meaning to his words.

"At Alissa's?" Martin eventually offered.

"Yeah, when I was taken… I was on my way to you. I couldn't bear to wait until you came home."

There was an odd hiccupping breath before Martin replied, "You were coming…"

"Back to you…yeah. We're not fine, nowhere near it. There's the stuff we need to sort out, loads of things, but…yeah, I want to try because…" Casey cleared his throat. "Damn it, I *hate* talking about this stuff. Because we're better together, and I can't stand being without you."

Except for a noticeable tightening of Martin's arms where they held Casey to him, there was no response. Casey quietly stood in the circle of his embrace and waited. He had some insight now of the vulnerability behind Martin's sometimes brash exterior, and there was a delicate balance to be held between the resolution of their issues and giving Martin a measure of security in Casey's faith in him.

Eventually, a hesitant voice whispered against his ear, "In spite of it all?"

Casey let slip a small laugh. "In spite of…because of— I don't know. It's all a bit mucked up in my head, to be honest. All I know is…" Casey thought before adding, "The problem isn't you, Martin. I've had a lot of time to think."

Casey smiled a little bitterly. "And I think, maybe, what I need, Martin, isn't less of you. It's more."

Martin pulled back slightly and looked down to Casey, confused.

"Sorry...sorry, that's not very clear. I'll try again." Casey dragged in a full lungful of air. "You've hidden things from me. I don't know why—"

Martin opened his mouth, but Casey hushed him with a finger. "I don't care why, Martin. But whenever I find out something else you've hidden, I freak out. Maybe I'm an insecure idiot, maybe I wasn't hugged enough as a child or something, but there it is. I panic. So." He looked down and then back up. "No. More. Secrets. That's my only condition." Casey suspected he was rambling, but he'd sworn that if he got the chance to have this conversation, he'd take it. And the only way he'd get through it was in one lump, so he forged on. "Look, I know there's stuff that doesn't matter, little stuff, big stuff, white lies...but the other things, you know the stuff I'm talking about, yeah? The stuff that matters...you need to tell me that stuff, okay?"

Casey stepped back, creating a little space between them. Enough to provide breathing space, but not so much to make Martin think he was distancing himself. He smiled warmly.

"And that's the most emotional speech I've ever made... So, I hope you realize how much you must mean to me that I made it."

Martin looked at him, mouth slightly agape and eyes a little moist. He closed his mouth and swallowed before opening it again. "Casey..." he said slowly. "I'm scared."

Of all the things Casey had heard come out of Martin's mouth—the wings, the risky strategies, the fact that he liked hot sauce on pancakes—this was the most surprising.

The simple words, uttered without reservation took Casey aback, and he paused before softly asking, "Of what, love?"

Martin's eyes widened suddenly at the word, offered without conscious thought and in the space of a heartbeat, and its importance. In response to Martin's unvarnished honesty, Casey in return, without even a moment's hesitation, had revealed Martin's real worth to him.

Swallowing, Martin continued. "I'm afraid that...if you know it all, it will be too much. I'm a lot to take. I know that. Everybody tells me, all the time. I thought if I could shield you from it, hide some of it, then it wouldn't be...so much."

Casey stepped back into Martin's arms and smiled as the enormous wings unfurled to mantle around them, enclosing them in a small, private space. "Martin, I could never get enough of you. Don't you know that by now? I know I fuss and complain and bitch about getting stuck behind enemy lines, but I need that. I need you, all of you, even the messy bits. And I need you to trust me with those bits, the messy, dangerous, and ridiculous, impossible bits. I need you to believe that I'm strong enough to handle it. And in return, I'll tell you that I can't live without you, because that's the truth, and you deserve that."

"Casey." The name came like a prayer on an exhaled breath.

"Where's your room?" Casey didn't need to add why he wanted to know. The meaning was clear in his tone.

Without another word, Martin took his hand and led him down the corridor.

The corridor that led to Martin's room ran through a small well-appointed lounge area. It was clear that Hurricane Bishop had passed that way on his path to

Casey's room, given that several strangers were stooping to pick up books and overturned furniture as the two men passed. In a red wingback chair by the fire, Leon looked up from his paper and gave them no more than a curt nod before returning to his reading. Martin grabbed a couple of sandwiches from a side table before they continued on their way.

"We'll leave the cakes for Leon," Martin whispered as he passed the platter to Casey. "He has a sweet tooth."

Casey hid his smile, but he was pleased to see the snarky sibling rivalry undiminished. The worst of Martin's rage at Casey's abduction had been spent on havoc in and around the estate, and Leon's share was to be no more than the ongoing childish feud that they'd engaged in for so many years. Although Leon's legal position as a Queen's Counsel had significant power, Casey wasn't naïve enough to believe he'd ultimately been behind Casey's incarceration.

"Here we are. I hope things are as I left them." Martin turned the handle on a nondescript door down an unremarkable hallway and held the door open for Casey to pass him and enter the room, before closing it behind them.

Bathed in light, Martin's suite was open and airy. Twin French doors opened onto a balcony containing a small table and two chairs. The room itself was dominated as much by a recessed area clearly designed for study and research as it was by the plush bed, freshly made with high-quality linens.

Casey stood for a moment and stared at the large, open space.

"What?" Martin moved up behind him as Casey assessed the room.

"It's nothing like your flat in London. I suppose I expected this to be just as cramped. I'm trying to work out why it's so different."

Martin sighed. "We may as well start now. In the spirit of..." He made quotation marks with paired fingers but rolled his eyes as he did so "...full disclosure, there is no hidden agenda about the differences between the rooms. My place in London is a small, poorly lit space housed in premium real estate. This is a light, spacious house in the countryside and the bedrooms match accordingly. This room is no more 'me' than London. You've asked for honesty, and I'll try. Don't look for mysteries where there are none, Casey. You'll drive us both mad."

Casey turned to regard Martin in the waning light, looking for signs of guile. The arches of his wing joints formed twin sentinels hovering above his shoulders, and for a moment, Casey found himself conflicted between the wish that he'd never been exposed to all this Avian madness and the miracle that was Martin's wings. Martin, in response to his look, turned so his back was to Casey.

With agonizing slowness, his wings pivoted and lifted at the tips. The quiet susurration of the feathers raised goose bumps along Casey's arms as the angle at the shoulder joint widened, and the broad planes of feathers spread. The light from the windows picked up on the whispers of indigo and emerald as the black feathers shifted and caressed one another. Martin stole a look over his shoulder, basking in the blatant admiration written across Casey's face.

And still, the wings spread, impossibly wide. Martin's strong shoulders flexed to bear the weight as his centre of gravity adjusted. Primary and secondary flight feathers, longer than a hand's-length, trailed from the lower edges, their highlights reflecting and diffracting in shimmering hues. Finally, reaching their fullest extent, they stilled, the only movement a slight vertical shift as Martin's breath moved supporting bones beneath the skin.

The silence of the room thickened, sweet and syrupy as the two men stood, effectively separated by a living wall of black feathers. Casey tried to keep his breath light and instead managed only to suppress stuttered, shallow gasps as the urge to reach out and touch threatened to overwhelm him.

"Can I?" Casey asked, his voice breaking as he reached toward the glossy mass of feathers.

Martin inched backward until Casey's fingers were buried and brushing pale skin beneath. Twin groans broke the remaining silence as Casey stepped closer and added his other hand to his exploration. Martin's gaze broke and instead his head lolled back on his neck as Casey's fingers threaded and stroked along the pinions, lost in the velvet feel of feathers and skin.

"Casey..." Martin mumbled, his voice hoarse. "You need to stop."

Casey slowed and then ceased his gentle stroking, gradually slipping his fingers away from Martin's skin. "Why? I don't understand."

Martin stumbled forward to rest a shaky hand on the doorframe, putting some distance between them as his wings lowered and visibly trembled at his back.

"Sorry." Martin's head fell forward, his forehead resting against the cool paint. "Sorry, that was my fault. I gave permission." He gasped. "I said you could touch. I just didn't expect..."

Casey stepped closer but kept his hands at his sides. "Didn't expect what? Can you explain it?" He ducked under the right-hand wing and close to Martin's side. It was warm and sheltered between Martin's arm, wing, and body, and Casey took comfort in the intimate familiarity. "No secrets, remember. Whatever it is, we handle it together, yeah?"

Martin tilted his head slightly to make eye contact. Casey's calm, direct gaze held his, silently asking for trust and honesty, and Martin nodded with a deep breath and a wry smile.

"We're not like you, Casey—the Avians. You know me, we don't make friends quickly. We keep ourselves distant. It's the way I cope, the way we *all* cope. You've seen Leon. He's much the same."

Casey nodded encouragingly and held firm barely a handbreadth away.

"Do you remember going through puberty? All those hormones and no self-control; the way every touch, every sensation was new, too much and yet not enough? Avians never grow out of it. The nerves in our wings are too close to the surface, apparently. It's like firecrackers going off if we so much as brush against a wall. When someone touches us with—" Martin blushed but continued. "—intent, it's..."

"So." Casey tried not to smirk as he whispered, "You're a bit sensitive, yeah?"

Martin shrugged. "More than a bit."

Casey reached out a gentle hand to cup Martin's face. "Martin..." he said roughly.

"Mmmm?"

"I *really* want to see how sensitive," Casey whispered, his nose brushing along Martin's cheekbone.

Martin's eyes widened a fraction. "I want that, too, but what if…"

Casey nuzzled up to Martin's ear. "None of the rest matters. The thought of you, under my hands, trembling, writhing, surrendering… I don't want to wait."

Martin sighed and leant into Casey's touch, surrendering to his firm hand at the nape of his neck and the sure one at his hip. "Then to hell with waiting. Touch me, Casey. Take me apart."

Casey backed Martin toward the bed, the broad wings drawing in slightly to avoid furniture before reflexively spreading again and beating once as Casey pushed him, slowing his fall onto the pale sheets.

"I can't believe you've hidden these all the time I've known you. How many times have we been chasing criminals and you've longed to just flap off after them?" Casey muttered, crawling onto the bed and up to straddle Martin's thighs.

Martin huffed a gentle laugh. "Not as often as you'd think. Metropolitan London isn't really conducive to midnight flights. Besides, if I'd flown off after them, I'd have had to leave you behind."

Casey chuckled easily. "And we both know how that usually ends up."

"Locked in a jail cell or bleeding out in an alley, mostly." Martin looked up at Casey, crouched over him, his shaggy blond hair falling around his face.

"Damn straight you would," Casey muttered in mock-chastisement as he settled in, nestled along Martin's side and lying on a smooth layer of feathers. "I feel like I'm laying on silk. It's soft and slippery, but dry. Is it uncomfortable?"

Rolling his shoulders slightly, Martin settled with a happy sigh. "It's good. I imagine it's a bit like having someone go to sleep on your arm. I'll let you know when I lose feeling in it."

"You imagine?"

Martin clarified with a chuckle, "I'm hardly a blushing virgin, Casey; not by a long shot, if that's what you're implying. But let's just say...*snuggling* hasn't featured much in my past experiences."

"Is that what we're doing? Snuggling?"

"What would you call it?" Martin curled an arm around Casey, pulling them more tightly together.

"I was hoping we'd call it foreplay, but if you're still healing, if you want to wait...?"

"Does it look like I want to wait?" He glanced down toward his crotch, tenting his trouser so tightly the fabric puckered.

Casey followed his gaze, and a quick lick of his lips cleared the saliva that suddenly pooled in his mouth. "Well, I'm not sure I can see properly with all that material in the way." Casey smoothed his hands down the soft fabric of Martin's shirt to hook his thumb under the waistband of Martin's trousers.

"I can remedy that." Martin lifted long fingers to the buttons of his shirt before Casey's own covered them and stilled their movement.

"What do you say you let me do that?" Casey looked up for permission, gaining a surprised affirmation as Martin lowered his hand once more to Casey's chest, silently rubbing at the soft T-shirt.

Releasing one snug button at a time, Casey whispered intimately, "I can't believe you've never had a lover. You're breathtaking."

Martin huffed in frustration. "I said you weren't the first—"

"I said *lover*, Martin." Casey levered himself up to pepper kisses on the pale skin as it appeared in the vee of the open shirt. "You may have had sex, but if you've never snuggled, then you've never had a lover. Certainly not a good one."

"I..." Martin gasped a stuttered breath as Casey nosed his way into the increasing gap in the shirt, still methodically unclasping buttons. "I...don't see the difference."

"I promise that by tomorrow you will." Casey reached the bottom of the buttons and pulled the fabric out of Martin's trousers, all the while continuing to murmur softly.

"You see, sex is about getting off." He smiled against Martin's belly button, his voice muffled. "I mean, *making love is, too, obviously.*" He lifted his head and grinned. "But making love is more, or it should be. It's about the other person, about caring about their pleasure." Casey gently unclipped the fastening on Martin's trousers. "And them caring about yours."

The sound of the zip was loud, and Martin reflexively clenched his fist in Casey's T-shirt.

"So, tonight, Martin, I'm going to see to your pleasure." Casey nuzzled at the black cotton briefs exposed under the trousers, his voice rough. "And I'm going to take my time about it, because that brings me pleasure. I'm going to take my time," he repeated soothingly. "And we'll slow down sometimes, and...and we'll speed up when you want. I'm not on any timetable here, and I don't have any expectations."

Martin looked dubious, and Casey wondered at the careless use he must have suffered in the past to leave him so jaded.

"No...expectations," Casey said firmly, smiling all the while, "because I get to have you here, in my arms. And that's something I never expected to have." He nuzzled against the black fabric again. "I'd never actually considered it, if I'm honest. I get to be here with you now, and that's a miracle. We don't know what the trial will bring tomorrow, so I'm going to fucking well enjoy myself, Martin Bishop. And that means—" Casey sat up and pulled his T-shirt over his head. "—that I intend to show you the time of your life."

CASEY WAS TRUE to his word. Over an hour later, Martin lay naked on the bed with an equally naked Casey Watson settled between his splayed legs, tonguing lazily at Martin's still erect cock.

"Casey... Oh, my God... Casey..." Martin's pulse visibly beat in his carotid artery at his throat.

"Mmmmmm..." Casey eased off again as Martin's breathing hitched and there was a warning spasm under his lips. He laid his head on Martin's thigh and looked up at him through lowered lashes.

"I...this..." Martin struggled to form a coherent sentence. "I had no idea."

Casey smiled. "Enjoying yourself? Want some more?"

Martin looked torn for a moment before shaking his head and reaching out his arms. "Want you up here."

Casey crawled up the bed and sprawled across Martin's chest, leaning in for a kiss. Whatever concerns Martin might have implied regarding his oversensitivity, he kissed like a champion. Martin kissed with passion, confidence, and more than a little advanced technique. It evened up what could have been a very unequal power play, and Casey joyfully gave himself up to Martin's lavish attention, groaning as Martin's agile tongue pushed between Casey's lips and began a slow seduction of his tongue.

Casey trailed his fingers across Martin's ribs and edged down toward his wings, still spread wantonly across the bed under him. Grazing fingertips gently between the crisp white secondary, he ran delicate nails across the skin hidden beneath them.

Martin gasped and pulled back. "Casey..." he said warningly.

"No?" Casey asked, stilling the movement.

"Just... slow...go slowly, or this is all going to be over very shortly."

"I can do slowly." Casey grinned and inched ahead with his fingertips again, watching Martin's eyes. "Slow is good. Just tell me what you need."

"It's good..." Martin's voice sounded distant, and the wings shivered under Casey's hands. "It's so good."

"Can you manage a bit more information? Harder, softer, higher, lower... Give me a hand here, Martin."

Martin groaned and shifted his hips restlessly. "That sort of depends on what you want?"

Casey chuckled, deep and darkly amused, and rolled his hips where they pressed, hard and self-explanatory against Martin's. "I think you can guess what I want."

"Yes..." he whined, eyes rolling back as his head arched back into the pillows. "Please, yes."

"Are you sure?" Casey hadn't come to bed with any assumptions on how far the night would take them, but now he was here, fucking Martin seemed an outstanding idea.

Martin's blue eyes opened and sought Casey's. Behind the desperation and arousal, there was an unshakable openness. Slowly, he nodded. "I want more. We don't know what tomorrow will bring. I want this. I want you."

"Then, tell me...tell me what you want." Casey kissed Martin's outstretched arm where it lay along the feathers, lax and pale.

Hesitantly, Martin leant to lick Casey's neck, pausing when he reached his ear and whispered, "I want you. I want your fingers sunk deep in my feathers while you're sunk deep within me."

Casey sucked in a rushed breath as Martin continued.

"I want to wrap my wings around you. Cocoon us together while you take me, and I want to forget that this might all end tomorrow.

"Yes..." Casey breathed, his head fallen back on his shoulders as Martin's words rumbled at his ear. "Oh God, yes, Martin."

It took some manoeuvring to arrange themselves to allow Casey to reach both Martin's wings and his arse, and yet more time as Martin curled against Casey, his pitiful whimpers warning Casey when the stimulation to his wings necessitated Casey slowing down.

Finally, Casey was content with his preparation, and he murmured a gentle "Come here. You're more than ready."

The way Martin crawled into Casey's lap was intimate and vulnerable, Casey's back against the headboard, and Martin straddling his hips, knees bent up at a seemingly impossible angle. Casey raised his knees, giving Martin some support at his back. The wings stretched wide before drawing in, Martin curving them around, enclosing them in a musky-smelling alcove all their own.

Casey's strong arms circled around Martin and down to settle under his thighs. As Martin rested his hands on Casey's shoulders for balance, Casey steadied him as Martin lowered himself, gently bringing their torsos together, so Martin was poised, Casey just rubbing against his sensitive, loosened hole.

"Easy, love, I've got you," Casey whispered, easing him down inch by inch.

Martin's eyes closed and his lips tightened minutely as he continued to descend into Casey's lap. As his arse touched the tops of Casey's thighs, his mouth fell open with a wordless *O* as Casey's hands moved and settled at his hips.

"You okay?" Casey's voice was hoarse with his struggle to resist the urge to move and the sure knowledge that with all the earlier teasing, Martin was balanced on a knife-edge of arousal.

Martin's eyes opened and sought Casey's. the flighty panic in his pale blue eyes settling as Casey's steady gaze held his. He panted a few deep breaths and nodded more calmly.

"Okay, okay, good." Casey cast a lustful glance at Martin's wings. "You think you can last a little while?" At Martin's doubtful face, he hurriedly added, "It's okay if you don't. I'm not going to last either."

"Casey..."

"Yes, love?"

"Thank you."

Tears burned at Casey's eyes, hot and sudden, and he wrapped his arms around Martin, holding him tight. "Nothing to thank me for. You're the best partner, the best friend I could ever have. Thank you for this."

Martin rocked gently against Casey, his hips making a tiny circle, and Casey responded with a slight thrust, steadying Martin with his hands. They set up a steady rhythm, slowly increasing in pace as Martin became more confident in his self-control. The arrangement wasn't ideal, putting Martin's head slightly too high for Casey to reach without difficulty, but they managed, exchanging sloppy kisses between thrusts.

As the tempo became increasingly frantic, Martin grunted, "Casey...my wings...touch..."

"Yes...oh...yes." Taking his hands from Martin's hips, Casey reached out to card his fingers through the giant feathers as they brushed close to his shoulders and face. The wings shuddered, ripples of pleasure washing through them as Martin rocked back and forth. Casey turned his head and buried his nose amongst the plumage, his panting breath stirring the skin underneath and Martin growled low in his throat.

"Christ, Casey...do that again."

Raking his fingers down the rows of feathers once more, Casey made a concerted effort to direct his hot breath onto the skin buried beneath them, and Martin keened, the sound sending a rush of ecstasy straight to Casey's cock, buried deep within Martin.

"Martin, oh, God, Martin...I can't...I...oh!" Casey thrust erratically once, twice more and reached to grip hard at the long bones along the top ridge of Martin's wings, spilling deep inside him. The combination finally broke what little restraint Martin had left, and he rocked forward into Casey, his release spreading wetly between them.

Casey took his hands from the quivering wings and wrapped them around Martin, shifting them both to lie more comfortably on the bed. They clung to each other, and their breathing steadied, strength returning to their limbs.

"I'll get a cloth," muttered Martin, trying to ease himself away.

"In a second, just stay here a bit."

"We're a mess." Martin chuckled, nose amongst Casey's hair.

"We're always a mess, that's nothing new." Casey giggled back.

In a couple of minutes, Martin tried again. "I'll...get a cloth."

"Shhhhh" came the sleepy reply.

When it became apparent that Casey had no intention of releasing him, he asked, "What are you doing?"

"Snuggling, Martin. This is snuggling," Casey slurred on the edge of sleep.

"Oh..." Martin replied with a smile and settled back into Casey's arms.

Chapter Thirteen

WHEN CASEY AWOKE the following morning, the sheets beside him were empty, and Martin had gone. After a quick wash and a run past his old room for some fresh clothes, he set off after his absent lover.

In other circumstances, Casey supposed the sudden disappearance of a partner the morning after sex might be cause for concerns, but this was Martin, and if he were honest, he'd have been more alarmed if he'd awoken to his head beside him.

A buffet had been set up in what he'd come to refer to as "the Study," and without an invitation, he loaded a plate and settled in beside Martin's brother.

"Agent Wicker. I trust you had a good night." Leon tone made it clear he was under no illusions as to what sort of night Casey had experienced.

Casey blushed but nevertheless answered without wavering, "Fine, thanks. You?"

"I always find the country air to be incredibly... stimulating. I'm sure you agree?"

Not rising to the bait, Casey changed tack. "I was wondering if you'd seen Martin this morning. I'd quite like to have a chat before the hearing."

"I'm sure you would. I must say, I'm pleased you and my brother seem to have settled your differences, although I fear it may be too little, too late."

In the high emotion of yesterday's dramatic events, Casey had pushed thoughts of the trial somewhat out of his mind. "But surely...the jewels have been recovered, after all."

Leon made a noncommittal noise at the back of his throat. "Let's wait and see, shall we? In any case, you wished to know where my brother is? You'll find him in the conservatory. He said there was—and he specifically asked that I used these exact words—*one last secret to share with you*. You'll find it down at the end of the hall, through the double doors."

It was clear that with these words, Casey had been dismissed and he took the hint, grabbing a few pieces of toast and a handful of grapes from his plate before excusing himself and making his way down the hall.

As he neared the end, the deep thrumming beat accompanying music became clearer. The faintly familiar melody resolved itself to something classical and opulent, luscious strings accompanying deeper woodwinds as they rose and fell. The double doors of the conservatory were open, and Casey expected to find Martin sitting and reading, or perhaps enjoying the watery crepuscular light that streamed through the floor-to-ceiling windows.

What he never expected was to find Martin dancing.

Lost within his own world, Martin danced shirtless, his wings the only accessory on his torso. A pair of gauzy beige trunks wrapped his lower body from hips to thighs, looking more like artfully draped scraps than any real clothing. He spun and whirled across the floor, bare feet flexing with each step and leap.

Casey stood in the doorway, entranced by the fluid grace of the man in front of him. The previous impression he'd had of ballet being in some way an effeminate sport was driven from his mind. There was nothing remotely feminine in Martin's movements. Each step, each bunch of thigh muscle translating into a seemingly effortless leap. Each lunge and roll before springing away spoke of strength and control and was charged with masculine fire. This was the dance of a man fully in control of his body and who knew exactly what he could do with it.

But what transported the dance from the mundane to the miraculous were Martin's wings.

Black and shiny as freshly laid pitch, they formed an integral part of the dance. As he leapt, they spread. When he landed, they curved to shelter his form from view. They enhanced and exaggerated each move, but with an indefinable subtlety that left Casey agape.

Martin turned and moved again, taking a handful of steps and pushing up into the air. What would have been an artful rotation for any traditional dancer was instead transformed into an elaborate roll as he ducked his head and swung his feet up and over his head. At the same time, his wings and arms counterbalanced to give him time to uncurl and land, continuing the move across the floor as if it were the most common dance move in the world.

As Martin spun, his wings stretching to their full width, the emerald and sapphire highlights catching the sunlight through the windows, the breeze from them brushed Casey's fringe away from his face. It was the most beautiful thing he'd ever seen, and he slid to the floor, admiring art made flesh in front of him.

Some sound as Casey's knees hit the timber floor must have alerted Martin to his presence because he turned his head toward him after completing a complex combination of leaps and turns and came to a gentle stop with the final bars of the music.

He grinned and stepped lightly toward Casey and helped him to his feet. "Nothing like stretching the muscles out early in the morning. Sleep well?"

Martin stood drawing deep breaths, his bottom ribs springing into stark relief against the dark skin of his abdomen as it repeatedly hollowed out and refilled below them.

"I had...no idea." Casey cast an appreciative eye down Martin's torso before dragging his gaze back to the sparkling blue eyes. "You can dance... I mean, you can *really* dance."

"I love it, Casey. I thought you'd like to know." A touch of seriousness made a valiant effort to break through his effervescent mood. "No secrets anymore. I gave you my word."

"I've never seen you dance like that...and you're unbelievable at it."

Martin grabbed a towel from the floor and wiped his face, the sweat making his hair shine in the light. Meanwhile, his wings arched back and flapped lazily, creating a musky breeze that flowed around them, further cooling the early-morning air. "My teacher would have disagreed with you, but I appreciate the sentiment."

Casey grinned and slid his arms around Martin's damp torso, pulling him close. "I suspect he wasn't as hopelessly biased toward the dancer."

Martin snorted. "We should get changed for the trial. It starts at nine."

"What do you expect will happen?" Casey pulled back a little and looked up. "Has Leon spoken to you?"

Martin's brow furrowed. "Only to say he'd do what he can. To be honest, he didn't sound hopeful."

"But you found the jewels. That's what they wanted."

"What they want and what it's worth can be very different things. Come on. I need a shower." Martin led Casey back to their rooms, neither of them asking the question that hung heavy in the air—what would they do if the outcome of the trial was bad.

NOON

The arguments had been made, the evidence presented, and witnesses to character, both positive and negative had been brought forward. Leon had clearly brought every ounce of his experience with the courts and, with all the finesse of a diplomat, argued Martin's case and the mitigating circumstances.

Throughout, Casey's mood had slumped from slightly optimistic to vaguely hopeful to a little concerned, and now sat somewhere around rather worried. Martin had made no secret regarding the severity of Martin's instinctive reaction to save Casey and thus expose the Avians, and everything he'd heard in court only made Martin's action seem more foolhardy. Casey was beginning to think, jewels or not, a miracle would be needed to get them out of there unscathed.

"Gentlemen," the judge began. "Martin Nathaniel Bishop, you have been charged with treason, to wit you knowingly exposed your wings and thus the Avian race to a human, one Casey Wicker."

Martin stood, eyes downcast as the verdict was read, his hands gripping the rail in front of him.

"The court has heard that this act was committed in a reflexive and, I must say, noble attempt to save the life of your long-time colleague and friend. One who has, in the past, saved your life on several occasions."

Martin's cheek twitched but otherwise portrayed no outward sign of stress.

"You are aware that the traditional sentence for treason of this type is death. However, as Leon Bishop has demonstrated, you have an extensive history of providing service to Her Majesty's nation, most recently in the recovery of the missing jewels, a matter of some importance to us."

Casey reached out and brushed a finger against Martin's hip in silent support.

"Therefore, it is the judgement of this court that due to the mitigating circumstances, death is an overly harsh punishment. Instead..."

Martin dragged in a silent breath and held it, eyes still on the floor.

"You are sentenced to the surgical removal of your wings. If you cannot abide by our laws, you will henceforth be denied the primary feature of our race." The gavel struck down, and its woody echo rang through the room.

Martin's knuckles went white where they gripped the railing, although not visible to those in the room, Casey saw his friend's knees tremble and threaten to give way before he righted himself and lifted his gaze to face the chamber. Leon turned and met his brother's eyes in concern, and to his surprise, Casey saw the glint of a tear in their corners.

Before Casey could fully process the verdict, the judge continued, "Casey Wicker..." Casey turned to stand, shoulders back and spine straight, focus firmly fixed on the judge who held his future.

"It has been explained to you that, as a human, you would normally be outside the jurisdiction of this court to charge. However, human/Avian law allows for situations such as this, where a person has been exposed to our population, and thus, you are being sentenced in accordance with the *Collateral Damage Act of 1896*, as a result of Mr. Bishop's treason charge. Whilst the court is aware that exposure to the Avians was in no way your fault, the fact remains that your inability to follow the directives of our council, to wit staying within the confines of the safe house at..." The judge looked down, referring to his notes. "Twenty-two Appleby Street, Camden, leads us to believe that you present a very real and ongoing danger to our people. Something of an 'unexploded bomb,' if you like, primed to go off without warning, and as such, this situation cannot remain unaddressed."

Casey's lips tightened, but he remained silent. He could feel Martin's stare on him, watching silently, but he continued to focus on the judge.

"The survival of our species must be held above the value of any one man, and it is, therefore, the judgement of this court that for the good of our people, the threat you present must be neutralized..."

Casey noticed Leon moving silently toward Martin as his lover gasped at his side.

"You will, therefore, be put to death immediately after the removal of Mr. Bishop's wings tomorrow. I'm deeply sorry, Agent Wicker."

He had just enough time to hear Martin growl angrily and vault the wooden barrier and Leon running to intercept him before hands grasped his arms from behind and dragged Casey away.

Chapter Fourteen

CASEY WAS ROUGHLY shoved through a door into an unremarkable room containing nothing more than a kitchen table, a couple of chairs, sink, and cupboard. For over an hour, he paced the room, occasionally testing the doorknob, which remained resolutely locked.

Eventually, his guards returned, and he was moved again, this time, back to Martin's room.

As the door closed behind him, he noted Leon sitting quietly, watching him from a wing-back chair nestled in one corner of the room, hands clasped on the arms in a mannerism he shared with his brother. Casey knew that however controlled Leon appeared, frustration was simmering just below the surface.

"Where's Martin?" The question was simple, direct, and the most fundamental of Casey's current needs.

"My brother is currently being brought here. He's been sedated."

"*What?*"

"After your sentence was read there was—" Leon winced. "—an incident. My brother may have...lashed out, somewhat."

Casey smiled. He could just imagine *the incident.* He hoped Martin had at least made contact with the judge before they took him down.

"I doubt this is the time for levity, Agent. Do I have to remind you of the judgements?" Leon's words were harsh.

"Is it any surprise that Martin's reaction was so... explosive?"

"They're going to take his wings," Casey whispered brokenly. "I imagine that explains his response."

Leon looked down his hawk-like nose and sighed. "Oh, Casey. Still so blind to my brother's heart. He might survive the loss of his wings. He'll never survive the loss of you." Leon dropped his face into his hands and added with the surprising sentiment. "I fear I've let you both down. I was supposed to defend you. They may as well have sentenced you both to death."

Casey looked at Leon's bowed head, suddenly so silent, and realized that the words were right. They'd come too far now for either of them to go on alone. Casey had begged Martin to never leave him behind again, and he saw with shattering clarity that the opposite was equally true. On hearing Martin's sentence, he'd thought nothing could be worse; he'd been wrong.

Before he had gotten any further with the thought, the door opened and several uniformed men escorted Martin into the room, although escorted might have been an exaggeration. With one arm draped over each man's shoulder, Martin was virtually dragged between them, head lolling low on his shoulders.

"Jesus." Casey sat up in bed. "How much did you give him?"

"Enough," Leon replied grimly, arising from the chair and walking over to lift the edge of the bedsheets as the two men unceremoniously dumped Martin face down.

"Thanks..." The slurred words arose muffled from where Martin's face was pressed to the pillows, and Casey leant over to roll him gently onto his back.

"I'll leave you two alone. Take care of him, Casey." Leon stopped by the bed and in an uncommonly loving gesture, ruffled his little brother's hair. "He needs you."

Casting one last glance down where his fingers lay on short dark curls, Leon carefully erased any sign of emotion from his face, lifted his hand away, and walked from the room.

Casey placed a finger under Martin's chin and lifted his face up so he could get a good look at his eyes. As expected, the pupils were dilated, and Martin was having trouble holding his head still as Casey checked him.

"Hiiii," Martin slurred. As he sat up, a hand came up sleepily to ineffectually cup Casey's cheek. "Are you going to...kiss me?" He ended the question with a comically exaggerated pout.

Casey couldn't resist a brief laugh. He knew he should be concerned by the Avians dosing Martin, but he couldn't find it within him to care, given the bleak future they had before them.

His immediate concern was to make Martin feel comfortable, secure, and let him sleep it off. "Maybe. If you're very good for me."

Martin's eyelids drooped in a way Casey suspected was intended to look seductive and instead just looked tired. "Oh...I can be very *very* good." Martin then swayed toward Casey who grabbed him by the shoulders and redirected the momentum, so Martin was again lying on the bed.

"C'mon, you, let's tuck you up, and you can have a nap," Casey said soothingly.

Martin reached up. "Nooo...need you here. Don't leave me, Casey." The plaintive tone cut to Casey's heart, and the touch of panic behind the words was clear.

"Shhhh, I'll stay. I'll be right here, love." Casey curled under the sheets and nestled up tight behind Martin. It wasn't the most comfortable of positions, wedged between the two wings, one below and one above, but time was running short for both of them, and as Casey curled his arms around to wrap against Martin's chest, he suddenly found that there was nowhere else he'd rather be.

Martin whimpered and clutched Casey's hands together on his chest. "They can't take you from me... I can't...I..." Martin lapsed into an uneasy sleep.

Watching the last rays of light dwindle through the large windows, Casey sighed sadly and wriggled slightly higher so that he could fit his chin on the curve where wing met shoulder. As heavy tears finally breached the barriers of his eyelids and rolled down his cheek, he sobbed silently, surrounded by the feathers he'd come to love as much as the man who bore them.

MORNING SUNLIGHT STREAMING through the window, Martin sat straight up in bed, dislodging Casey from his nest buried amongst the feathers, and shouted, "*Unexploded bomb!*"

Before Casey even rubbed his eyes and sat up, Martin had sprung from the bed and was heading for the door, pulling a robe around his shoulders as he bolted.

"Martin? *Martin!*" Casey was slower to disentangle himself from the sheets and hopped from foot to foot as he tried to pull on shoes before heading after the manic Avian.

After a modified game of cat-and-mouse where the mouse remained oblivious to the cat as he barrelled down corridor after corridor, Casey finally caught up to him, grabbed him by the arm, and stilled the headlong rush.

"Where..." Casey grabbed some much-needed air. "Where are you going?"

"The vault, Casey...the estate vault! Come on." He tugged Casey's restraining hand off his arm, anxious to resume his journey.

"What? Why? Oh, tell me on the way." As he released his grip, Martin took off again, pulling his mobile from his pocket and tapping out a text while at a steady jog.

"See, this is what happens when you're not with me. I miss the obvious things. It should have been obvious," Martin muttered to himself.

Casey kept pace, knowing better than to push for information. He was better served to save his breath and to let Martin lay it out in his own time.

"The jewels, Casey. They were too easy to find. Stupid..." he berated himself. "We were supposed to recover them, but they needed them found. They wanted them back in the tower."

"I don't think... Oh!" Casey slowed minutely in realization and then picked up his pace again to catch up. "When you said unexploded bomb. You think there's a bomb in the jewels?"

"I *know* there's a bomb!" Martin turned and grinned as they approached a dull grey desk manned by an officious-looking woman in a suit. "Open the vault."

"Don't be ridiculous, sir. I have no intention of..."

"Do as he says..." Leon's voice came from behind them. Casey turned to see Martin's brother, flanked by some of the senior council members.

"Yes, sir," she said meekly before pushing a button.

As Leon stepped up to stand beside his brother, he muttered, "I don't know what you're doing, Martin. But I hope you have a plan."

Martin made a dismissive noise before stalking into the open vault and crouching by the padded case containing the recovered fake jewels.

Delicately he opened the lid and leant to sniff at them.

"Casey, come here," he called over his shoulder, and Casey joined him on the floor. "Smell that?"

"Smells like motor oil," Casey recalled his bomb training. "C-4?"

Martin nodded grimly. "Get the people moved back, Casey."

Casey rose and ushered the small audience out of the room, briefing Leon in low tones as Martin gently eased the two halves of the Sovereign's Orb apart, careful not to disturb the arrangement of wires inside.

"*Casey!* I need you over here." The call brought him running back to Martin's side.

Casey leant in close, looking down at the simple mechanism cradled in Martin's hands and whispered, "Looks straight forward, simple trip switch activating a timer."

"I know..." Martin muttered close to Casey's ear, "but I need you to make a show of disarming it."

"Why?" Casey whispered back.

Martin spared him a glance loaded with meaning.

"Oh." An unpleasant thought occurred to Casey. "Just promise me it wasn't you that hid the bomb in the first place."

Martin snorted. "Of course not. Great idea though. I wish I'd thought of it."

"Shh, this is serious. We have a bomb in our hands." Casey cleared his throat with a cough and bent over the device. "So...pull the blue?"

"Good to see you passed *Introduction to Simple Bombs*."

"Just checking..."

"Let's add a little drama." Martin raised his voice so he could be clearly heard by those outside the room. "Thank God you're here, Casey. With the timer so short, there would have been no chance to evacuate."

Casey sighed as Martin continued.

"There's no way I could have done this myself, it needs your delicate touch," he called loudly.

"Can I do this now?" Casey asked in a murmur. "My knees are cramping up."

Martin looked back and nodded. Casey deftly tugged at the wire, disabling the amateurish device. Whoever was behind this, they were obviously relying on it being returned unseen, rather than resisting any attempt to disarm it.

Martin rose to his feet, the two now-separate halves in his hands, and Casey joined him as they went to greet the assembled group.

"There you go, Leon. A souvenir. Just as well we were on hand to save your feathered skins." Martin blithely tossed the orb to his brother as they pushed through the crowd.

"Come on, Casey," he added in a loud voice. "I think we still have a couple of hours before they kill you and mutilate me. I feel like a walk in the garden."

The assembled council watched them walk away, silent with mouths open.

Martin pushed past the double doors leading to the expansive gardens, rare English sunshine filtering through the scattered clouds.

"Good day as any to die, I suppose." Casey stretched his shoulders and walked out onto the grass.

"I'm hoping our efforts this morning might at least make them think about softening your sentence."

"What about yours?"

"If I can only have one or the other, you know which I'd choose, Casey. I'd do anything to save you." Martin looked at him, the affection evident beneath the sadness.

"Still, after all you've done for them..."

"It's our law, Casey. I can't claim ignorance when I jumped after you. I knew the penalty and was willing to risk it, and gladly. It just seems somewhat ironic that the price of saving you is for me to be responsible for your death. You don't deserve it. You've done nothing wrong."

They walked on toward a grove of fruit trees for a while before Casey broke the silence. "You could run, you know, or fly. Get away from here; save yourself."

"As if," Martin replied.

"Yeah, didn't think that would work."

"Generous of you to try, though."

"You know me. I'm a saint. What do you want to do with our last hours?"

Martin stopped and arched his back, spreading his wings in the summer sunshine, the delicious greens and violets shining in the light. "I can't think of anything I'd rather do than share them with you. Ideas?"

"Actually...one. If you wouldn't mind," Casey began timidly.

"Anything." Casey had Martin's full attention now, brown eyes locked on lighter blue.

"Fly for me, Martin. I still haven't seen it, and I'm never going to get another chance," Casey asked, a touch of bittersweet to his tone.

"Really, that's what you want?"

Casey nodded with surety. "Really. Come on, Martin. Impress me."

Martin smiled and unbuttoned his shirt, reaching behind to unlace the loose ties that kept the fabric closed below his wings. Casey hadn't given much thought to the intricate tailoring required to allow Martin to remain clothed while his wings were visible. He'd become so accustomed to Martin in his fitted shirts that the majestic wings protruding from the back seemed a natural extension of his friend's wardrobe.

Sparing one last look back at Casey, Martin turned to face ahead, and with three quick strides with matching solid downbeats, he pushed off the ground as if diving into a pool. The difference was, of course, that he simply didn't come down. With each strong beat, he lifted higher as he pushed up through the air. Clad in nothing but his tailored trousers, his dark hair, tanned skin, and wings like a shadow on the sky, relieved only by the flash of white feathers hidden on the undersides and the gemlike reflections on the darker feathers.

Even from a distance, Casey could see the broad grin on his face, teeth shining whitely as he reached the top of an arc and paused before tucking his wings to dive, then spread again to swoop horizontal with the ground. He wondered what it must be like to have such a gift and so rarely be able to use it. Martin clearly loved being in the air, and Casey silently swore that, if by some miracle they made it through this, he'd find a way for Martin to revel in his ability more often.

Martin curved away and gained height again before swinging back toward Casey and soaring over him, shouting something that was lost to the wind as he passed.

"*What?*" Casey shouted back.

Pausing in an unsteady hover high overhead, he pointed down to Casey and gestured with his arms overhead.

Casey shook his head. *"I don't understand!"*

Again, the determined motion of Martin raising his hands over his head and Casey unquestioningly mimicked the gesture as Martin nodded enthusiastically.

In a moment of clarity, Casey understood what was planned. Hurriedly planting his feet evenly to provide a stable base, he reached up with more commitment and opened his hands, ready to grip Martin's as he went past.

As Martin dove toward him, reaching down, eyes alight with reckless adrenaline, Casey had less than a handful of seconds to realize that it was unlikely that Martin had ever tried to lift another person before, much less a full-grown man. Casey cast his doubts aside as Martin's wrapped strong hands around his forearms, sliding briefly to lock at his wrists. There was a deep grunt from Martin, a violent wrench and Casey was momentarily airborne before his feet touched the ground. Martin released his grip and curved away again.

Casey looked up. Martin hovered in the same spot above him, gesturing to raise his arms again.

Martin rolled his shoulders to loosen them before beating his wings, and Casey suspected that when this second attempt came, it was going to be hard and fast.

His conclusions proved to be correct. Martin rushed toward him. A slap stung against his forearms as he was gripped, held, tugged, and then suddenly, magically lifted aloft. He found himself hanging below Martin a mere foot from the ground as Martin's wings carved long, forceful slices through the air. A glance up showed his lover's face etched with determination, a light sheen of sweat springing on his forehead as he battled with gravity and inched higher.

Slowly, Martin adapted to the extra weight, and they gradually gathered height. The stress cleared from Martin's face and his eyes opened.

"You're bloody heavy." Martin grinned down to where Casey hung from his hands.

"I thought you worked that out in the barn." Casey grinned back.

"I won't be able to keep us up here for long, but I thought you'd like the chance to see the world from my perspective."

Casey looked down. They were now over roof height, and he was able to see the actual size of the estate he'd been confined in. Enormous didn't begin to describe it, and Casey idly wondered who owned it. Turning his head, he looked out over the groves and fields.

"It's amazing."

"If we'd had time, I'd have shared more with you," Martin said sadly over the sound of the wind.

"We shared enough, Martin. More than I ever hoped. Whatever happens, it's been enough."

Martin lowered Casey to the ground before landing and turning to face him, frustration in his eyes. "It's not sufficient. I'm greedy, Casey. I wanted more. I wanted so much for us. I wanted years of travelling, and missions and driving the hierarchy insane. I wanted to get us in so much trouble that they threatened to kick us out of the Service. I wanted to find time to argue about which Marvel movie was the best, and I wanted you to get so frustrated with me that you threw that ugly coffee mug that you love so much at the wall. I wanted us to be together for so long that agents no longer spoke about Martin Bishop without adding Casey Wicker at the end of every sentence. I wanted...I want..." Martin sat heavily on the grass and put his face in his hands. "I want more time."

As Casey sat beside him and put a hand on Martin's shoulder, neither of them heard Leon approach from the house until he cleared his throat behind them.

Martin raised his head, no longer caring if his brother saw the tears in his eyes. "Have you come for us?"

Leon looked at Casey and then Martin and cleared his throat. "You've given the council a lot to think about, little brother. They've called an extraordinary meeting tomorrow morning. You have another night." His eyes flicked between the two men sitting on the grass again. "Make good use of it, gentlemen."

Mercifully, Martin and Casey were left in peace for the remainder of the day. They seemed destined to spend it in a mixture of quiet contemplation and simple togetherness, never wanting the other to stray farther that an arm's length. To Martin's frustration, Casey insisted on setting some time aside to write short letters. Casey knew that when agents were lost, the months ahead could be hard for those left behind and he was, therefore, determined to soften the blow however he could.

"Martin?" The question came, a little after six. They'd just finished a simple meal of sandwiches and soup together in their room, unwilling to join the other Avians in the dining room.

"Mmmm?" Martin looked up from a thick sheaf of papers.

"What did Leon mean?"

"When? He says rather a lot, and most of it is a waste of air."

"When he said we should *make use* of the extra night. Was he implying...?" Casey waved his hands vaguely, cognizant that the room might be bugged.

"That we should try to escape? No. Leon's smart enough to know we wouldn't get far. I suspect his motives were far more straightforward. I think he's suffering from a simple case of guilt."

"For what?"

"He's very much aware that were it not for him, you'd likely not have left the safe house. On our way here, he admitted that he underestimated you, or at least the depth of your feelings for me. When you announced that you were"—Martin's voice cracked, the memory clearly still raw—"leaving, I believe he confronted you with the footage from Alissa's to hurt you. He now concedes that was a mistake. He was, in a rare display of brotherly protectiveness, wanting you to see the consequences of your actions. What he didn't anticipate was your headlong flight, attempting to reach my side." Martin smiled. "He's never been much good with interpersonal relations."

"So, he just means..." Casey's brow furrowed.

"In his own awkward way, I think he was saying we shouldn't expect to be disturbed tonight."

"Oh." Casey's tongue reflexively darted out to wet his lips.

"So, I'd appreciate it if you could put that pen down." Martin stood, reaching his hands over his head and arching his back, so his ribs sprung into relief against the tight skin of his chest. Looking directly at Casey, he began a somewhat predatory journey across the carpet. "And come here."

Their lovemaking swung between desperate and hungry to gentle and reverent that night. There were all the usual sounds of the bedroom; the sighs, the moans, and the broken cries of surrender. But there was also laughter and tears. The emotional roller coaster finally burning its way to the top and expending the last of its reserves in twisted sheets. Neither of them held anything back, celebrating and mourning the end of a journey they knew had taken too long to reach the summit and yet unable to believe the beauty when they'd arrived.

The dawn found them huddled in blankets as the sun rose on their private patio. Squeaky clean from the shower, Casey sat caged warmly within the confines of Martin's arms and legs, Martin's pointed chin perched upon Casey's still-damp blonde hair as they watched the sunrise across the lavish lawns.

"Is it wrong to be happy?" Casey asked sombrely.

"It's a little bit wrong, but I forgive you." Martin nuzzled his nose against Casey's crown.

Casey chuckled within his woollen cocoon. "Sorry. Just, look at us, we got to have this. I wanted you for so long."

"How long?" Martin asked softly.

"Since the start, I think. Ever since I pulled you out of that burning building in Denmark."

"I think you called me a maniac." It was part statement, part question.

"Yeah, I did. But even then, I was in awe of your bravery. Those people would have died if not for you. I'd known you for two weeks, and yet, the thought of losing you—I don't think I've ever been more terrified."

Casey snuggled in a little tighter. "That was when I knew, I think. That maybe the experimenting I did with a guy at Uni might be more than a one-off. You knew, of course, that I fancied you. Even though I usually picked up women?"

"Of course."

Casey nudged an elbow backwards playfully. "Don't be narcissistic."

"Ow. You asked."

"What I meant was—"

Martin placed a gentle kiss amongst the drying strands of Casey's hair. "I know what you meant, Casey. You weren't ready, neither was I, so I never mentioned it. I just left the possibility open and hoped you'd act on it one day. I just didn't think it would take us so long. Or that our time would be so short."

Casey sighed and changed the topic. "Martin, what's going to happen today?"

Martin's arms wrapped a little tighter. "I don't know. But I give you my word, whatever it is, we face it together."

"AGENTS BISHOP AND Wicker, you present us with something of a quandary," the judge began.

Martin and Casey stood side by side in the makeshift dock. Unlike the first hearing, a substantially larger crowd had gathered. Word had spread regarding the events of the previous day, and the Avian community at least suspected history might be about to be made.

"The scale of our debt to both of you has been significantly increased."

Martin shifted slightly at Casey's side in response to the comment.

"However, the risk of having a human, at large, with knowledge of our community remains unacceptably large."

Leon turned to make eye contact with Martin, his expression firm as he mouthed the words... *wait*.

"The elder Mr. Bishop has therefore proposed a rather...unorthodox solution." The judge said the last as if the words tasted rank in his mouth.

Martin raised a quizzical eye toward his brother. "Agent Bishop." His name being called brought Martin's attention back to the presiding council. "Have you ever heard the term 'bonding'?"

The flicker of surprise was quickly masked, and Martin silently shook his head. He clearly had heard the term but wanted the council to surrender whatever additional information they had.

The judge continued. "It is an ancient ritual. I won't pretend to suggest that we understand either the process or the finer details. However, your brother seems to think that it stands the best possible chance of resolving this situation in a way that meets everyone's best interest."

Martin nodded for the judge to go on.

"Our legends say it provides a way to link together a human and an Avian on something akin to a spiritual level. If successful—" The judge looked to Leon who was rigidly staring at his feet. "If successful, the two parties are bonded so tightly psychologically that betrayal of our people would be unimaginable."

Without a word, Martin reached out to clasp Casey's hand in his own. Martin was apparently trying to recall any details he remembered of the process and needed the contact with Casey to keep him grounded.

"However, let me be clear, gentlemen. There has not been a successful bonding in living memory. The only successful bonding we have on record occurred over five hundred years ago. We have no idea why the more recent ones have failed, or what is required for success."

Casey raised a tentative hand, feeling like a schoolboy.

"Yes, Agent Wicker?"

"What happens if the bonding isn't successful?"

"In all cases, both parties have died, quickly and in excruciating pain."

Leon finally lifted his head, and Casey saw a look he never wanted to see on the QC's face ever again, desperation.

"SO, IT'S *ALL-or-nothing* time, is that what you're saying, Leon?" The three of them sat alone in the study, Casey asking questions, Martin deep in thought. They'd been given an hour to make a decision—accept or refuse the offer.

"I'm sorry, Casey. They were absolutely immovable with regards to your sentence. This was the only option available." Leon sipped at his whisky.

"So, to save my life, you risk your brother's. Charming." Casey's anger was palpable.

"Leon knows my life is forfeit with yours." Martin reached to place a large hand over his. "You know that. Regardless of the council's *mercy*, I have no wish to outlive you." Martin looked at Casey, clear of obfuscation or doubt. "And Leon knows I don't intend to."

Casey made a frustrated noise. "So—" He sighed. "—tell me what they'll do."

Martin gave his hand a squeeze. "Not much to tell, I'm afraid. The bondings are usually conducted behind closed doors. The histories provide details on the process, but are pathetically inadequate on the actual experience, and nobody talks about the ones that fail. All that it says is that there is a degree of pain for the human. It's unclear how or why the Avians die."

"Only that they do?" Casey looked down at their joined hands.

"Invariably."

"Invariably," Casey repeated, shaking his head. "So, what do we do?"

"Simple." Leon put his glass down with a clunk, and the two men looked up. "You don't die."

Interlude

Mum,

By now, the Service will have informed you that misfortune has befallen Martin and me. I hoped I'd never have to write a letter like this, and I find myself at a loss as to what to say except how sorry we are that I didn't get a chance to say goodbye. Things all happened in a bit of a rush towards the end, and time caught us out.

I expect everything will be kept pretty hush-hush. You know how the government is. I hate to ask this of you, but there's some things best taken care of by family.

Can you pick up a few things from my flat for me? There's nothing that will cause a stir, just some items that I hope you'll understand that I'd prefer to be in the hands of people we trust.

My commendations are in the side table next to my bed, I'd like you to keep those. Just pretend you didn't see the other stuff in there, I'm embarrassed enough about that for both of us.

You're welcome to anything else you fancy or give it all to charity, whatever you think is best.

You'll also find the spare key to Martin's flat on the hook in the kitchen. His brother offered, but Martin has told me there's something he'd like you to do for him.

He says there are a couple of photos of me on his mantel that he'd like you to have. They were taken overseas, and they're his favourites. I know we couldn't tell you much about the work we did, but if it helps, I had the chance to do things that I never dreamed. And I think we made a difference. I really do. Dad would have been proud.

Sorry, I'm getting a bit maudlin. I promised myself I wouldn't. But you need to know, Mum, how happy I was; how happy I am, right now, even facing what we're facing.

One last thing, and I hope it helps you make peace with all this. That thing we discussed at Christmas, about Martin and me. You were right, and Martin and I were together at the end.

Properly together, so it's all fine. I want you to know, we were fine.

Casey

Chapter Fifteen

ONCE THE DECISION had been made to proceed, things moved quickly. A team came to lead Martin away to be prepared elsewhere. Meanwhile, Leon escorted Casey back to Martin's room. While they waited, Leon explained what little they knew of the bonding to come.

"You must understand, Casey, we have little more than medieval whispers and rumours to indicate what you should expect. As you know, I'm not given to coddling and platitudes—"

"I'd never noticed." Casey smiled wryly.

Leon raised his voice slightly and continued. "Nevertheless—" He gave Casey an exasperated look. "—I'll tell you what I can. The ceremony involves a mixing of yours and Martin's DNA. My brother is currently being medicated with a cocktail of drugs designed to interrupt the process by which his wings appear."

"Interrupt how? It won't damage them, will it?"

"No. The drugs simply take the process out of Martin's control. Our understanding is that the process is slowed, potentially even halted. Martin will be restrained, as the drugs can potentially also cause other physical issues. We don't want him hurting himself."

"And my job, do I just stand by and watch all this?"

Leon's face softened, a hint of regret shadowing his features. "I wish it were that simple, Casey."

"WELL, THIS IS cosy." Casey was draped over Martin's bare back. Both stripped to the waist, the position would have been intimate if not for the crowd assembled around the edges of the room. His wings absent, Martin had been tied face down and spread-eagled to a padded structure.

"Nice of you to join me. Comfortable?" Martin turned his head as best he could to glance over his shoulder to where Casey's face was tucked into his shoulder.

Casey rocked his head from side to side and made an undecided noise. "Well, you know... I'm always up for trying something new. Although we should probably have discussed mixing bondage and public sex before we just... leapt into it."

Martin snorted. "Stop making me laugh. This is serious."

Casey stifled his giggling by pressing his nose into Martin's shoulder. "Really? I hadn't noticed. What gave it away? The arrayed Avians or Leon's disapproving stare?"

"Both." The word was interrupted by a pained hiss, and Martin's light tone broke. "Listen, Casey. It's starting; I can feel it. Listen to me, whatever happens..." Another gasp and Martin tried to arch against his constraints. "This wasn't your fault, none of it. Do what you need to do to survive. No regrets, okay? No regrets."

Casey clasped his arms around Martin's chest a little tighter and repeated. "I have no regrets."

He held tightly to Martin as he'd been instructed, terrified at the prospect of what might happen when Martin's wings appeared. Positioned as he was, clasped with his chest against Martin's back, there was nowhere for the wings to go but through him. Muttering soothing platitudes to himself, he leant in and waited for the worst.

He'd anticipated the now-familiar tingling rush of arousal, ready to welcome it to alleviate whatever else would come, but even the brush of lust against his nerves did little to soften the sudden and crippling pain.

The shout was torn from him as sudden and excruciating pain lanced through his chest. "OH.... MY... GOD, NO!"

He could hear Martin, coming from somewhere below him, mired in the fog of pain. "Casey! *Casey!*"

He could do nothing but keen as the excruciating pain continued. It echoed through the chamber, reflected back from the high ceiling overhead.

"Casey!" Martin again, desperately trying to give him something to focus on through the madness. "Stay with me. Breathe...breathe for me."

"I can't!" he gasped, the simple task of drawing breath threatening to make him black out. "Oh, God, Martin...the pain...they're inside me...tearing... I'm—I need—have to..." Casey began to pull backwards, instincts screaming at him to escape the agony. He released his clawed grip around Martin's chest.

"*Casey!* NO...please...no... My wings—you'll tear them out. Oh, God, Casey... Please..." The desperation was evident in Martin's shattered voice. "You'll kill us both."

Casey struggled, torn between the agonies, clogging, suffocating denseness, and Martin's pleas, and the truth behind them. He threw his head back and screamed, a weak, shredded thing, and forced himself to settle his hands more firmly against the skin of Martin's chest.

The sounds changed. Casey's breathing became a gurgling struggle for air, taking on a more stuttered, gasping quality. "I can't—I can't breathe... Martin.... I can't... help me...please...help me."

With the usual progress of Martin's wings appearing paused, they were stuck in a quasi-state between translucent and substantial, the skin, bones, and feathers of his wings invading Casey's lungs and robbing him of air. As Casey gasped desperately, Martin's made a decision.

"Casey! Pull away, Casey..." he begged. "You need to get away. Don't worry about me. It's not worth it. I don't matter. Try and save yourself...please. Just try...try to escape."

Something in the phrasing—*I don't matter; I'm not worth it*—penetrated the panic and fear and reached Casey deep within his nightmare of his pain.

With a final breathy whimper, he settled his head against the nape of Martin's neck and pressed desperate gasping kisses. "You're worth it...always...loved you...love you...Martin...worth it...together...never leaving."

"Casey. Oh...Casey?" Tears ran unheeded down Martin's cheeks as his lover lay limp against his back, exhausted and running out of air.

"It's okay, Martin," Casey's breathy whispers continued. "It's okay...no regrets."

"Casey..." Martin pulled against the strapping that confined him, struggling desperately. As the wings finally began to fade and Casey's arms fell to hang loose at his side, he whispered, "Stay with me, please stay. I love you."

"It's fine," Casey murmured almost too quiet to hear. "Just...going to rest here...for a bit, Martin... I'll just...rest."

Casey became a dead weight as he lost consciousness and Martin's shattered cry rattled the windows in the room as the Avians looked on in horror. "*Casey!*"

Chapter Sixteen

ALISSA STOOD SILENTLY by Leon's side, looking down at the two men entwined on the floor, unconscious. "Oh, God, Leon, what have we done?"

"Sometimes, Miss Satterfield, it turns out there is no winning move. Take them back to their room." Leon knelt to feel the pulse in both men's necks.

"How are they?" Alissa crouched at their sides, the tracks of tears still bright on her cheeks.

"They seem...fine." Leon laid the back of his palm on his brother's sweaty forehead. "They're both breathing easy. Although God knows how that should be the case, given what Casey's been through."

Alissa glanced up. Leon rarely referred to Casey as anything other than Agent Wicker, and the gentleness with which it was uttered now surprised her. At her look, the openness on his face disappeared, and he made haste to explain himself.

"Is it such a surprise, Alissa, that I can be grateful to the man who was willing to sacrifice himself for my younger brother? I may be cold, but I'm not heartless."

She blushed and looked away, gesturing for someone to help carry the unconscious men back to their room. She stood silently in the corner as both were stripped to their underwear and settled into the bed. Leon entered without a sound to check them one last time and rolled his sleeping brother so that the two of them were nestled together. He suspected that when they awoke, the immediate presence of the other would be more cathartic than all the medication in the entire house.

IN THE FUZZY world of the half-conscious, it was Casey's whimper that tipped the scales and dragged Martin back to wakefulness. Acting on instinct, his arms were around his partner even before he opened his eyes, pulling Casey farther into his embrace, the warmth and pliancy of the skin dragged a relieved groan from Martin even before he knew he'd done it.

"Casey…" he whispered, kissing the hair beneath his lips. "I thought I'd lost you."

Casey tilted his face up, seeking out the lips with his own before mumbling, "I figured you had too. God, Martin…that was awful. I can see why so many fail. I don't know how I survived."

"I don't care… I just care that you did, that we both did."

"So, that's it, then, that was the bonding? I don't feel any different." Casey stretched gently, as far as Martin's arms would permit.

"Nor do I." Martin loosened his grip on Casey and took a quick peek under the covers. "Nothing seems amiss under there."

"I half expected to have wings."

"Sorry to disappoint you. No wings, I'm afraid." Martin ran fingers along Casey's spine, delighting in Casey's shivered response. "You remain my perfect example of winglessness."

Casey curled his own arms around Martin, running them up the smooth expanse. "So, are you at the moment? Are they gone for good, do you think?" Casey asked, a little fearful. "Was that the price of our survival?"

Martin looked thoughtful as he concentrated a moment. "Hmm, I can't call them forth, but I can still feel the drugs in my system, so it could be temporary." The frown deepened. "Would it make a difference to you... if I was normal?"

Casey barked a short disbelieving laugh. "I doubt anyone would ever describe you as normal, Martin...wings or not." Martin looked insulted, and Casey reached for him. "You know what I mean."

"Yes, I know."

"Come here." Casey gathered him in, pulling them together and nuzzling into his neck. "Come here, my *normal*, beautiful maniac."

"God, Casey. I can't believe it's over, that we've made it." Martin edged a leg between Casey's and rolled them, so he was settled between them. "That we can keep this."

Casey arched up, their hips aligning and rapidly filling cocks settling against each other. "And by this, I assume you mean me?"

"Us, Casey. I mean us. But—" Martin circled his hips down again, and then paused, sniffing thoughtfully. "—I stink, and, forgive me...so do you."

Casey laughed and took a long theatrical drag of air in the general area of Martin's armpit. "Forgiven. Nearly dying is bound to work up a sweat. Join me for a shower?"

Martin threw back the covers and rose gracefully from the bed. "Thought you'd never ask."

"JESUS, MARTIN, RIGHT there. Christ, don't stop." Casey stood, palms pressed against the tiles as the water beat down on them both, back bowed as Martin continued to thrust into him over and over again with such force it threatened to lift him off his feet.

"Casey..." Martin panted. "You're so good. I can't..."

"Don't you fucking dare come yet. Don't. You. Dare." Roughly grabbing at his own cock, he stroked quickly but too desperate for much finesse, groaning in relief as Martin's large hand joined his and helped the rhythm.

Martin began muttering amongst the swear words, and Casey caught enough to realize that he was being serenaded with a list of European nations through gritted teeth and interspersed with the occasional colourful profanity as Martin tried desperately to stave off the inevitable.

"Close...close..." Casey grunted as his muscles began to tense.

"Christ, Casey, will you...just..." Martin leant in with the intention of nibbling gently at Casey's neck only to be blind-sided as Casey's orgasm finally crested, and he instead bit down, eliciting a startled gasp and flinch from Casey as he shuddered under him.

"Fuck! God. fuck...did you? You bit me!" Casey managed even as he continued to climax, clenching around Martin's cock.

The statement barely registered as Martin was driven to his own orgasm, Casey's internal muscles gripping and pulling at him.

"Christ...sorry. *nnfff*...sorry..." Martin muttered, ineffectually trying to raise a weak hand to Casey's neck with little coordination, even as his legs threatened to give way.

Casey went quiet, the shudders of ecstasy subsiding and just when Martin expected Casey to turn and shout at him, the tremors started up again, and Martin realized Casey was laughing. Open, honest laughter that held nothing back, bouncing off the tiles and Casey pulled away and turned to joyfully wrap his arms around Martin's neck.

"That was ridiculous! When you...and I told you not to come...and..." Casey leant against Martin's chest, weak with dissipating adrenaline and laughter. "And...European nations, and then you bit me, and you apologized... you...apologized—" Casey sank to the floor of the shower, giggling helplessly. "—while still in my arse. Oh, my God, Martin."

As always, Martin found Casey's laughter infectious and soon they were sitting back to back on the floor, ribs aching and the water around their arses cooling rapidly. "Not like in the movies, was it?"

"That wasn't even good enough for a bad porno." Casey chuckled. "God...now, my chest hurts again."

Martin waited until silence settled before reaching behind himself to capture Casey's hand where it rested comfortably near his hip. "Casey..."

"Hmmm?"

"I love you," Martin said gently.

"I know," Casey replied automatically. "I love you too."

"No." Martin gripped the fingers more firmly. "I don't mean it like that, in some amorphous trite way that people say when they're sleeping together."

Casey stilled and swivelled to face Martin. "Then what do you mean?"

"I mean, I'm in love with you, Casey Wicker. I just need you to know that. That I've fallen hopelessly in love with you."

Casey met Martin's gaze. There were dark rings around them from too many days with too much stress and not enough sleep. The extra pigment gave his eyes an usual vibrant, sapphire glow, making them seem more vivid and unusual. All traces of the reserved mask Martin usually wore to hide from the world were finally gone. Sitting on the cooling tiles of the shower, this was Martin at his most raw, his most authentic, and as Casey reached out to lay a gentle hand on the man's cheek, the words came easily in reply.

"Good... That makes both of us."

"MARTIN..." THE QUIET voice came inches from his nose in the huge fluffy bed. "Martin, get up. The sun's coming up."

Martin rolled over and groaned. "Who cares?"

"I care! I didn't think we'd see today, so I want to see all of it. Come on!" Casey tugged at a long, fair arm before begrudgingly letting it fall and strolling into the chill morning air of the balcony.

Martin looked up from the sheets at Casey's nude form framed by the window. Martin was again struck by the quiet strength in his partner.

Usually hidden under unassuming shirts and jackets, Casey had unexpectedly broad shoulders for his build. His ribs tapered to solid hips, his tight arse set off by twin dimples on either side of his spine.

The sudden tingling and feeling of pressure at his back were a new sensation for Martin. Usually, his wings were consciously summoned with a dark rush of energy and a sense of oneness with the world. For the first time, it was as if his wings were a separate entity, making their presence known and asking for permission to materialize. With joy, he closed his eyes and breathed a deep, relieved breath, surrendering to their feathered call and celebrated their return. Martin's pale eyes opened, and they wordlessly grinned at each other in thankfulness.

"Now, will you get up?" Casey asked from the doorway.

"Try and stop me!" Martin vaulted from the bed, ran past Casey, and leapt into the air, the downdraft stirring Casey's blond hair as he laughed elatedly and applauded in delight.

"CLOTHES, MARTIN...YOU might consider clothes." Leon had silently appeared at Casey's side and was watching his brother as he tumbled and arched in the morning air.

Well beyond caring about personal modesty anymore, Casey stood naked and unmoved beside Martin's older brother. "Morning, Leon."

"Casey...I see my brother's aloft again." Although trying to sound ambivalent, there was a bright note of relief in Leon's voice as he watched his younger sibling dive and bank in the chill morning air.

"I think everyone can see that." Casey let out a light-hearted giggle as Martin whooped and laughed as he frolicked in the early-morning air above the estate, and for once, Leon joined in.

"The cold air's not doing his reputation any favours." Leon's laugh was rich as he smiled, his chin tilted up to watch. "Although, from this distance, I suppose there was never going to be much to see."

Casey turned to Leon in surprise at the joke and then laughed openly. He extended a hand, which Leon took warmly. "Truce?"

"Truce. You're good for my brother, Casey. I'll admit I've had my doubts."

"You were trying to protect him," Casey interjected.

Leon nodded. "However, I'll admit that I misjudged you, and that doesn't often happen. You make my brother—" Leon tilted his head searching for the right word.

"Better?" Casey suggested.

"Happy, Casey, which seems more important after all you've been through." Leon stepped forward, cupped his hands on either side of his mouth and shouted into the clear air. "Martin! Come down."

Martin wheeled to hover upright and dramatically gestured with one finger, eliciting a bark of laughter from Casey.

"Martin! Come down, or I'll come up after you!"

Casey remembered for the first time what Martin had said about Leon's flight ability. *Too much deskwork.* Obviously, he'd been exaggerating if Leon's threat was to be believed. Looking at the tall litigator next to him, he wondered, not for the first time, what Leon's wings were like. However, considering the arousal that an Avian summoning his wings caused, he had no desire to see them appear.

"Martin," Casey called to the sky. "Please!"

Turning back, Martin nodded and dove, landing beside Casey. He stood tall, naked, and unapologetic, holding his brother's eyes unflinchingly.

"Leon," Martin said tersely, the brotherly aloofness firmly in place.

"Martin," he responded, equally dispassionate.

"Well," Casey began. "If this reunion gets any more emotional, I might cry. Should I leave you two alone?"

"No, stay, Casey. This concerns you too. The council have conceded that although they have no idea what the effects of the bonding will be or how it prevents Casey from endangering them in the future, you have met the conditions of the sentence."

Martin frowned. "How generous of them. Please pass on my apologies for not having the good manners to just expire on the council floor."

"Martin." Casey inched closer to his partner, warning him to keep calm.

"No, Casey. You nearly *died*. When you lost consciousness, when you couldn't breathe..." Martin's voice cracked. "I should never have let you..."

Leon tactfully turned away and gave the two men some privacy, walking back into the room as Casey stepped forward and wrapped his arms around his lover, on the verge of tears.

"No regrets, okay? We said no regrets. I'm fine." Casey tucked in tight against Martin, his head turned to slot against the other's neck. "I'm fine."

Martin whimpered softly. "I can still hear you screaming, gasping for breath." Martin laid a large hand on Casey's head, holding him to his chest. "I think I'll probably always hear it."

"I know," Casey said gently. "I know. Whatever it was, it was an illusion. I'm fine."

"Promise?" Martin pulled back to look down at Casey.

Casey smiled back. "Promise. Now, I think we've probably traumatized your brother long enough, hugging naked on the balcony."

Martin's eyes brightened. "Spoilsport." Nevertheless, he put some clear space between them and looked through the doors to where his brother was studiously rearranging the writing desk. "What exactly did you want, Leon?"

Looking up at the sound of his name, he made his way back. "What I came to say was that although free to leave at any time, there is an alternative to an immediate return to the Service that I'd like to offer if you're interested."

Martin folded his arms over his chest. "I'm listening."

"DI Carrington—"

Martin smiled knowingly. "Jared."

"Quite so." Leon flashed a warning look at his brother. "Jared...Carrington—"

"Your lover," Martin continued to press.

Leon's eyes flashed angrily as Casey glanced between them, shocked.

"Wait, *what*?" Casey looked at Leon open-mouthed.

Leon rolled his eyes and sighed. "Couldn't leave it alone, could you, Martin?"

"I've promised Casey no secrets, Leon. And after all, Casey's family now."

"Very well. You've begun now. Tell him before his brain explodes."

"You..." Casey stared at Leon. "You and Jared? Detective Inspector Jared Carrington? The bloke from Scotland Yard?"

Leon sighed again as Martin smiled smugly. "Years, Casey... Years! Oh, and you should know...it's not an interracial relationship."

"I don't underst— Oh, for God's sake... Is *everyone* but me a fucking bird?"

"Avian," Martin corrected, still grinning.

"Not helping, Martin," Leon said. "I'm sorry, Casey. I know it seems like you've been surrounded by some sort of secret society, but it's simply that we tend to gravitate to each other."

"Birds of a feather, as they say..." Martin sniggered until Casey threw him a filthy look.

"*Anyway!*" Leon interrupted. "Jared...Carrington—" He shot Martin a warning look not to interfere again. "—would like to know if you and Casey would be interested in a trip to the Orkney Islands. There's a case up there, and as you know, there's plenty of, let's say, open sky to explore."

Martin was nodding thoughtfully. Casey took the opportunity to drag on some jeans and a shirt, then grabbed some clothes for Martin.

"Interesting case?" Martin asked.

Leon smiled. "Very."

Chapter Seventeen

IF THERE WAS one thing Casey had learned to be thankful for, it was capable helicopter pilots. As far as he was concerned, as he gripped the armrest a little too tightly, doing something was a far cry from being comfortable with it.

Perhaps it was just as well that a pair of magical wings hadn't sprouted from his back after the bonding. He reached over his shoulder to idly scratch at his scapula. He'd never been at home in the air. It always seemed, well, too far off the ground.

The exception had been when Martin had lifted him into the air. He'd been so engrossed in the sheer miracle that Martin was flying with him that he had completely forgotten about the distressing distance of the ground below him.

No such luck now, he thought as the helicopter carried them over the short space of water between the Scottish mainland and the seemingly tiny dot of an island ahead.

Martin nudged him with his shoulder, the sound of the rotors making conversation almost impossible, and when Casey turned, Martin nodded down to his thigh where his hand laid palm upward. Moving his own off the armrest, Casey gratefully gripped the long fingers, accepting the unspoken comfort wordlessly.

Fifteen minutes later, the rotors were slowing as they stepped out onto a flat, sparsely grassed field a little distance from a grey-stone cottage.

"Well, this is home for a while." Martin grabbed their coats from the seat beside him and jumped down to the ground, holding out a hand. "Shall we?"

Casey hoisted the backpack, which had been delivered to them at the estate during the preceding night, over his shoulder, adjusting it to sit more comfortably. "Looks cosy."

The chopper lifting off behind them threw up dust and grass, and they covered their eyes against the grit as they made their way to the small brick-red door.

Pulling a key from an inside pocket, Martin swung the door open and ducked under the lintel, reaching for the light switch just inside.

"Hmm, not bad. Hasn't changed much." Martin moved around the room, pulling back the curtains to let the thin northern light in. Dust motes floated in the air.

"You've been here before?"

"Leon owns it." He paused before adding, "Although I suppose, technically, I own half too? We used to come here as children. Haven't been here for...oh...thirty years, I guess."

Casey's head was immediately filled with images of a small raggedy boy accompanied by his older brother, exploring the rocky outcrops and beaches. Perhaps Martin laughed more in those days; maybe Leon's face hadn't yet acquired its perpetual scowl.

Banishing the thoughts for more immediate concerns, Casey stretched and glanced around the dim room. The central room held little more than a lounging area, complete with fireplace. Set off from this room, a tiled area contained a small but well-equipped kitchen. Made to look vintage, the brushed-steel doors of a French-door fridge belied the effect of the timber cupboards, and Casey noted the induction cook-top and oven in the space where the old woodstove likely held pride of place in years past.

"Loo?" Casey looked to the two doors leading from the central area.

"On the left. The bedroom is on the right. Sorry." Martin grinned wickedly. "Only one bed. We'll have to share, I'm afraid."

As Casey headed for the door, he snorted and tossed the backpack toward Martin, giving a silent cheer at the sudden outrush of breath as it hit his partner in the chest.

"DID LEON GIVE you any details whatsoever?" Casey strode beside Martin as they made their way from the car to the Murray Arms Hotel.

Martin rolled his eyes. "What do you think, Casey? When presented with the options of providing his brother with all the necessary information or alternatively retaining the illusion that he's sole custodian of secrets fit only for the highest echelons of the legal system, which do *you* think he chose?"

Casey smiled. "So, we have nothing."

Martin held the door to the pub open and ushered his partner inside. "Virtually. We're meeting the local Inspector from South Ronaldsay. Hopefully, he'll be more forthcoming than my dear brother."

"You must be Mr. Bishop?" The man was out of his seat with his hand extended before Martin had a chance to remove his scarf.

"Agent, but please, call me Martin. This is my partner, Casey Wicker." Martin grasped the offered hand.

Casey paused a moment and considered the descriptor—*partner*. The introduction was the one they'd always used, but now it had new, more intimate meaning, and there was something in the way the word had rolled from Martin's mouth with a new feeling that unexpectedly warmed Casey's heart.

The Inspector, younger than Casey had expected, switched his focus from Martin and repeated the handshake warmly. "Yes, I can't tell you how grateful we are to have you both here."

Casey glanced around the room. "Happy to help. What can you say, Inspector?"

"Gordon, please." The man indicated a small table tucked toward the back of the large room and gestured for drinks. "Take a seat."

In a long-practiced motion, Casey circled the table to take a seat so he was facing the room. While Martin was listening for the next half hour, he'd be focusing more on the others around them. Through experience, they'd developed an efficient routine where Martin interviewed whomever they were with, and they shared their findings later. Casey would nod at appropriate intervals, and there'd be the occasional kick to his shin under the table if he'd missed something, but otherwise, Martin left what he called *"the people watching"* in Casey's capable hands.

The Inspector continued. "Gentlemen, as I'm sure you're aware, we are a tiny, isolated community here in South Ronaldsay. The isolation and, let's just say, prevailing winds make this an attractive destination for some, and home for others."

From the corner of his eye, he saw Martin's mouth twitched up at last, but he kept his primary focus on surveillance of the room.

"And by some, you mean?" Martin prompted quietly.

"I mean those with...." And the Inspector gave a dramatic circling shrug of his shoulders. To the layperson, it would be interpreted as a man at the end of a long day, stretching out tired muscles. To Casey, however, the pantomime flexing of invisible wings made the meaning clear.

"Oh." His attention drawn back by the idea of an entire community of Avians, Casey drained the pint glass in front of him. "Go on, Gordon."

Nodding, he continued to lay out the facts. "Right, well, locals have been turning up dead. The pattern's not one we can advertise, for obvious reasons. Things were getting a bit desperate until your Inspector Carrington contacted Agent Bishop's brother."

Casey nodded, as another glass was set in front of him. "So, all the victims were—"

Martin interjected and looked pointedly at Casey, adding, "People with 'aching shoulders.' Yes, very common in these parts. As you know, Casey, it's a condition I suffer from myself."

"And you, Inspector? Do you suffer from 'aching shoulders'?" Casey toyed with his glass, finally looking up to make eye contact.

Gordon was smiling broadly. Clearly amused by the terminology they'd adopted, he leant in and quietly said, "No. I'm a nester. But my family all have—" He paused to look between the two men. "—aching shoulders."

Martin leant in close so his voice could only be heard by Casey and elaborated. "Nesters are children of Avians who have been born without wings. They're exempt from the death sentence as they carry all the right DNA and their offspring are often born with wings."

Casey suspected he could live to be a hundred and still not get his head around the complexity of Avian society. Instead of miring himself further in the quagmire that was apparently Avian law, he opted instead for "So, how many victims?"

"Eight in the past twelve months." Gordon's face was grim. "That's more unnatural deaths than we've seen in the preceding decade. We have a serial killer, and we have no idea who it is, or why he's killing."

"Jesus." Casey's shocked reaction was instinctive, and as he glanced to the side, he could see Martin was similarly affected. "And there's no pattern?"

"I've brought you a copy of the file, it's all there. You'll get all the help you need, and I'll be honest with you both." He looked between the two men. "We could use it."

THE TWO MEN sat cross-legged on the floor of the cottage. Strewn over the space between them were the contents of the case file, several empty mugs, and a plate containing a half-eaten jam sandwich. Casey loved this part of any mission—gathering the information, working it all through, devising strategies, and guiding Martin away from the more dangerous ones.

Earlier, Martin had drawn the line at Casey's suggestion they affix the several dozen documents to the pristine wallpaper with pins he'd tucked into his coat pocket. The resulting half-hour strop had ended only after Casey had looked up to see Martin watching him with undisguised fondness.

Confused as to the reason for the look, Martin had explained that watching him act like a maligned toddler was something he'd always loved. For some time afterwards, the file and the obstinacy had been forgotten for a passionate and very pleasant snog on the couch, leaving the floor littered with evidence.

"I still don't understand why I can't pin all this to the wall." Casey dug through the papers to bring two photos together next to a plastic mug with a picture of a cartoon cat on it.

"Don't start that again," Martin warned with a grin.

"Surely, you must see that it—"

"No. You're not putting holes in my wall, and that's all there is to it. Take your shirt off," he added, without preamble.

His eyes twitched. "What?"

"Your shirt, you've been scratching at your shoulders most of the day. There's clearly something irritating them, ergo shirt off."

At the mention of the itching, Casey realized that his hand was indeed idly rubbing at the cloth over his left shoulder. He switched to undoing buttons. "Probably just the washing powder they were using at the estate."

"Let's prove your hypothesis, Casey, just to be sure."

Turning his back to Martin, Casey eased the shirt off his shoulders, realizing for the first time how irritated they actually were. The sensation was not unlike prickly heat or sunburn, and he flinched as Martin's fingertips came to touch the skin gently.

"Hmm," Martin said.

"What the hell is that supposed to mean?" Casey tried in vain to crane his neck to look over his shoulder. "What's back there?"

The gentle touches continued, ranging from close to his spine to as far out as his elbows on either side, then down across his ribs.

Finally, when Casey thought he was likely to go mad with waiting, Martin sat back on his heels and cocked his head to the side. "Well, there's no sign of wings erupting from your back, if that's what you're wondering."

In fact, that was *exactly* what Casey had been wondering. Following all the dramatics and pain of their bonding, the consequences so far seemed to be negligible. Perhaps his initial proposal of an adverse reaction to soap powder was the right one after all.

"So, what is it?"

"In layman's terms, I think I'd call it a rash."

Casey released a breath he hadn't known he'd been holding.

"Except for one thing..." Martin continued.

Casey tensed all over again.

Martin rocked back and stood gracefully, holding out a hand to Casey. "It might be easier to show you."

In a daze, Casey allowed himself to be helped to his feet and guided into the bathroom. Martin left him momentarily to roll a large floor mirror from the bedroom so Casey could use the reflection to see his own back in the long mirror.

Martin hadn't lied; the skin of his back was inflamed, turning his normally fair skin a rosy pink. However, imprinted within the angry red boundaries was something both beautiful and mysterious.

In fine black lines, which shifted and shimmered in violet and emerald hues as he moved and flexed his shoulders was an almost perfect rendition of Martin's wings, accurate down to the blaze of white feathers near his spine on his ribs.

Casey looked up from the reflection to Martin, who was standing close but not touching. "What do you think it means?"

Martin's brow creased as he looked from Casey's back to his eyes. "I have no idea, but I think we can safely say the bond has been successful."

Chapter Eighteen

CASEY STOOD IN the open air, the sea salt stinging his nose. As is often the case in dreams, colours looked oddly bright and everything appeared strangely oversized or distorted. He was standing on a pier, its wooden planks uneven under his bare feet, and it struck him that he was seeing the world through the eyes of a child.

He looks around for his mother, suddenly wary of being alone in such a busy place. People are wandering in all directions, laughing and jostling each other, and he feels exposed and vulnerable.

From nowhere, the giggling of boys reaches his ears, and before he can react, he's being grabbed by the arm and swung around. They're tugging, not in a friendly way, and he feels childish tears spring to his eyes as he again calls for his parents.

He's pulled farther down the pier by the boys, and before he has a chance to muster the courage to try to fight back, they've pushed him, and he feels his feet slip from under himself and he's falling...falling... The safety of the timber pier is gone as he falls toward the water.

Casey startled awake and instinctively reached out to the bed beside him. Surprisingly, the lean form of Martin was still there, nestled against his side and breathing deeply. Rolling, he slotted himself against the curve of Martin's body, taking comfort from the way his smooth, muscular back fitted against his own abdomen and chest as if made for him.

In truth, he was still getting used to sleeping in the same bed as Martin. Endlessly restless during the day, Martin, unfortunately, had brought those traits to the bedroom. Even while asleep, he fidgeted and twitched long after his body succumbed to sleep. Casey's logical brain knew Martin had no control over his autonomic system, but his more primitive brain was tempted to shove his lover onto the floor each time another twist or flinch disturbed Casey's sleep.

But now, Martin's endless energy had burnt itself out and the man was settled and pliant. Casey burrowed closer, half hoping the man would stay asleep so he could snuggle a while longer, and half-hoping Martin would stir and perhaps this early morning cosiness would turn to more. Even at the thought, the thrum of desire shook him, and he snuggled more firmly against Martin's arse.

As if in answer to his prayer, there was a deep, contented rumble from the man at his front as he arched his back, drawing in a deep, waking breath before resuming his comfortable spot enfolded in Casey's arms.

Casey placed a gentle kiss at the nape of his neck, nosing against the dark skin where the musky smell of sleep was stronger.

"Morning, Marty," Casey murmured against the skin.

There was a brief tensing in the muscles as Martin sleepily snorted. "Are we doing pet names now? Should I find something equally ridiculous to call you when we're alone?"

It was Casey's turn to laugh. "Only if you want me to use yours in public."

Martin's hand, draped over Casey's arm where it encircled his chest, rubbed idly back and forth. "I can't see that ending well, can you?"

Casey fell quiet for a moment. "Oh, I don't know." He paused again. "You might enjoy it."

Martin measured Casey's statement before rolling in his arms so that they faced each other.

Martin's eyes were still heavy from sleep, and his voice rough from a night of disuse more than wilful effort, but the effect was the same as he leant to whisper, "You mean, *you* might."

Casey shivered at the tone. Whatever else, Martin knew him so well. Pulling Martin closer he pressed their lips together with clear intent. "You think you're so smart."

"You love it," Martin countered, a soft smile on his lips.

"Yes, I do."

Casey rolled to lie over Martin, beginning a concerted assault on his jaw and neck, layering kisses as if determined to leave nothing untouched. Martin lifted his hands to rub at Casey's flanks, took his wrists, and without a word or stopping his attention on Martin's collarbones, Casey pressed Martin's hands down on his pillow, either side of his head.

When he released them, Martin immediately tried to bring them back into play, and Casey repeated the gesture, this time, pressing more firmly, indicating that they were to stay where they'd been put. Martin's eyes were wide, and his mouth opened with a slightly awed "Oh."

Casey had never really considered the idea of dominance in the bedroom. He'd never seen the allure, but this is Martin, who gets a thrill from danger, and as Casey sucked gently on a nipple, licking it to a sharp nubby peak, he considered the fact that part of their dynamic was the constant struggle for dominance that pervaded every aspect of their lives.

Images of their lives flashed in his mind. *"Run, Casey... This way"* ... *"Get DOWN"*... *"Catch him."* There's no doubt Martin exuded an aura of dominance, and that Casey all too quickly submitted in the field. But the opposite is equally true. *"We're not doing that"* ... *"Don't forget the documents"* ... *"Don't go off on your own, you idiot."* Yes, exerting control over Martin certainly had appeal.

As Casey switched to the other nipple, Martin's hands strayed to his hair. With a grin, he lifted his mouth from Martin's skin and soundlessly rose from the bed. There was a distressed whine from Martin that quickly stuttered out as Casey pulled the belt from Martin's dressing gown and returned to the bed.

Straddling Martin's narrow hips, he held up the silky tie. "Do I need to use this?"

Martin began to shake his head and move his hands back to the pillow before something changed his mind and he instead turned it into a pouting nod, full of restrained belligerence.

Casey's breath caught and he muttered, "Right, then."

On some level, Casey knew Martin was controlling this as much as he is, but his cock seemed blissfully unaware of the deception as he loosely tied Martin's wrists to the headboard. It gave a delighted twitch, and Martin groaned as a pearly drop of pre-cum dripped on his abdomen.

"Ever used a safe word, Martin?" Casey asked roughly, his face inches from his lover's.

Martin nodded and whispered, "Syria." The serpentine word coiled around Casey like smoke.

"Good man." Casey kissed him before edging back down his body. "We're not going to do anything we haven't done before, and you know you can get out if you need.

But...” Casey looked up and made solid eye contact. “I *want* you to stay there. Understand?”

Martin bit his bottom lip and nodded. This might be for show, but Martin was not unaffected by being forced to submit. There was a growing nervous energy around him, and a subtle twitching was visible on the long muscles of his thighs.

“You’re beautiful like this. So much skin, the black hair, and of course, this.” Casey leant down and pressed the most delicate of kisses to the tip of Martin’s rigid cock. “And you’ll do whatever I say, won’t you?”

Another nod as he struggled to angle his hips closer to Casey, obviously desperate for more friction. “Anything, Casey. Anything.”

“Lovely.” Casey took his time, roaming freely and lavishing attention as if he didn’t have a care in the world. All the while, he continued to talk. “You know, when that thing appeared on my back last night, those wings—” More kisses, and long lapping strokes where hips met thigh. “—so like yours, I wondered if they meant I somehow belonged to you.”

Martin was actively wriggling now, begging without words for attention.

“And I wondered how I felt about that, and you know what I’ve decided?” Pausing with his hands holding Martin’s hips to the bed, Casey hovered above Martin’s erection, his breath ghosting over the turgid flesh. “I’ve decided this isn’t about ownership.” He swirled his tongue briefly around the crown of Martin’s cock, and the man underneath him moaned in abandon. “It’s about partnership.” Casey gave a quick teasing suck before pulling off. “It’s about us both getting what we want... What do you want, Martin?”

"You, Casey, I want you, your mouth." The words tumbled out in broken tones. "God, please, Casey, please..." The words were gasped, stuttering, on the verge of tears.

"That's the way, beg me." At Martin's words of surrender, Casey dipped his head to take Martin entirely in his mouth, sinking down until he felt the rosy head nudge the back of his throat. Drawing back up, he sucked gently and with more intent as Martin pulled at his restraints and moaned long and low.

Casey settled more comfortably, crouched between Martin's legs, bent low over his crotch. The angle gave him total control, adjusting speed and angle whenever he desired, keeping Martin on edge for long minutes as he bobbed his head, saliva beginning to edge it's way past his lips to trail down Martin's cock. The distinctive taste of pre-come on his tongue signalled that this couldn't go on forever, and, in any case, the muscles in Casey's forearms had started to ache from the strain of maintaining this position.

Casey knew Martin wouldn't last much longer; his stamina was better when his wings weren't present, but Casey had teased him long enough that he was close. Casey hummed happily around the cock in his mouth, and there was another hitching breath and shiver as Martin desperately tried to maintain what little control he'd been left.

Casey realized that Martin's hands were free and buried in his hair again, but he barely had time to consider berating his lover before his head was being dragged off Martin's cock as his partner arched up from the bed to pull himself upright into Casey's arms.

Martin buried his head in Casey's shoulder, his arms reached urgently around to clasp them together. With a cry, he came against Casey's stomach, as a sudden and violent shiver of light and heat burst around them, and Martin's wings sprung into existence, quivering and ruffled. The familiar rush of lust took Casey, and he threw his own head back with a shout, his own release joining the mess on their bellies.

Casey found himself holding a shaking and exhausted Avian in his arms when he came back to himself enough to catch his breath. Martin was sobbing silently on his shoulder, utterly wrecked and exhausted, and Casey smoothed his fingers through sweaty curls and murmured gentle endearments.

"God... Oh God..." Martin finally managed.

"You okay?" Casey asked as he tried to pull a blanket up around their entwined bodies.

"My wings, Casey..."

"I know... You called them."

Martin lifted his head and cupped a shaky hand on Casey's cheek. "That's just it, Casey. I didn't... I think you did."

Chapter Nineteen

"WHAT?"

"I didn't call them. To say I was far beyond concentrating enough to summon them would be an understatement."

"And yet, there they are." Casey reached up a hand to pat down the ruffled feathers that fluffed up farther at his touch.

"Yes, here they are." Overly sensitive post-orgasm, Martin nevertheless leant into Casey's touch as the wings twitched and flexed. Martin winced even as he smiled. "God, that's just—"

"Too much?"

"I think so." The wing flexed away before returning within Casey's reach again. "No. Yes. Hell, I'm not sure."

Casey chuckled and adjusted his light grazing tough to a firmer stroke, pulling his arms around to fold them against Martin's back, pinning the lustrous wings in place. "Better?"

Martin sighed against Casey's neck. "Oh, that's nice. That's very nice, indeed. How did you know to do that?"

"I'm not sure. It just made sense, I suppose." Casey clasped his arms a little tighter, running firm hands in long strokes down the folded plumage. "Tell me what it feels like."

"It's difficult to describe. Did your mother ever brush your hair when you were young? Not to remove the tangles, just to soothe you?"

Casey nodded in remembrance, a smile tugging at his lips. "Yeah, I get what you mean. But however nice this is, we need a shower to get this mess off, or we're going to regret it."

"Agreed." Martin pulled back slightly. "You go first. There's only the most rudimentary of showers, and I want to stretch my wings out for a while."

"Thanks, won't be long." Casey eased off the bed and stood up, turning to head out the door.

"Casey!" Martin was off the bed and behind him before he reached the door. At the note of alarm in his voice, Casey began to turn around before Martin stopped him.

"What? What's wrong?"

"Your tattoo, or whatever it is. It's gone."

"What do you mean it's gone?" Casey twisted his arms so he could see the underside. Martin was right. They were bare again.

"I mean, it's completely gone. The redness, the markings, it's just...gone."

They made their way back to the cramped bathroom where the long mirror was still set up from the previous day. Sure enough, Casey's back was pristine again. Not a trace of the strange markings remained.

Casey huffed in irritation. "Well, what does that mean? Where has it gone? Will it be back? Did we, I don't know...fuck it off me?" He threw his hands in the air as he paced in frustration.

Martin laughed openly. "Fucked it off? The sex was good, but it wasn't—" He grinned wickedly. "Come to think of it, it *was* exquisite."

Casey turned on him, skating the thin edge of anger. "You can't seriously believe—" He looked at Martin's sparking eyes and the frustration dissipated. "It's not funny."

Martin was still chuckling. "It's a bit funny, you must admit. The idea that good sex—"

"Great sex," Casey interjected.

"All right, *great* sex...could make it disappear." Martin stopped and thought for a moment. "Actually, maybe you're on to something."

Casey looked at him as Martin proceeded to pace the very short length of the bathroom, stark naked, wings proud on his back. In Casey's mind, the already laughable scene was taking on a truly epic level of grandeur.

He sighed in defeat and sat on the closed toilet lid. "Go on, tell me."

"What if the two are connected?"

"What, my tattoo and sex?"

"No." Martin rolled his eyes. "Try and keep up, Casey. What else happened?"

Casey glanced down at the dried mess on his abdomen.

"No. Well, yes, but I was thinking more..." Martin flexed his wings in the small room.

Realisation dawned "Oh! So, my markings have gone and—"

"My wings are back." Martin grinned in triumph.

"Seriously?"

"Do you have a better idea?"

Casey conceded that he didn't and stepped into the shower while Martin went hunting for towels and put the kettle on.

Casey had just put the shampoo bottle down as Martin strode back into the room. Pulling open the screen, he crowded into the tiny cubicle, jamming Casey up into the corner.

"For fuck's sake, *Martin*!" Casey shouted, trying to push him out again. "There isn't enough room in here."

Martin put his hands on Casey's face, forcing him to pay attention. "I know. Concentrate! I've been trying to dismiss my wings, nothing happened and then I had an idea."

Casey ineffectually tried to shove him away.

"There's not enough room. What would give us more space, Casey…? *Concentrate!*"

Casey's lips tightened, his temper rising at Martin's tone, and suddenly, Martin's wings shimmered and dissipated.

At their departure, Martin also frowned, looking deeply disturbed. "Well, that's going to complicate matters."

Still angry, Casey asked roughly, "What is?"

"I have no control over my wings anymore. None at all."

Casey's eyes widened in realization, and he asked, awestruck, "But I do?"

Nodding, Martin confirmed, "But you do, and if we needed any additional evidence—" Martin put his hands on Casey's shoulders and turned him around, grunting in confirmation. "—your tattoo's back."

WHATEVER THE PROBLEMS they were facing with Martin's wings, the ongoing murders necessitated action.

"So, tell me again, why we are going to church, Martin?" It felt good to stretch his legs, Casey thought as he walked beside Martin along the gravel road.

"Small, remote community. There are a couple of places people gather to swap gossip and check in on each other. One's the pub, the other is—"

"The church. I see. So, it isn't really about religion?" When Martin had announced they'd be attending the Sunday service, Casey had done some quick mental math and estimated it was over ten years since he'd attended church, much longer since he'd been to a proper mass. The instinctive Catholic guilt that settled in the stomach at the prospect had been distressingly familiar.

"Don't worry, Casey; I won't make you go to confession. I suspect neither you nor the priest has enough time set aside for that today." Martin smiled as his long strides ate up the distance.

"Oh, funny." Casey's brisk pace kept him at Martin's side. "I'll have you know that on the scales of heavenly justice, I think I'm doing all right, thanks."

Martin slowed to a stop and turned seriously to Casey. "No lingering self-doubt or Catholic shame at being in a relationship with a man?"

Something in Martin's eyes gave Casey the impression that his answer carried more weight than a casual chat exchanged on a country road, and he reached out to lay a gentle hand on Martin's arm, pausing to take a few extra moments to choose his words with more care.

"None. Look, Martin, I'll admit I was raised a certain way, to believe certain things. And I struggled against that for a long time." Casey set off again at a more sedate pace, and Martin fell in beside him. "Too long. But I've decided that the church can't have it both ways. Either their God is a loving, forgiving, all-powerful being who can come down in person and explain to my cock that it shouldn't find my infuriating, amazing, courageous partner the most fucking gorgeous thing it's ever seen. Or God and anyone else who has a problem with it can get the fuck out of our bedroom."

Martin stopped, and Casey turned back to see him standing in the road blinking at him, a grin on his face.

"What?" Casey asked, arms wide in confusion.

"Just the image of God standing by the side of the bed, telling you to get your cock out of my arse."

Casey grinned back before stepping up and taking Martin's face between his hands. "And even then, he'd have a fight on his hands. It's a very nice arse."

"So you've said." Martin dove in for a kiss before straightening. "We're going to be late."

"Sorry we're late, Father. My partner and I were just having an intimate discussion on the subject of gay sex. Yeah, not a great first impression." Casey chuckled as they headed off again.

They walked in silence for a few minutes before another thought struck Casey.

"Martin?"

"Hmmm?"

He glanced around them to make sure they wouldn't be overheard. "Can we talk about my tattoo and the link to your wings?"

"We *are* talking about it, I would think." Martin sunk his hands into his deep pockets as he walked.

"You're proposing that whenever your wings appear, my tattoo disappears, right?"

"It would seem so, on current evidence."

"And that since the bonding, it isn't you calling and dismissing your wings. It's me."

"Yes."

"But you called your wings that first morning after the bonding when I was on the balcony."

"Did I?" Martin didn't turn his head toward Casey. He only asked the question, and Casey considered it.

"Didn't you?"

"Think back, Casey. You were on the balcony, I was in bed. What were you thinking about?"

Casey's steps slowed but didn't stop as he cast his mind back to the light, airy room, the relief that they were both still alive, and how he'd be able to see Martin flying again and—

"Casey," Martin said urgently, "whatever you're thinking right now, stop it. Think about taxi cabs, dismembered corpses...anything!"

Casey turned to find Martin had stopped dead in his tracks and was hunched over, grasping at his knees. When he lifted his face to Casey's, his expression was stricken.

"Jesus," Casey muttered. "I nearly did it again, didn't I?"

Martin nodded. "It wasn't your fault. It was my suggestion. No harm done." He was panting slightly. "At least I felt them coming that time. I think I slowed it down, but I'm not sure."

"We need to sort this out. God, imagine if I did that in public."

Martin stood and approached Casey, gathering him close. "It'll be okay. We'll work it out." He eased back. "So, you *did* think about them, back at the house?"

"Yes, I think I probably did," Casey said slowly, "but I didn't have this tattoo yet. How does that factor in?"

"I don't know. Maybe it just took longer to appear. It's not as if there's anyone we can ask about this. If it helps, you're not the first to struggle with controlling their wings. We all go through it at puberty."

"But... they're not my wings," Casey replied.

Martin smiled thoughtfully. "They beg to differ, I suspect."

"AMEN." THE HUSHED repetition echoed around the tiny church. Martin thought there were maybe two dozen people clustered in the pews. A good turnout for a midsized community, and more than a few lingering glances were set in their direction, assessing the new arrivals in their parish.

The congregation was seated in tightly grouped sets. Couples, children, parents, here and there a single person silently hoarding the vacant space either side of them. Casey sat quietly observing the gathered populace.

The family of four, marriage looks rocky from the body language but statistically likely to weather the recent infidelity for the sake of the children. There's the other participant, with his own wife, no kids there, they're both blaming each other.

Newlyweds, new to the village. Can't wait to get out of here and back home to bed, but their parents would want them to go to church. Avians, then, children of local families, returning to raise their own brood.

An older couple, look well into their 80s. Look at the way he keeps his eye on her. Probably had a bit of a scare, but they look okay now. They'd be worth chatting to later. They probably know everyone in the village.

A nudge from beside him brought his attention back to the room.

"Do we do communion?" Casey asked.

The withering glance Martin gave put paid to that, and they sat quietly, watching a handful approach the front and kneel, accepting first the wafer, then the wine.

"I don't recognize the priest," Martin murmured into his ear. "He must be new."

"In the name of the Father, the Son, and the Holy Spirit... In the name of the Father, the Son, and the Holy

Spirit..." Casey watched solemnly as the priest made his way along the line, performing the familiar ritual.

Martin leant in close. "Next...pub. Now that we're 'part of the community,' people will be more willing to talk to us."

"Do you see the old couple? I think they'll probably know every intimate detail of the past sixty years."

"Dolly and Stuart." Martin nodded. "They babysat Leon and me as children. She makes the most amazing hummingbird cake."

Casey nodded, a small smile tugging at his lips. "Good to know. Did you learn anything from the service?"

"I found out that my initial impressions of Sunday service when I was young were correct."

"And they were?"

"Pointless and dull, but interesting from a sociological point of view. Shall we?" Martin eased himself from the pew and slipped out the door.

"I NEVER THOUGHT we'd see you again. You've grown up, Martin. Hasn't he grown up, Stuart? And working for the government, how exciting! We never see you anymore. How is your brother? Is he still a lawyer? And who is this? Are you here together? How are you? You're gaunt, Martin. Have you not been well? Doesn't he look thin, Stuart?"

Martin managed to get a word in after only three minutes by launching himself toward Dolly and hugging her warmly. It was a similar approach used by his mum with equal success. Tugging the old couple to a table, Martin motioned for Casey to retrieve drinks and sat down for a chat.

By the time Casey returned, the conversation had descended to local gossip, heads conspiratorially tucked together in the middle of the table.

"Just be careful, young man. No walking around alone at night. It isn't safe." Dolly tapped a wrinkled hand on Martin's long fingers.

"I will be, I promise." He nodded with mock seriousness. "Oh, Casey, this is Stuart and Dolly. They were like a second family to me."

"Pleased to meet you. I've ordered tea and cakes."

Dolly winked at Stuart. "That one won't be single for much longer, Stuart. Casey knows just how to turn a lady's head."

Stuart shook his head but smiled in spite of himself.

Martin snorted and eased a silent hand to cover Casey's on the table, saying more with the motion than words ever could.

Dolly's eyes widened slightly as she spotted the move and then smiled kindly. "Well, look at that." She reached to take Stuart's hand in her own. "He's already taken."

Although they hadn't discussed "going public." Casey's next move happened without hesitation. With a smile to his lover, he turned his wrist and interlinked his fingers with Martin's, the grin on his face saying everything.

They chatted amongst themselves amiably over the following hours, talking about people moving to the area, people moving away. Of marriages, and infidelities, of births and deaths. They spoke of the local bakery owner, whose leg had been amputated after a car accident, and of the priest's mother, ill with cancer and her son balancing his ministry's needs with hers. They talked about the impact of the economy and how so many locals were opening their houses as bed-and-breakfast hotels. They talked about Dolly's knee replacement and Stuart's failing eyesight and about how Martin and Casey began working together in the bright lights of London. Dolly enquired after Leon and "that lovely silver-haired gentleman he brought up here sometimes," and Martin asked about Dolly and Stuart's two children over in France pursuing careers and family of their own.

By the time they were debating whether to stay on for dinner, Casey had been unofficially accepted into the family, and left to her devices, he suspected Dolly would be planning their wedding before dessert.

Casey dramatically stretched and looked to Martin who raised a questioning eyebrow.

"Time to get going?" Martin asked.

"Yeah, my leg." Casey gestured at the table top.

"Of course." Martin rushed to explain. "Old war wound. It bothers Casey on the cold northern nights, and we have a bit of a hike home."

Dolly's eyes widened in sympathy as Stuart rubbed his own knee knowingly. "Oh, then you must go. We've already kept you too long. Will we see you around?" She sounded hopeful.

"Not sure. We're playing it day by day at the moment, but it's been lovely to meet you." Casey rose and shook both their hands, emitting a short squeak as Dolly pulled him into an expansive hug.

"Casey!" Martin was calling him from the door, having already paid the tab.

"Sorry, must dash... Wouldn't want to leave him alone in the dark." And he made a quick escape through the door to join his partner in the gathering gloom.

Chapter Twenty

HOT...SO HOT. The Middle Eastern sun beat down on him as he crouched amongst rocky outcrops, rifle cradled in his hands. Even in his dreaming state, Martin knew he'd never been there. Likely the landscape was a mental patchwork put together from years of documentaries and anecdotes from Casey's time in the armed forces. Further adding to the strange tableau was the presence of his wings at his back, black and gleaming in the sun, arched slightly to shade his head from the baking rays. Around him, his troop clustered, all human, and nobody so much as blinking at the feathered appendages on their leader's back.

Whispered instructions, supplemented with urgent hand gestures had the team moving eastward toward a small house. Scrubby trees and livestock nestled around it, and the team moved quietly so as not to raise the alarm. More concerning was the battlefield inside his head. A plethora of thoughts and images bombarded him without the usual control or constraints he managed to apply. Some distant part of his consciousness understood that these were Casey's thoughts, Casey's scattered ideas, and while comforting to have his friend with him, the bedlam was distracting.

Suddenly, a shot rang out, then a second, and two of the team fell with a choked-off cry. Diving to the dust, Martin rolled and sought what little shelter could be found in the barren landscape. The heavy weight of a first-aid kit appeared in his hands, and he looked down. He recognized the hands as Casey's; shorter, stockier, and fair instead of his own dark skin.

Crawling to his fallen teammate, he crouched protectively over him and pressed the gauze firmly against the messy wound, the blood slick on his fingers. With sickening prescience, he knew what was coming next. He looked up just as the shot hit him in the thigh, wrenching him away from his patient and into the sand, screaming... his voice lost amongst the gunfire.

"Martin...*Martin!*" Casey was roughly shaking him awake, his firm fingers gripping too tight on his biceps in the dark room.

He screamed desperately, then it tapered off in his own ears; the blinding pain shooting through his leg was slower to dissipate. He could feel the shattered crunching of the bones and the aching numbness closing in on his toes. He tried to flex his foot and failed, his leg stubbornly refusing to respond to his commands.

"Christ, Martin, I thought you were dying!" Casey moved a hand to his face, prying open his eyes to check the pupils.

Martin tilted his head forward, shaking it to try to clear his thoughts, scattered between memory and reality. "It wasn't me. It was you."

"I don't understand." Placing a hand on Martin's forehead, Casey did a basic test for fever.

"I was there, in Afghanistan. I was shot, or rather, you were." Martin tried to roll his hips, wincing at phantom pains. "I'd be tempted to think it was just a dream, but with the bonding, I'm just not sure."

"Drowning," Casey whispered, earning him a wide-eyed look from Martin.

"What did you say?"

"The other night... I dreamt of falling off a pier or being pushed, actually. At first, I thought it was just a bizarre mash-up of memories and imagination but—"

"I was pushed off a pier by some bullies when I was six," Martin whispered, hushed and hesitant. "I nearly drowned. I was in the hospital for weeks. Do you remember anything about the beach?"

"No, not really. Could have been anywhere."

Martin was nodding. "Still, sounds close enough. I don't know what this means, or even if it's useful."

"Just one more complication." Casey rubbed a soothing hand up and down Martin's back. "We should try to get some more sleep if we can."

The sound of gunfire and the hot flare of pain still skittered at the edges of Martin's mind.

"You go back to sleep, I'm going to see if I can spot anything new in the files."

The following days passed uneventfully. Having covered the floor, dining table, and bench-top with information, Casey began layering papers and photos on the chairs. When he pegged notepaper to the curtains, Martin finally capitulated, taking the car into town to source a large pinboard and a flip chart. Casey's delighted reaction made the long trip worth it.

Martin stood before the arrayed information and scrubbed a hand through his hair in frustration. "There's nothing here! There's no pattern, no theme, no sequence. Whatever the thread is to tie these together, we don't have it!" He kicked at the table leg. "This is *impossible*!"

Casey looked up from the autopsy photos he was analyzing for the fourth time. "You need a break."

"I *need* more information!"

Casey pursed his lips. "You *need* a change of pace. C'mon…" He stood up and grabbed his coat.

"Where are we going?" Martin asked.

"You're going to teach me how to operate your wings."

"*NO, CASEY, NO.* Concentrate!" Martin shouted.

"*I am concentrating!*" Casey yelled back.

"Not well enough, because as you can see…*no wings!*"

"I can *see* you haven't got wings, Martin. I *am* trying, you know."

"You're useless at this. Any Avian over the age of three can learn it!"

The two of them were standing in the gravel yard at the front of the cottage. Hidden from the road, they had only secluded open fields to their back, ending at the sheer cliffs that descended to the North Sea. For over an hour, Martin had been standing shirtless in the cold air, prompting Casey with suggestions on how to summon his wings in a controlled way. The results had been less than successful.

"I don't know if you've noticed, Martin, but I'm *not* an Avian."

Martin made a rude-sounding noise of dismissal. "Well, that's obvious."

Casey turned his back and began a slow count of ten, his fists balled at his side. "I don't know what you expect me to do!"

"*I expect you to learn,*" Martin shouted before reining in his temper. "You don't seem to understand, Casey. If we can't get this in hand, if you can't control this, everything we've been through, everything you've had to suffer, will be for nothing." A note of desperation crept into Martin's voice. "They *will* lock us away. Is that what you want, for us to be incarcerated because I can't be allowed in public?"

Casey turned back, frustrated anger flushing his cheeks. "Of course, I don't *want that*! For Christ sake, Martin... *I'm. Trying*. It's not as if I *like* having to manage your wings for you!"

"Well, it's no fucking *picnic* for me either! Perhaps you *like* being in charge? Exerting authority over me. Pretending you're in control!"

"*I am in control!*" Casey shouted.

"*Nobody controls me!*" Martin shouted back.

They stood breathing hard and silently glaring at each other, not really angry, but trapped by the situation.

"I'm going for a walk," Casey finally announced, turning to walk across the field. "Clear my head."

"Casey..." Martin called, suddenly desperate.

Casey turned back, anger burned away to tired sadness. "What?"

"Don't be long," Martin offered, his voice soft and vulnerable.

Casey's lips quirked in a defeated smile. "'Course not. Put the kettle on."

BY THE TIME Casey returned, a remarkable transformation had taken place in the living area of the cottage. Space had been cleared on the floor, and a large blow up mattress had been installed, sheets and blankets neatly folded on it.

Casey looked at the bed, distressed. "Umm, I hope our argument hasn't resulted in my being banished from the bed. Would it help if I said I'm sorry?"

Martin turned from the mugs. "Don't be ridiculous. We're expecting guests."

Casey took one of the mugs gratefully. "Anyone I know?"

"Oh, I should think so." Martin smiled. "Carrington and Leon are coming to stay."

Casey paused, before carefully putting down his mug. "Your brother."

"Yes."

"And Jared Carrington."

"Yes. Well, it's a weekend, so obviously they'll be together."

Casey paused again before his next question. "Why?"

"Because they spend every weekend together."

"Not what I meant."

"Oh, right. Because…" Martin sipped at his drink, not making eye contact. "We need help."

With those words, Casey realized that this was Martin's way of apologizing too. For him to reach out to his brother, admitting that they couldn't handle this alone must have taken an enormous toll on his usually self-assured partner. He walked around the island bench and closer to Martin's side.

"We'll make this work. We'll find a way for my boring little non-Avian head to wrap itself around the whole 'wing-thing,' and we'll be okay. After all—" Casey nudged against Martin "—we do know one sure-fire way for me to summon them already."

Martin blushed and laughed into his mug before he could stop himself. "Yes, but getting each other off isn't really practical in all circumstances."

Casey grinned, his voice just a touch husky. "I dunno… Could be. How long until your brother gets here?"

Martin put his mug down and turned to his lover, eyes dark, and said, "Hours."

Casey's mug joined Martin's on the bench as he moved in close. "Just enough time then."

"Shall we take this to the bedroom?" Martin whispered, his hands already sliding under Casey's shirt.

"God, yes."

Chapter Twenty-One

"LEON?" JARED CARRINGTON'S voice echoed off the timber wall moldings as he closed the front door behind himself.

"In the study," came the distant reply from down the hallway.

After shrugging off his coat, he hung it on his accustomed hook in the front entrance and dropped his briefcase to the floor. The moment the physical weight left his hand, a similar lightening of mood swept through him.

It was a well-known rule of Jared's. Once the clock hit 7:00 p.m. on a Friday night, he was "off air." His phone was on silent, emails remained unanswered. Short of a disaster that risked the security of the nation (which he assured everyone that he'd hear about through other channels), his weekends were sacrosanct, and Scotland Yard would need to take care of itself.

The payoff for his team was that for the rest of the week, he was focused, engaged, and available virtually any hour of the day.

"I'm just getting a beer," he shouted down the hall.

"They're chilling in the fridge."

The kitchen was filled with the delicious aroma of Moroccan spices, emanating from the general direction of a slow cooker tucked in the corner of the bench. Jared lifted the lid and peered inside. Tantalizing glimpses of chicken and chickpeas bobbed into view with the gentle simmer, and he replaced the cover to keep the heat in. In the well-stocked fridge, he found a six-pack of his usual beer pushed well to the back of the top shelf where they'd get the most benefit from the chill-zone. He pulled one from its cardboard restraint and made his way down the rest of the hall.

With a cleansing sigh of relief, he walked through the open door of Leon's study. A contrast of dark and light zones, the pair of wingback chairs nestled in companionable dimness near the open fire, their cushions almost lost in the shadows. Meanwhile, Leon sat head down at his desk on the other side of the room. Brightly lit with two fluorescent lamps, the area was clearly designed for efficiency, and from the pile of files stacked next to the man at the desk, it needed all the efficiency it could manage.

Without raising his head, Leon welcomed his visitor. "I won't be long, just about finished."

Jared walked across the room to the man's side, close but not touching, and responded, "Take your time. I know if you don't wrap up whatever it is you're doing, you'll just end up back here."

Leon briefly leant into Jared's solid presence before returning to his focus. "True."

THIRTY MINUTES LATER, Leon finished saving his files, unplugged the USB key, and tucked it into the top case before snapping it closed and flipping off the twin lamps.

Suddenly night-blind, he made his way toward the chairs by the dim firelight, smiling when flickering light reflected off a scotch glass on the side table. He was about to thank Jared for the thoughtfulness when he noted the slumped form and gentle snores from the other chair.

Sitting, he took the opportunity to consider the sleeping man opposite. It was nearly two years since he and Jared Carrington had entered into what they called their "marriage of convenience." In truth, they were neither formally married nor would a homosexual relationship, should it become public, be considered convenient for either of them. And yet...there they were—two men, defenders of the realm, in public office and prominent figures in their circles.

Jared snuffled and mumbled something that might, possibly, have been about asparagus, and Leon's face softened into an adoring grin. That expression was one very few had seen. Also in Jared's safekeeping was the expression Leon made when he had the chance to sit and really enjoy a meal, the one where he'd just woken up after a long sleep-in on a Sunday morning, and the one where he was on the sharp edge of self-control and blissful oblivion. Leon wasn't exactly sure when he'd agreed to surrender so many carefully hoarded moments of vulnerability, but he knew with a bone-deep certainty that his secrets were in the safest of hands. There was nobody Leon trusted more than Jared, and he couldn't imagine life without him.

Leaning forward in the chair, Leon whispered softly, "With hollandaise or vinaigrette, DI Carrington?"

"Mmmmmmm..." Jared dragged a long breath in through his nose, and his head lifted from where it had settled on his chest. "Sorry. Long week."

"No apology needed. I take it as high praise that you feel comfortable enough to drift off here."

"With these chairs and that fire, I was a goner before I sat down."

"As long as it isn't the company boring you, I'll forgive you." Leon drained his scotch and stood to refill the glass. "Another beer?"

"Sure."

As Leon left the room, Jared stood and stretched out tired muscles. His plans for the night indeed included sleeping together, but he wanted that to include *all* the usual meanings of that phrase. Although he and Leon had agreed to make this relationship something of a casual-fuck-on-Friday-night thing, somewhere in the past two years, it had become significantly more. It was to Jared, at least.

As his lover returned, beer in hand, Jared considered again what it was that had prompted such a strong bond with the superficially officious litigator. Indeed, Leon wouldn't be considered classically handsome. In fact, neither of them would be fending off offers if he was honest. Well on the wrong side of thirty, long office hours, and set in their ways, they certainly weren't "ripe for the picking." But there was something about Leon Bishop, the way he held himself, the self-assurance, the unshakable belief that good would triumph, tempered with a cold pragmatism. Combined with intelligence, which, quite frankly, Jared had never seen anyone come close to, resulted in an almost magnetic pull. Jared couldn't imagine life without him. But he just couldn't seem to find the courage to say the words out loud. Leon had made his feelings quite clear, *no strings.*

They returned to the chairs by the fire. "I thought we might have some supper," Leon offered.

It was always like this at first. Small talk, cagey flirting, both of them a little uneasy and awkward. Even after all this time, it seemed that these little insecurities crept in. Sometimes it was Leon, other times it was he. It was as if they were both afraid that one wrong word or a misstep would spell the end of the odd relationship they had. This peculiar emotional dance was the only part of the weekend he detested.

With any other man, Jared would just throw caution to the wind and push for what he wanted, but Leon was different. He couldn't afford to lose Leon. For that alone, he'd tread carefully.

"Yes, supper sounds great."

Things settled into a more comfortable dynamic over bowls steaming with rice and Moroccan stew. Leon had opened a bottle of wine, and as the level dropped below the halfway point, the awkwardness dissipated, and the conversation flowed more freely.

"So, Martin and Casey got to South Ronaldsay all right?"

"Yes. They got there yesterday, but there's a problem. They've asked if we could fly up tomorrow."

Jared chewed thoughtfully, lost in memories. "I love that cottage. Why don't we go there more often?"

"We lose three hours each way on the plane—" Leon paused, then added, "and there are other things I usually prefer we do with the limited time we have."

There was always a moment...a tipping point. Every Friday, it was exactly the same; a look, a touch, a word. The moment that would set the tone for the evening. Some weeks, the flint would strike a spark and the flame would flare and consume them both. Clothes would be shed hurriedly, and the night would end in sweat-drenched satiation. Other nights, there would still be a spark, but the tinder would smoulder rather than erupt. The heat was still there, but it would curl and lick at them, warming them deep into their bones.

Tonight, as Jared lifted his face to Leon's, the answer was written in the dark rings under his eyes. The first hint had been the dipped head in front of the fire, and the exhausted slope of his shoulders was the final clue.

Leon put down his bowl. "Come here," he murmured, holding out his arms as he stood.

Jared's bowl joined his on the table as he gratefully moved into the circle of his arms.

THIS, JARED THOUGHT, *simply...this*. This was why he came back, week after week.

"Come to bed, Jared. You need sleep."

"Sorry," he murmured, his mouth against the smooth fabric of Leon's shoulder.

"For what? Isn't this what we do, give each other what we need?" Leon's voice was smooth and calming against his ear. "Come on, leave the dishes. You're practically asleep on your feet. You work too hard." Leon murmured endearments as he slipped each shirt button through the hole, sliding the cotton down Jared's arms. "Now, summon those beautiful wings, and you can relax."

Jared nodded and stepped back slightly. Closing his eyes, he dropped his shoulders and pulled in a deep breath. With a whisper of sound, a ginger-tinged glow and the smell of fresh-mown grass, his wings shimmered into existence.

Regardless of the fact that Avians didn't succumb to the bliss that humans were subjected to, Leon still found Jared's wings a wonder.

Crisp and beautiful, they put his own grey plumage to shame. Jared flexed his shoulders and, for the first time since the previous weekend, stretched the strong caramel-coloured hawk wings out as if stretching his arms. Flecked with black, they were clearly raptor wings, and Leon had always thought them terribly appropriate for the man who bore them.

"Gorgeous. Now, bed." Leon regarded his lover.

"You're joining me?"

"Well..." Leon smiled openly. "It is *my* bed."

"And I sleep better with you in it. Will you summon your wings for me?"

"I'll have a shower first and then crawl in after you. I doubt I'll wake you."

As Jared crawled between crisp sheets and his head hit the pillow, he mumbled, "I doubt it too."

Twenty minutes later, hair damp and wings folded against his back, Leon quietly lifted the quilt to lie down and stare fondly at his sleeping lover.

This, he thought, unaware that for the third time that night his thoughts were echoing Jared's own. *Simply this...* This is why they came together week after week. If it were up to him, they'd be sharing a bed and a house every day. He'd known for some time that he wanted this man in his life forever. But that wasn't what they had agreed. It would be too complicated, too messy. And if it meant that he got to keep at least this much of Jared, then he'd keep his thoughts to himself.

Chapter Twenty-Two

THE KNOCK ON the door came as Casey was toweling off his hair.

"That was cutting it a bit fine, don't you think?" He looked back at Martin, fastening the buttons on his shirt as he strode into the room.

"I was actually hoping they might catch us *in flagrante delicto*." He smiled wickedly. "It'd serve my brother right."

"They're here to help us; it wouldn't hurt you to make an effort."

Martin rolled his eyes and opened the front door as Jared raised his hand to knock again.

"Martin... Not interrupting anything I hope?" Jared's grin was infectious, and he gave him a quick wink as the DI pushed past and dumped two suitcases on the rug.

"Not at all, we were just..." Casey gestured at a mug as he switched the kettle on.

"Taking a shower in the middle of the day... Yeah, happens all the time." Jared continued to nettle them, moved to his side, and flicked his eyes up at Martin.

"All right, Carrington, we get the point. You're pleased that Casey and I have consummated the next phase of our relationship." Martin held the door open for his brother before closing it against the evening chill behind him.

"Well, you settled some idle speculation around the Yard from when you two were working for us. There may have been a betting pool started."

Martin looked up, aghast. "Good God. They barely knew us?"

"What can I say? You were a bit obvious."

"I was *not* obvious." Martin turned to his brother, and to the surprise of the room, they shared a surprisingly warm hug. Dropping his voice, Martin said earnestly, "Thank you for coming, Leon."

His brother broke the embrace somewhat awkwardly. "Well, Martin, whatever else we may be, we *are* family."

Casey and Jared shared a glance before taking the four mugs back to the lounge room to set them down on the coffee table. Casey settled on the floor at the foot of one of the armchairs and Jared joined them. Jared sat on the edge of the air mattress, leaving the remaining armchair for Leon.

"So, little brother… Tell me how I can help," Leon said with all sincerity.

Martin sighed and rubbed a hand through his unruly curls. "We expected some consequences from the bonding. Even though we had no idea what they'd be."

Jared held up a hand. "Lee filled me in on the ceremony. Sorry I couldn't be there, by the way. He said there have been some…complications?"

Casey smiled, he'd never thought anyone would call Martin's brother Lee. Martin nodded. "We may as well start with the obvious. Casey, you may as well show them."

Standing, Casey shucked off his shirt, revealing the vivid marking across his back and shoulders. If anything, the lines and colours had deepened over the past couple of days, making the similarity to Martin's wings even more clear.

Jared released a low whistle. "Wow, well, that's… impressive. Anyone in the community would be able to tell who you're bonded to."

Leon stood and stepped closer, reaching out before pausing mere inches from Casey's skin. "May I?"

At Casey's nod, Leon traced the lines with his fingers. "They're hot to the touch. Do they burn, Casey?"

Casey glanced over his shoulder, shaking his head in confusion as Martin joined his brother, reaching out to place his own hand over the marks.

"They don't feel warm to me. Jared, can you check, please?" Martin let his fingers fall away to make room for the Detective Inspector.

"Yeah, Lee's right. It's hot, almost too hot to leave my hand there. You really can't feel it, Martin?"

Testing the skin again, he shook his head. "Just another item to add to our list. Seems benign, at least."

"We may as well show them how the tattoo is linked to your wings while I have my shirt off." Casey turned to Martin.

Leon looked at Martin, confused. "I thought you said he couldn't summon them?"

"Not reliably. We have a technique, but let's just say, it's not practical in polite company." Martin blushed. "If you'll excuse us a moment." Martin gestured to the bedroom.

Casey snorted and muttered, "Prude" before shepherding Martin to the bedroom.

With the door closed, Leon and Jared were left to guess at what was happening until a very flushed Martin and Casey returned to the room, Martin's wings now clearly in evidence.

Jared looked between them both, taking in the tented state of their trousers and stifled a laugh with the back of his hand, laughing harder at Leon's still bemused face.

Clearing his throat, Jared asked with an almost straight face "Purely for scientific purposes, I think you should describe what happened, preferably in graphic detail."

Casey and Martin shared an awkward glance before Martin finally blurted out, "I stuck my hand down his trousers, all right? I get Casey worked up, and *hey presto*... wings! Can we leave it at that?"

Leon buried his head in his hands and Jared collapsed into schoolyard giggles as Martin continued, "Yes, I know. Can we just never mention that again?"

"Agreed," mumbled Leon, shooting Jared a nasty look as his partner's laughter only gained in volume.

"*Anyway*!" Martin interrupted the exchange. "Casey, turn around, if you would."

Sure enough, Casey's back was clear of marks and, after a quick check, clear of the distinctive heat present before.

Leon rubbed a thoughtful hand across his jaw. "So, the problems with summoning your wings, that's the only symptoms?"

"There's the dreams..." Martin mentioned quietly.

"You think they're connected?" Casey queried.

"Don't you? We're having dreams; imagery that could only belong to the other person. They're muddled together, vivid...strange." Martin explained what little he knew.

"Anything else?"

"Not that I can think of. Can you, Casey?"

A shake of the head and Leon looked at them both thoughtfully before asking, "Jared, would you mind summoning your wings?"

Casey paled and took a step back. "Hey, wait a minute. Not that you're not a good-looking bloke, but I think we've established that I'm with Martin now. I really don't want to find myself unexpectedly humping your leg—" He turned to Leon. "—or yours!"

Leon smiled benignly. "And to be frank, Agent Wicker, that image alone is enough to give me nightmares. But if you'll indulge me, I'm testing a hypothesis."

Martin stepped behind Casey and placed a steadying hand on his shoulder. "I suspect I know what Leon's thinking. Let him try." He leant in close and whispered in Casey's ear, "And I promise the only man you'll be humping is me."

Casey shivered and leant back as Martin's arms circled his chest, finding comfort in his warmth as Jared apprehensively shed his shirt.

"You're sure?" Jared looked to Martin. "I've heard the stories...changing in front of humans."

"I'm sure. When you're ready, Jared."

"Can we just get it over with?" Casey muttered, leaning his head back against Martin's shoulder and gritting his teeth.

Casey was used to the heat and light that he associated with Martin's wings, so he was surprised at the almost serene calmness that accompanied Jared's as they shivered into existence. There was a gentle susurration and the sharp smell of rain on grass. The dim light of the room took on a distinct caramel tinge, and Jared's hawk-like wings seemed to settle into place on his shoulders like a king putting on a robe. It was no less beautiful or magical than Martin's. However, there was none of the crippling lust that had assailed Casey before their bonding. He released a long breath, and the tension slipped from his frame, still held within Martin's arms.

"Okay?" Martin whispered in his ear.

"Yeah, fine. Looks like you're the only Avian for me." Casey chuckled.

Leon was nodding as Jared idly brushed fingers through ruffled plumage. "I thought as much. Your bond has negated your human response to our changing."

"It's probably the only useful side effect so far," Casey murmured.

Leon's eyes widened slightly. "The only good one? From what you've told me so far, all the changes have benefits."

Martin looked briefly angry but then thoughtful. "I can see you plotting, Leon. Explain what you mean."

"In the morning. We've had a long day and a longer flight, and from the look of our luxury bedding you've *so* kindly arranged for us, I doubt we'll be getting much sleep." He looked distastefully at the inflatable mattress on the floor.

Jared stepped up beside his partner. "Could be worse."

"How?" Leon asked tersely.

"Casey and I could make you share with Martin."

The twinned looks of horror on the Bishop brothers' faces was worth any payback.

CASEY AND MARTIN lay facing each other in the generous bed, listening to the awkward squeaks and rustles as their guests tried, and failed, to make themselves comfortable in the lounge. Martin's wings lay folded behind him, taking up the equivalent of an extra person's space as they talked quietly in the dim room.

"We should have offered them the bed," Casey murmured.

"Don't be ridiculous, Casey. Why would we have done that?"

"You're a terrible host, Martin, and a worse brother."

"If I treated him any differently, he'd suspect I was plotting his demise." Martin smiled in the darkness.

Casey shuffled closer, reached out a gentle hand, and ran his fingers down Martin's neck, eliciting a gasp in response before Martin's hand came up to settle at his waist, tugging them together.

"We'll have to be quiet. Your brother's in the next room."

Martin rolled Casey onto his back and nuzzled into the hollow of his neck. "I can be quiet. I can be silent as the grave. You, on the other hand..." He reached to run a thumb over an already pebbled nipple and delighted in the groan that resulted.

"Maybe this wasn't such a good idea." Casey chuckled, pulling Martin's errant hand away from his chest and sucking a mark onto the pale skin under Martin's ear.

"I think it's an excellent idea." Martin tilted his head to expose more of his throat, while his hand strayed lower, carding through short, wiry hairs below Casey's navel.

Casey bit down gently to smother the noises threatening to escape his mouth as Martin slipped his hand lower to ghost over his erection. Fingers brushed light enough to tease yet not provide the desired pressure and friction, and Casey whimpered.

"Shhhhhh...quiet, Casey. You said quietly." Martin pulled away and began a tortuous descent down Casey's body, his wings spread, allowing the long flight feathers to brush against the undersides of Casey's arm and his chest, then licking at the goose bumps that rose on his skin.

LEON AND JARED had settled as best they could onto the uncomfortable inflatable mattress.

"I hate my brother," Leon muttered.

"You don't. We wouldn't be here if you did." Jared lay sprawled face down, arm draped over his chest, toying idly at Leon's chest hair with his fingertips.

"Well, then, he hates me."

"That's not true, either, and you know it." Jared chuckled.

Leon heaved a sigh. "And listen to that, now they're having sex in the room next door. This is unbearable."

"They make a good couple, you have to admit."

There was a noncommittal grunt as Leon shifted again.

Jared's quiet chuckles threatened to escalate, so he instead leant over to press his lips firmly against Leon's. "Bet I can take your mind off them," he said.

"I am *not* having sex in the room next door to my brother." Leon sounded aghast.

Jared kissed him again, brushing his tongue against Leon's pursed lips. "Not even a little bit of sex?"

Leon relented and smiled against his lover's lips. "There's no such thing as a 'little bit of sex' with you, Detective Inspector."

"Then we should have a *lot* of sex in the room next to your brother." Jared nibbled and then sucked Leon's lower lip between his own. "Lots and lots of noisy, messy sex," he muttered.

"SHHH...STOP...STOP for a second." Casey placed a hand on Martin's head, now somewhere in the vicinity of his navel and still travelling southward.

Martin lifted his head from Casey's stomach and stilled for a moment. "What?"

"Listen." Casey held up a hand and waited. Sure enough, the clear sound of moans and an air mattress moving against wooden floorboards carried into the dark room, and Casey giggled quietly.

"Oh, God!" Martin buried his face in the skin of Casey's abdomen.

Casey grinned. "If I'm not very much mistaken, Martin, that's the sound of a challenge being made."

"How *could* they?" Martin's tone was despairing and somewhat disgusted.

Casey ran fingers through Martin's curls. "Much the same way we were...and are about to."

Martin looked up, horrified. "You're not saying—"

"If you can't beat them..." Casey flexed his hips. "Unless you're not interested anymore."

Martin rolled his eyes and poked his tongue in Casey's navel as retribution. In retaliation, Casey ran firm fingers between the layers of feathers edging Martin's wings.

JARED'S HAND JOINED Leon's where it was already wrapped around them, encircling both and stroking firmly. This position allowed Jared to look directly into Leon's eyes as they leant their foreheads together, their hips moving against each other.

Suddenly, Jared's look of passionate concentration broke into a foolish grin, throwing off Leon's rhythm.

"What?" he huffed, breathing the same moist warm air between their faces.

"Can't you hear them? I haven't heard Martin laugh like that since we were kids."

"Can you...*not* talk about my brother when we're having sex," Leon huffed without any real malice.

"Sorry..." Jared thrust in the way he knew Leon liked. "Sorry. It's just...Casey makes him happy. You can see how much Martin loves him."

"I'm...pleased for them." Leon adjusted the angle just slightly, knowing just what Jared needed. "I'll be pleased...for them...tomorrow...I promise."

"You should know, you make me happy, Leon. I want you to know that." There was a hint of something unsaid, and even in the throes of passion, Leon rarely missed things. His rhythm faltered, and he stared into Jared's eyes, shining in the dim light of the room.

"You make me happy, too, Jared. You have no idea how happy."

AS CASEY'S BACK arched and he jammed a fist into his mouth to stifle his cry, Martin swallowed once, twice, and again as Casey came in his mouth. He glanced down to see his hands buried amongst Martin's ruffled feathers and knew from their quivering that Martin was perilously close to the edge himself.

"Come up here. Want to try something," Casey whispered, voice raspy from panting.

Martin crawled up the bed and allowed himself to be turned so that his wings were sandwiched between his back and Casey's chest.

"Further...a little more." Casey curled in behind him, his now softening cock against the small of Martin's back, and he reached an arm under Martin's folded wing to take him in hand.

"Tell me how this feels." Casey tilted his head down so he could direct his breath down over the edges of Martin's wings as he stroked with his hand.

"God, Casey..."

"I'll take that as a positive reaction." Casey brought his free hand up to smooth down the length of the wing right in front of him as Martin arched and wiggled in his arms.

"You are... you...are."

"I'm what, Martin?" Casey blew warm air amongst the feathers, never ceasing his stroking. "What am I?"

"Everything..." Martin mumbled brokenly as he trembled and shivered. "You're everything."

Casey carded fingers through glossy black feathers, feeling them flex and lift from the skin in a way he now knew meant Martin was right on the edge.

He picked up the pace of his strokes, paying attention to the sensitive underside as he whispered, "You're the most amazing man I've ever met, Martin...and you're mine." With the last, he lowered his face to the wing under his cheek and nuzzled amongst them, inhaling the clean, fresh scent and placed a sucking kiss against the skin there.

Martin came with a cry, never even sparing enough thought to try and suppress it. He shuddered in Casey's arms and then fell limp against him, doing no more than curling even closer against him.

THE TWO MEN in the other room were so wrapped up in each other that a minor war would need to be declared to drag Jared's attention away from Leon.

They were cuddled together under the blankets on a mattress that now seemed strangely larger given the spare space around their tightly clasped forms.

"You're very quiet." Jared laid a heavy hand on Leon's chest.

"There's something I want to say. It's needed saying for some time, and I've been avoiding it."

A chill ran down Jared's spine. Surely, Leon wasn't ending things. Not now. He cast his mind back over the past weeks. Had he been too clingy, too demanding?

"You don't need to say anything," Jared ventured quickly, not wanting to hear it.

"I do. I can't go on like this, Jared. I'm not...it's not enough."

"Leon—" Jared could barely get the word out.

"No, let me finish, I wanted to say..."

At a stuttered sound, Leon turned his head to discover Jared's eyes were wet, his face stricken. "Oh, God, Jared, no. You've misunderstood. Please, love." He leaned to pepper Jared face with kisses, wiping away the tears with his thumb. "Let me finish."

"Don't leave me," Jared mumbled. "I'll do anything, please. We can cool things down, just...please."

"What? Leave you? What are you talking about? God, I'm making a mess of this. Don't cry. Please don't cry. I'm not leaving you, quite the opposite."

"I don't understand. I thought..."

I don't want this to be a casual thing anymore, Jared," Leon blurted the words. "I want this to be the opposite of casual."

"This hasn't been a casual thing for me for ages," Jared replied, leaning to wipe away the last of his tears.

"It could cause problems. People won't like it," Leon said.

"We're good at solving problems. It's what both our jobs are about. Stop worrying."

"Because I have such a successful history of not worrying." The sarcasm wasn't lost on Jared.

"And I'm good at telling you to stop. Look, if I'm honest, I doubt this will come as much of a surprise to most people."

"What makes you say that?"

"Your PA's been sending me birthday gifts for years. She even knows what brand of underwear I buy."

Leon's laugh was open and bright and more carefree than Jared had ever heard. "I'll have to thank her. You know what I meant earlier, don't you?"

There was a long pause before Jared's response. "That I make you happy too?"

"Yes...that I love you."

Chapter Twenty-Three

BY THE TIME Jared Carrington had gotten his coat on and joined the three men in the expansive back field, Martin and Leon had already bailed Casey up and were assailing him with a steady litany on concentration methods *guaranteed* to control the summoning and dismissal of Martin's wings.

Jared thrust his hands deep into his pockets and strode toward the little group.

"No." Martin turned on his brother. "We tried that, Leon. What he needs to do is—"

"Martin!" Jared's uncommonly authoritative tone drew all three sets of eyes to him in surprised silence.

A fierce frown appeared on Martin's face, and he opened his mouth to take control of the situation again.

"No." Jared held up a single hand, demanding silence again. "Look, I know you two think you know what you're doing, but take it from me, you don't. So I'm asking you both to go over there—" He pointed across the field. "—and leave Casey with me."

A doubtful look was exchanged before Jared nodded more gently to Leon, silently begging for trust, and Leon guided his brother away with a hand on his back between his still-present wings.

Jared watched them meekly walk away before he turned and smiled at Casey. "God, I *love* when I get to push those two around. Nothing like it."

Casey stared after them, already bickering between themselves with animated hand motions.

"Right...Casey, I know you and I don't know each other particularly well, so this is going to be a bit of a leap of faith."

"Martin and Leon seem to trust you, so that's in your favour."

"I'll take it. First things first, whatever tripe those two have told you, forget the lot of it." Casey's mouth opened and then closed as Jared continued, "They're experts, the both of them, in their own fields, and I daresay they think that makes them the authority on this, too, but when it comes to us ordinary blokes, what works for a Bishop doesn't work for us."

A tiny smile had begun to quirk up at the corner of Casey's mouth, "Right. Yeah, you're right."

"So, chuck out all that *concentrate* bullshit that they instinctively seem to take to. I'm going to go old-school with you, okay?"

Casey nodded. "Thank God! Martin says *concentrate* like he's expecting me to pull a fucking rabbit out of my arse."

"Yeah, Lee's the same." Jared took Casey's shoulders in his hands and turned him, so he was facing away from the two men far down the field, out of earshot. "Lesson one. Stop thinking so hard. Ever done any meditation?"

"Not since University, but I remember enjoying it."

"Good, so we're gonna do a bit of that stuff, and then when you've stopped concentrating on the one hundred and one other things we pathetic idiots have going on in our heads all the time, we'll...umm... Look, let's get that going first."

Half an hour later, Jared and Casey were seated cross-legged on the cold rocky ground, knees just touching, breathing in time. Over and over, Jared had drilled him on how to centre his thoughts, drifting out and back to imagining a blank, white page.

"Okay, break time." Jared looked past Casey's shoulder and grinned. "Look at our boys, will you? Bloody idiots the both of them, but magnificent, all the same."

Casey stood, brushed the gravel off his jeans, and turned around.

Leon and Martin were playing some complicated game of aerial tag. Martin had a scarf in one hand and was dodging and diving as Leon wheeled and spun to try to grab it from him.

"Wait a second... Martin said Leon couldn't fly." Casey shielded his eyes from the sun as they engaged in a bizarre Avian dogfight.

"What? Of course, he can fly. What Leon lacks in speed, he compensates for in manoeuvrability."

Casey could see what Jared meant. Unlike Martin's iridescent black plumage, Leon's wings resembled the shorter, more compact wings of a pigeon. Touched, like his brother's, with opalescent violets and greens, they were a soft dove-grey, which seemed to match the lawyer's personality perfectly. While Martin had more power, Leon clearly cornered faster, and Casey grinned as the older brother secured the scarf and spun to arc away with desperate haste.

Jared stepped up behind Casey, twin faces turned to the sky, watching the siblings in the Avian equivalent of a wrestle on the carpet. "It's good to see them relax away from prying eyes. It strips away all the posturing, and they remember who they are to each other."

Casey nodded thoughtfully. "Okay, let's get back to it." He turned away and resumed his spot on the ground.

Jared looked up once more, as his lover hovered and tumbled with carefree abandon. "Right, let's get settled. But I need to get Martin on the ground in case you get it right first time."

Casey swallowed and nodded in realization. "Got it. Visualise but don't apply." Casey settled on the ground.

"Okay, so now you can get to the mental place you need to be in a matter of moments."

"White paper, yes...got it." Casey nodded.

"So, now, if I remember my first year right, there's two basics we need to get right. One is to summon, and the other to dismiss. Hang on... I'm going to call Martin down. Wait here."

In a familiar rustle of copper brown and the smell of grass, Jared's wings appeared, and he was aloft. For the first time, Casey wondered at the speed and ease of Jared's summoning.

There was no doubt that the process was faster for Jared than Martin, and even when Casey had unwittingly summoned Martin's wings, it seemed faster than when Martin had control. *Keep it simple*, echoed in his head in Jared's voice, and with a sigh, he filed it away with the other mysteries he might never solve.

The draft of wings announced their return, and he was suddenly surrounded by the seemingly impossible sight of three grown men, men he'd worked with but with wings proudly stretched the length of their back. Casey found the not-unfamiliar hysterical giggle bubbling up from deep in his chest before clamping down on it again.

"All right, Casey, graduation day. Ready?"

Casey remained seated, not yet ready to test his newfound skills while standing, but nodded confidently.

"Okay, Martin, come here." Jared took his arm and led him to stand behind Casey, out of his line of sight.

"Casey...white paper."

Summoning the image of the now-familiar blank page, he nodded silently.

"Now, imagine a picture of your tattoo on the page. Replicate what's on your back on the page. That's the image of your wings on your back."

Casey thought for a moment and visualized the ink covering his skin replicated on the page. He nodded again. "Got it!" The entire process had taken less than half a minute.

"Now," Jared said confidently, "rub the picture out!"

Casey knew the outcome from Jared's joyous yell and stood to see the result of his efforts, opening his eyes.

Though the gaps in Martin's shirt remained, the wings had gone. Martin was staring at Casey, delighted and a little proud. "You did it! Casey, you did it!" He briskly covered the few strides that separated them and pulled his lover to him, engulfing him in a crushing embrace. "You *did* it."

Casey struggled to nod within the confines of Martin's embrace, giggling with relief as Leon stepped around them to embrace Jared with similar pride and enthusiasm.

"We're not done yet," Jared managed to mumble through the heavy twill of Leon's casual shirt. "We need to make sure he can get them back."

"Of course." Leon pulled back and returned to Casey's side, tugging his brother away from him. "Although, I daresay Casey has the knack of it now. Go ahead, Casey."

All eyes rested on Casey as he stared into Martin's intense eyes. He took a breath, imagining the piece of blank paper once more and, with a slow blink, visualized the tattoo on the page again. The air shimmered around Martin, and Jared and Leon took a step to either side as Martin's wings returned to their rightful place at his back, neatly folded and smooth.

Martin took a step forward again and looked down into Casey's face, serious for a moment and unguarded as to the emotion in his voice. "You, Casey Wicker, are amazing. You are brilliant, you are astonishing, and you...are *everything* to me."

"So, just keep your mind on the page, and I think you'll be fine." Jared placed an encouraging hand on Casey's shoulder as they entered the lounge.

"Yeah." Casey considered thoughtfully. "I think I've got it. Look, thanks for your help. I slept better last night than I have for... Oh, for God's sake, what are you two doing?"

Over the breakfast table, Martin and Leon were engaged in an old-fashioned game of rock-paper-scissors. Twin sets of brows creased in concentration, their stares never wavered from each other.

"*Damn!*" For one brief moment, Leon's concentration had wavered to glance sideways at Jared, and Martin's scissors had toppled his hastily thrown paper. With a smug grin, Martin unfolded himself from the chair and stood, stretching his shoulders.

"So, that's decided." Martin picked up his coffee cup, draining it quickly. "You and Jared are on gossip duty at the church and pub."

Leon flashed a distasteful look to Martin and stalked past him to change out of his casual fleecy pants and cable jumper. Jared trailed after him silently.

Once Leon and Jared had departed to gather the latest town gossip via the church grapevine, Martin and Casey settled in for a quiet morning, Martin with the morning's paper, Casey with a novel he had been dying to spend some time with.

Quiet reigned in the small space until Martin suddenly blurted, "Well, yes, but we'd have to be quick."

"What?" Casey looked up, startled.

With a look of confusion, Martin responded, "Yes, I think there probably is time for you to give me a blowjob..." Martin blinked. "But we'll need to be quick if you want me to get you off as well before Jared and Leon get back."

"I didn't ask..." Casey looked equally confused.

"Yes, you did. I heard you."

"No...no, I didn't." Casey considered a moment and then held up a finger, asking for silence as he closed his eyes.

Martin, what's eight times eleven?

Martin's eyes widened. "Eighty-eight," he whispered.

And is Pluto a planet? Casey opened his eyes and smiled.

"Yes, funny." Martin grinned before the expression dropped away. "This is fascinating."

"So, can you hear all my thoughts? That could be awkward. Can I hear yours?"

Martin closed his eyes and concentrated. When no response came from Casey, he opened them again and looked for confirmation. "Nothing?"

"Nothing. It's either one way, or you haven't worked out how to do it yet."

OVER THE FOLLOWING two hours, they tested their new ability. Martin could clearly hear Casey through closed doors, over a significant distance, and even through water—tested with Martin holding his head deep in the laundry trough. It appeared that Casey had to at least be thinking about Martin or to Martin. Otherwise, his thoughts remained his own.

By the time Jared opened the door to the cottage, Martin held copious pages of notes and was delighted by what he considered the first useful side effect of their bonding.

"Hi, Jared," Casey greeted him happily. "You won't believe what Martin and I have—"

Jared glanced around the room and frowned. "Where's Leon? Isn't he back yet?"

TWO HOURS EARLIER

Leon knelt before the railing to receive communion. As his head tilted back and the priest placed the wafer gently on his tongue, Jared quietly murmured *amen* in silent brotherhood with his lover.

He wasn't entirely sure how he felt about Leon going through the motions. They were both far from what the Catholic Church would consider in a state of grace, but he'd always considered faith to be a very personal matter, and if Leon felt no qualms about the ceremony, he wasn't going to question him.

Returning to his side, Leon sat quietly and bowed his head in silent reflection for a moment before looking to Jared and smiling serenely.

"I'd never taken you for a particularly religious man. Did I miss something?"

"I like the simplicity," he replied. "The routine, the repetition, the predictability. I always know what's going to happen here. There are no surprises."

Jared nodded. "And it doesn't bother you, that they—"

"That our lifestyle's not really...approved? I rather suspect God, if he or she indeed exists, is far more liberal-minded than the agents on Earth."

"I hope so." Jared smiled. "So, what's next? Home?"

Leon shook his head. "Martin wanted us to check in with Dolly and Stuart at the pub, but I might ask you to head there alone if you don't mind. I'm feeling a little faint. I think I'll go back to the cottage."

Jared laid the back of his hand on Leon's forehead. "You do look pale. You sure you don't want me to come with you?"

"No, I'll be fine, Jared. Go, have a beer, and then a scotch for me, and I'll go and disturb my brother, who's no doubt poking through our personal belongings in our absence."

Jared snorted and took Leon's hand, well out of view of the congregation. "I won't be long. Then perhaps we can go home and have one night to ourselves before we head back to work tomorrow."

"Sounds perfect." Leon leant in. "Now, get out of here, Detective Inspector, before I assault you and scandalize these kind people."

BACK AT THE COTTAGE

"I'll think I should go back to the church and see if the Father Campbell saw him leave." Casey pushed his arms into his coat.

"And I'll head back to the pub. Maybe Leon changed his mind and tried to catch up with me there." Jared was shifting from foot to foot, obviously anxious to be gone.

"I'm sure he's all right, Jared. I'll drop past Dolly and Stuart's. See if he's trapped between Dolly's cake and a cup of tea." Martin's tone was light, but Casey knew his expressions well enough to see the tension behind his eyes. He was worried and attempting to hide it.

The three men parted ways at the doorway, Martin heading off across the open field, Casey toward the church, and Jared making his way back to the village. As he walked, Casey tested his connection with Martin again.

I know you can't answer me, so just listen. You're worried but didn't want Jared to see. If you get wind of something, call me. Casey put as much force behind the images as possible. *You don't go in alone, you hear me, Martin? Do NOT go wading into trouble without me...or so help me, I'll kill you myself!*

CASEY QUIETLY PUSHED open the door of the church, scanning the dim interior for Leon's distinctive figure in the pews without success. He was about to turn and leave when a noise toward the back caught his attention.

Martin, something feels wrong at the church. Don't know what. Better head here.

Edging silently down the aisle, the noise came again. Distant muffled shouting from somewhere below. At the top of the stairs, Casey crouched to listen.

"Couldn't believe you came back... Thought I'd missed my chance... It's a sign."

Martin...trouble...hurry.

Casey eased a foot onto the top stair, sending a wordless prayer that it didn't creak as the ranted diatribe continued.

"Don't you understand? I need more time... Mother hasn't repented yet... Too soon for the Rapture..."

Taking another two steps gave Casey enough room to crouch and peer down, assessing the basement of the church.

Stalking from side to side, a long blade in his hand, was Father Campbell. In front of him, strapped to a makeshift frame, was Leon Bishop.

MARTIN! Leon's here. We're in trouble. Wings visible. Need you here... HURRY!

Leon's head lolled to the side, still conscious but gagged and bound. Casey remembered what Martin had said to him weeks ago about it being impossible for a human to force an Avian's wings to appear, and yet, Leon's dove-grey plumage was visible behind him, his wings cruelly roped to the supports of the frame.

"The angels will herald the Lord's return... I'm sorry...no...not yet. I have to slow His return."

Risking a glance back up the stairs, Casey saw no sign yet of Martin. There was no time. If he delayed further, Father Campbell apparently planned to take matters into his own hands. With the calmness of the battlefield, Casey made a decision and acted on it.

"*What have you done? You think you speak for our Lord,*" Casey shouted, striding down the stairs.

The knife clattered to the floor as the priest turned, paling at the fire in Casey's eyes, the determination in his words.

"You would treat His beloved angel so?" Casey narrowed his eyes, trying to convey the displeasure of a vengeful God. "You are no priest of ours."

The priest fell to his knees with a shudder, staring at the floor.

"Why? Why would you disrespect our God this way?" Casey played for time, needing Martin's backup to ensure the priest's successful apprehension.

"My mother...so sick...redemption...she needs redemption...the voices...the voices told me...stop the angels...he said...delay His return...give her time."

Casey blinked, thinking fast. The man was deluded, mad, and desperate. But dangerous?

Father Campbell mad...thinks Avians are angels...trying to delay the second coming, apparently.

Several things happened in the space of the next several heartbeats.

Father Campbell looked up. A spark of clarity cleared his eyes, and in a flash, he reached for the knife.

With a shout, Martin came careening down the stairs, shrieking like a banshee.

Casey summoned Martin's wings.

Martin might not have been an angel, but the flash of light, the heat, and Martin's makeshift sound effects together with his massive shining wings instantly reduced the priest to a whimpering pile on the floor.

A whirlwind of dark and light, Martin took the hint and loomed over the cowering man, shouting down at him, *"You have betrayed your God. You...will be...damned."*

Martin's wings bristled, looking every part the avenging angel of legend as the man cowered and Casey bound his hands with a spare rope coiled near the frame.

Once secure, Casey moved to check on Leon, lifting his eyelids and calling gently to him.

Martin meanwhile messaged both Jared and the local inspector.

Martin looked over his shoulder. "Is he all right?"

"Drugged. Not sure with what. I'd like to get him down. Can you give me a hand?"

With Martin's help, they untied the ropes and lowered Leon's pliant body to the concrete floor. Casey did his best to fold his wings neatly against his body, wondering again what the priest had done to summon them forth.

"Leon...Lee, can you hear me?" Casey tapped him gently on the cheek. "It's Casey. C'mon, wake up a little bit for me."

There was a grunt and a weak hand came up to grab at Casey's wrist.

"Good man. Listen, Lee, we've got you. You're safe. But I need you to put your wings away. People are coming. Come on, Leon, you can do it."

There was a frown of concentration, but the wings stayed stubbornly where they were, and Casey looked despairingly to Martin, concerned at what would happen if local law enforcement arrived, some of whom were human. Sirens already sounded in the distance.

With a huff, Martin walked over and crouched down near his brother. "Leon! Don't be such a baby. Put your damned wings away and stop showing off, or I'll tell Jared that you used to dress up as Margaret Thatcher when you were a child."

Leon's eyes cracked open, and he shivered hard, concentrating again. His wings shimmered and disappeared, and as Martin breathed a sigh of relief, Casey dismissed Martin's wings too.

"Martin?" Jared's voice came from above.

"Down here. We're all fine. Bring them down."

THE THREE MEN sat clustered around Leon's hospital bed as one of the most drugged-up and influential lawyers in the country mumbled happily about an enormous flamingo that was invading the houses of parliament.

"What sort of fucked-up priest kills angels?" Jared shook his head in disbelief.

Martin sat, his hands in a temple under his chin. "One who'd do anything to save his mother."

"Still." Jared leant forward to lay a hand over Leon's.

"Never underestimate what family will do for one another. It makes idiots of everyone." He looked pointedly at his brother, who slept on, oblivious to Martin's teasing.

"What will the council do with him—the priest, I mean?" Casey asked quietly. "After all, he knows...or at least, he knows something."

"Likely nothing. In the unlikely event that he ever regains anything resembling sanity, anyone he tells will simply think he was delusional. Plausible fiction, Casey, plausible fiction. He'll spend the remainder of his days in some sort of institution. I have no doubt of that."

"So, that's all it was? One crazy priest desperately trying to give his mother time for salvation?" Jared asked.

"Perhaps," Martin replied.

"What?"

"How did he identify the Avian...and where did he get those drugged wafers that forced their wings to appear? Doesn't seem a very likely skill-set for a small-town priest," Martin mused.

Casey stood and paced. "You think he had an accomplice?"

Martin looked up tiredly. "Not an accomplice, Casey. I believe he had a puppet-master.

Chapter Twenty-Four

THEY MANHANDLED THE bags through the door of Martin's flat and closed it behind themselves with a weary sigh.

"Finally!" Casey pulled off his coat and uncharacteristically dropped it at his feet. "I've never been so happy to get home."

"Nor me. It does seem like a lifetime ago, doesn't it?" Martin's voice held an odd, pensive note.

Casey paused for a moment before remembering the last time they'd been together in the safe house. The scene played back in his mind—accusing Martin of lying, telling him that it was over, that he was too much, Martin leaving to find solace at Alissa's, Leon's USB footage. Then the kidnapping, bonding, and...well, everything.

It had been a whirlwind of adrenaline, pain, and discovery, but mixed in, there'd been moments together when Casey felt like he'd finally found the missing piece of his life, his heart, and his soul. Turning, he found Martin purposefully avoiding his eyes, perhaps afraid of what he might find there.

Casey reached out a hand as he walked toward his lover and best friend. "Come here." Sliding an arm around to tug him toward his chest, he used the other hand to tilt Martin to face him. "Tell me what's bothering you."

Martin's lips tightened, tiny frown lines appearing between his eyebrows. "I'm wondering, what now?"

"What do you mean?"

"For us. What now? Things are...different." Martin pulled away from Casey's arms to pace nervously. "Even before Leon abducted you, you said you'd had enough. If anything, things have only gotten more complex, more confusing since then. You wanted space, and I've dragged you further into the mire of Avian society."

"Tell me what I'm thinking, Martin." Casey held his gaze.

"What?" Martin stopped and turned back.

"Read my mind. You can do that now. So, do it. Read me." Casey's arms fell loosely to his sides, feet planted wide.

Martin took a step closer, and Casey smiled at the way that Martin's focus seemed to narrow down to the finite space that Casey occupied in the centre of the room. His head tilted minutely as he seemed to sift through Casey's thoughts before his eyes widened with unexpected surprise.

"You're happy. No, you're...ecstatic," he said. "You're tired, but it's like the tiredness after a long run. You're... content." The frown was back. "Why are you content? What's changed?"

"Because now I know what I'm dealing with, Martin." Casey smiled and took another step, encircling Martin's waist again. "That's what I was trying to tell you at the estate. I needed more, and you gave it to me. For the first time, I feel like I'm on solid ground. With you, with...*this*"—he waved a hand between them—"with the whole Avian *thing*. Sure, this bonding still has some mysteries to solve, but I feel like I'm standing by your side, instead of running to catch up all the time."

Martin looked down at Casey, shaking his head in wonder. "You amaze me, Casey Wicker. When everyone else is running away, you retain your sanity by attacking head-on."

Casey chuckled and reached to pop a button through its hole. "So, you asked *what next?*"

Martin nodded, his breathing picking up as Casey moved to the next button.

"Now...I think I'll take you to bed."

LIFE RETURNED TO normal for Casey and Martin, well...as normal as things got. All was forgiven at the Service, following a glowing report by a certain Detective Inspector. Martin slept in, stayed up late, and Casey's underwear found a home in the top drawer of Martin's dresser.

Casey continued to practice his meditation, honing his control over Martin's wings. Meanwhile, by hard-won inches, Martin gained a tenuous ability to slow, if not stop their materialization.

Casey initially interpreted this as Martin rebelling at his loss of control until, one dark night, Martin had looked up from his chair, eyes dark and seductive, and rumbled the word *wings*.

Casey felt his pulse pick up as his cock throbbed at the prospect. Rising to his feet, Martin stepped closer, untying and letting his robe slip from his naked shoulders.

"My pleasure." Casey put his newspaper aside and joined Martin in front of the fire, running his hands up Martin's chest to thumb at dark nipples.

Martin growled low in his throat. As he'd become more accustomed to Casey's touch, they'd found a balance between control and his seemingly overwhelming tactile need. With fingers far more confident than mere weeks ago, he reached to pull Casey's jumper up and over his head, then made short work of the button-down beneath.

"Wings," he murmured again, more aggressively.

"Hang on...hold your horses." Casey chuckled roughly, picturing the white paper upon which he'd draw Martin's wings.

As Casey had become more skilled at summoning and dismissing, he'd been able to relax into the process, and was once again able to lose himself to the fizzing bliss that came with the midnight feathers. He felt the process begin, the familiar tug of heat at his groin, accompanied by the heat and shimmering light. It rose like a tide within him, rippling out in all directions until his toes were curling with pleasure. He opened his mouth to pant as he mentally drew Martin's glorious wings on the page in his mind.

Then suddenly, just as the wave of ecstasy should have begun to calm as Martin's wings settled into place, he felt the crest level out. With effort, he opened his eyes to find Martin's locked his own, concentration evident in the lines of his forehead. With a whimper of need, he realized what was happening. Over Martin's shoulder, he could see the wings, frozen in a quasi-state, fuzzy and translucent in the air as Martin slowed the process. He was holding Casey's arousal at its peak, allowing the bliss to roll Casey in its foamy waves.

Without a word, Martin stepped into Casey's space, his large hand reaching to palm Casey through his jeans before granting him relief by lowering the constricting zipper. Casey sighed as Martin took him in hand, stroking gently in time with the thrum of his passion.

"Martin..." Casey groaned, reaching for the man with shaking hands.

"Touch me, Casey," Martin grunted, pupils were blown wide even as he held his control with an iron will.

He needn't have asked. Casey couldn't resist touching, even if Martin had forbidden it. He took Martin's arse in his strong hands and pulled their bodies together. Trapped between them, Martin shifted his grip to hold them together, widening his stance slightly to better brace himself. There was a shimmer of light as Martin's concentration wavered and Casey keened as his orgasm, held back by the thinnest of threads, threatened to overcome him.

With a grunt, Martin steadied and returned to his rhythmic strokes, and Casey was forced to pull his mouth away to drag air into his lungs.

"Martin..." he gasped. "Read my mind, Martin... See what you do to me, know what I feel? Hurry."

With a rumble, Martin leant his forehead against Casey's, as desperate as Casey. What little control he had in reserve, he turned to delve into Casey's mind, connecting them in yet another intimate way.

Whatever he saw, it was enough to tip the balance; with a wide-eyed gasp and a shattered groan, the Avian lost his battle, and his wings stuttered into existence on his shoulders, leaving Casey to come with a shuddering cry, coating Martin's hand with his release and turning his legs to jelly.

Martin's arm tightened around Casey's back as his own orgasm overtook him, and he managed to stagger backwards, guiding them both to an ungracious tumble onto his chair, breathing hard as Casey continued to tremble in his arms.

"You're a..." Casey managed weakly. "You're a maniac...you know that, right?" He raised a weak hand to push Martin's sweaty curls off his forehead.

Martin cleared his throat as he caught his breath. "You knew what you were getting in to. I've always been the crazy one."

Casey giggled as he tried, and failed, to lever himself off Martin's chest. "I've been in denial."

Martin's rumbling chuckle joined Casey's as he held their bodies together with strong arms. "Then I hope you like maniacs."

Casey eased his arms around Martin, finding his way between feathers, skin, and the leather of the chair. "I like this one."

CASEY GRABBED FOR his mobile as it threatened to vibrate off the table. "Jared, hi."

There was a pause, and Jared talked to someone in the background before his voice became clear, "Casey, yeah, sorry. I'm— Hang on just a sec." The muffled sounds continued, Jared clearly frustrated at someone at his end. "Sorry, I'm at Leon's. I know this is gonna sound weird, but can you two come over?"

Casey frowned at the tone in Jared's voice. There was an odd mix of concern and frustration. "Yeah, sure. I'll just get us into some clothes, and we'll be right over." Casey's attempt at humour fell flat, and after a pause, he added, "Everything all right?"

"Yeah..." Jared replied in a drawn-out way that indicated that it absolutely was not all right. "I'd like your professional opinion on something. Family stuff, you know..."

"Right. Okay." The intonation of "family" rang alarm bells in Casey's head. In terms that would be overlooked by most monitoring systems, Casey suspected Jared meant Leon, and it was Avian in nature. "Martin! Get some clothes on. We're going out."

Chapter Twenty-Five

"I HAD NO idea houses this size existed in London." Casey whistled in admiration as they pulled into a graveled drive.

"He needs it to accommodate his enormous legal library and his equally massive ego." Martin passed some bills to the cab driver and followed Casey out of the car, stones crunching under their feet.

"Seriously, who has a lawn this size in London? How does he get it so green?" Casey knelt to confirm it was actual, living grass.

Martin was striding toward the door. "I expect he waters it with the blood of his fallen enemies. Keep up, Casey."

Jared opened the door before Martin had a chance to knock and ushered them both inside the rich timber-panelled hallway. Light from the leaded windows along the top of the door cast everything in warm jewel tones.

"Couldn't bring himself to ask me for another favour directly, Detective Inspector? Told you to use Casey to badger me into something? That's a new low, even for my brother." Martin was in fine form, having been deriding his brother for most of the trip over. He brushed an invisible thread from his suit jacket as if it shared common DNA with Leon.

But something in Jared's eyes made Casey place a gentle hand on Martin's arm, gesturing him to silence with a look. "Jared...why are we here?"

Before he could answer, Alissa emerged from a door somewhere down the long hallway, her worried expression losing some of its tension as she saw who it was in the hallway.

"I thought I heard the dulcet tones of the younger Bishop brother." She walked confidently toward them, stripping off latex gloves as she approached.

Martin spread his arms, a quick worried look darkening his features as Alissa came to a stop out of reach, shaking her head.

"I'm still in scrubs, sorry." She glanced to Jared. "You haven't told them yet?"

"Haven't had a chance." He shook his head. "Perhaps we should move to Leon's room so we can cover all the questions in one place?"

"Alissa?" Casey's alarm was increasing by the second.

"Best we just show you." The look Alissa shared with Casey sent chills down his spine, and he fell into step behind her as she led the group back down the hall.

"WHAT NEEDLESS DRAMATICS... What—?" Martin's planned patronizing comment died away as he walked through the doorway and beheld the elaborate setup.

More than half the room had been encased in thick plastic sheeting complete with a hospital-grade quarantine double-seal door. Inside, Leon Bishop paced restlessly, mobile phone to his ear, barking instructions to some unseen lackey at the other end. To the casual observer, he appeared perfectly fine, albeit clearly frustrated.

Seeing his brother, Leon huffed a frustrated breath, tipped his head toward Alissa, and continued his conversation, leaving the questions to her.

"You can see he's the ideal patient," Alissa muttered.

"Must be in the DNA." Casey chuckled back. "But, Alissa... Quarantine? What's happened?"

Alissa fell into a clinical tone, crossing her arms over her hospital scrubs. "We don't really know. Leon's been exhibiting some rather...distressing symptoms since you all came back from Scotland, and they're getting worse. Martin?"

Without a word, Martin had drifted silently to the plastic wall separating the two halves of the room. Lifting a hand, he laid his palm softly against the transparent wall, and as the others watched, something in Leon's face changed and softened, and he quietly hung up his mobile, moved to join his brother, and matched the position of the hand from the other side of the barrier.

"Are you all right?" Martin asked softly, sounding much younger than his thirty-two years.

Leon paused and shook his head slowly, his stare never leaving his brother's. "No, Martin, I'm not sure I am." He looked up at Alissa. "Should I show them?"

There were the beginnings of tears in Alissa's eyes as she watched the unexpected moment between the brothers and then swallowed roughly and nodded. "We need to check if there's been much change overnight. Go ahead."

With little ceremony, Leon unbuttoned his suit jacket, followed by his shirt. Folding both carefully and placing them on a chair, he looked to Jared with something like dismay in his eyes before he took a deep breath and turned around to display his back to the spectators.

The air in the room rippled as Leon summoned his wings, and Jared's breath caught in a stifled cry beside him as they began to form at the bureaucrat's back.

Leon's efficient, dove-grey wings materialized as tattered, broken things. Large sections of feathers were ruined or missing, and in some spots, the skin was broken and bleeding, with the unhealthy yellow and green of infection showing deep in the recesses.

Casey raised the back of his hand to his mouth, unconsciously moving to block out the smell of purification that couldn't permeate the quarantine envelope. At his side, Jared was struggling to swallow distressed sounds, and Martin was leaning heavily against the back of an armchair. Alissa was weeping openly, fat tears rolling silently down her cheeks as Leon turned to face the room.

"They're worse, aren't they?" Leon's voice was muffled by the plastic, but his expression held stark fear at the looks on the faces in front of him. Alissa nodded in despair. "A lot worse?" he asked.

Jared approached the barrier and stood in front of his lover. Martin stepped close to place a hand on his shoulder, and Casey noted silent support inherent in the motion. "No lies between us, yeah?"

"No lies, Jared." Leon stood a little straighter, steeling himself.

"Yeah, they're a lot worse," he said, a hitch in his breath breaking the statement.

"Mmmm, I thought so." Leon nodded stoically, only the barest hint of a tremor in his voice. "They feel worse."

Alissa coughed and pulled herself together. "Is the pain worse, Leon?"

He nodded, flinching as the movement jostled them. Looking to his feet, he bent and picked up a feather, tinged with his own blood and held it carefully.

As he turned the ruined thing over in his fingers, he asked, "Remember our mum being so angry when you pulled out a flight feather? You said you wanted to look at it."

There was stark horror on Martin's face. "She said they never grow back. God, Leon, what happened?"

Instead of answering his brother's question, he winced and looked at Alissa. "Can I dismiss them? I think they've seen enough for now."

She nodded, and in a pained shiver, Leon's wings were gone again. With a resigned glance at the half-dozen stained feathers that remained on the floor, Leon quietly redressed, buttoning the jacket as if donning a suit of armour. "Now..." Squaring his shoulders, Leon was once again the officious, distant litigator. "Let's deal with the questions."

"ALL WE CAN assume is that there was something in the drug that crazy vicar dosed him with up in Scotland." Alissa was walking them through the facts as Casey tried to make sense of the medical records and Martin continued with a barrage of questions.

They dragged chairs over, setting them as close as possible to the plastic wall, and Leon had done the same on the other side. It somehow seemed important to them all, for different reasons, to be close together, even if they were unable to physically touch. Of the five of them, Jared seemed to be struggling the most. He spent long minutes seemingly lost in his own head before Martin or Leon would ask him a direct question, consciously pulling him back to them before he mentally drifted too far away.

"What's this marker here, the one you've circled?" Casey pointed to an entry detailing the chemical makeup of the communion wafers confiscated from the church basement.

Alissa looked at the entry. "That's the one we think is interfering with the process. From what the experts have been able to test, his DNA is degrading each time Leon calls or dismisses his wings. We're trying to limit how often we call them, but it's impossible to track the progress when we can't see them."

"Like making endless photocopies, each one loses something in the next run," Casey said thoughtfully.

Martin looked up suddenly and snatched the file from Casey's hand, flipping through pages.

"Hey!"

Martin grunted an apology as he scanned the file. "It's worth checking..." he mumbled.

"Checking what? You've thought of something. Share with the class, Martin," Casey pushed.

Lost within the pages, Martin nevertheless took a moment to outline his thinking process. "I'm just wondering—" He paused as he flipped over several pages and then back again. "—where someone might get their hands on a drug to interfere with the wing-summoning process."

Martin looked up and held Casey's eyes. "Perhaps something like you and I recently went through."

Casey frowned and then his mouth dropped open as he caught onto Martin's line of thinking. "The bonding? You think this drug is similar to the drug the Avians used in our bonding."

Martin smiled grimly as Alissa gasped.

"An Avian wouldn't do this," she said, appalled. "It's horrific."

An uncomfortable silence had settled on the room before Martin spoke up, "And yet..." He didn't need to add that it made perfect sense.

THE WALLS OF Martin's flat were thick with papers—diagrams, spreadsheets, medical reports, and photographs. Martin divided his time between the internet, phone calls, and stalking between one sheet and the next.

Casey split his time between meeting their physical needs—food, sleep, comfort, and heading off interruptions. He'd made a difficult call to their superiors to ask for some unexpected leave until further notice, and had advised everybody they knew that they were heading out of town. That had allowed Martin free rein to lay out material about the Avians that should typically be kept hidden.

They slipped into a period of relative calm, both taking a few minutes to grab tea and a sandwich to keep their strength up. Martin had sworn that he wouldn't rest until he got to the bottom of whatever was affecting Leon's wings, and Casey had no reason to doubt or dispute it.

"Ideas?" Casey asked quietly from his armchair.

There was a short and frustrated shrug as Martin jammed virtually the entire sandwich into his mouth. "Nothing, but I'm close. I can feel it."

"Who would do this? I mean, I think you're right. It *has* to be someone connected with the Avians, but what sort of Avian would engineer a virus that could destroy his own wings?"

Martin shook his head, face downcast. "I don't know. Someone with nothing to lose. "Someone who'd already lost"—Martin's head tilted up, eyes wide—"everything!"

He was out of the chair suddenly and riffling through papers on the desk, hunting desperately for something.

"What?" Casey asked, joining him.

"It couldn't be. But...it makes sense." He crouched and pulled out the drawer of a filing cabinet, dragging out page after page.

"*What*? Talk to me, Martin!"

Martin paused and stood up, turning to Casey. "You'd better sit down."

Casey blinked and sat as instructed. He'd learned by now that if Martin considered news likely to be a shock, it probably was. "All right, what *else* don't I know?"

Martin knelt in front of Casey, hands on his thighs as if ensuring he wouldn't leave. Another secret had the potential to fracture Casey's trust most of all. It was bound up in so many things that had happened recently and like a house of cards stood every chance of coming tumbling down around them.

"Now, Casey. I want you to remember that when this happened, I *couldn't* tell you about the Avians."

Casey nodded slowly, a patient frown firmly in place.

"And that technically this wasn't my secret to share, not *really*."

"Jesus, Martin, just get on with it."

At little more than a whisper, Martin mumbled, "Someone else survived a bonding."

Casey's eyes widened briefly before the impassive patient face fell back into place. "I'm sorry... I thought you said *you lied to me!*"

Martin's lips tightened, not taking his eyes off Casey.

"The bonding, the one that *nobody has survived in living memory*? You're telling me that there's another couple out there like us?"

"No. Not like us."

Casey was out of the chair in a heartbeat. "Then what are they like, Martin? This *other* couple. These people who could have *helped* us when we needed it, because right now...I need some *fucking advice*."

"You're overreacting," Martin said calmly.

"Really? *Really?*" Casey shouted at him. "Because I *really* don't think I am."

Martin dodged Casey's arms and leant forward to clasp Casey to him hard, tucking his head under Casey's chin and holding them together, saying the first thing that came to mind.

"You're here."

Shocked into sudden silence, Casey's wild flailing ceased as he tried to look down at Martin, pressed against his chest. "What?"

"You're here, Casey. I'm here. I'm with you. And neither of us is going anywhere. I'll tell you everything I can, whenever I can. Whenever I remember something I haven't said before, I'll tell you...because *you're still here!*"

Casey tried to make sense of the words, as his shaking hand came up to run through Martin's curls. "I...I know that, Martin. What's that got to do with...?"

"Because he's not. Because they didn't both survive. Only the Avian survived," Martin blurted out, gripping Casey hard. "There will always be things I didn't tell you. But whatever those things were, they don't matter. *We* matter, Casey. One day, fifty years in the future, we'll know it all. You'll know every dull, dreary little fact about me, and I'll know every fascinating nugget about you. We have time for that now, Casey. Time. Because we both made it." There was finality in words, and in the strength of his arms around Casey.

Casey sighed. "Tell me what happened."

"Their bonding..." Martin lifted his head away and looked up, haunted eyes meeting Casey's. "It went wrong. It went terribly wrong. And it drove the Avian mad."

Chapter Twenty-Six

THREE YEARS PRIOR

"It is the ruling of the council that if you are to live with this Sebastian Brooks—" The judges looked unsympathetically at the man in the dock. "—then you must submit to this."

"We won't. You can't make us," Yates spat petulantly.

"Then Mr. Brooks will simply...disappear."

Yates glared at the judges' panel with open hostility. Once a difficult child and now a virtual outcast, his jet-black wings bristled at his back. "I'll take you all down with me, if you do."

"Mr. Yates," the primary judge said firmly, "whether you like it or not—"

"I don't—"

"*Whether you like it or NOT,*" he continued, "you are a member of this society, and you will abide by our laws. You will undertake the bonding, or your relationship with Mr. Brooks will end. There is no alternative."

The aftermath of that critical judgement had been horrific. At the crucial moment during the ceremony, when years later Casey would submit to his fate and settle against Martin's back, Sebastian had desperately tried to flee. He'd wrenched himself away, breaking the half-formed bond and suffering catastrophic damage to his lungs. He'd died, broken and suffocating on the stone floor, while Matthew Yates had writhed against his bonds, desperately trying to get to his failing lover.

When Yates had been released from the bindings in the centre of the chamber, he crouched sobbing, cradling the body of the man he loved in his arms, the framework of his wings holding the tattered remains of feathers and flesh, and cursed them all. He'd never been spoken of in Avian society again.

PRESENT DAY

"Jesus," Casey whispered, "you were there?"

Martin shook his head, swallowing thickly as the bile rose in his throat. "I was overseas with you on assignment. We broke him, Casey. My society ruined his wings, killed his lover, and drove him mad, all for loving a human."

Casey clung to Martin. "That could've been us, you know?"

"I know," he murmured.

Casey looked at the numerous sheets on the wall. "God, Martin. I hate what's happening to Leon...what could happen to you all? And I agree, Yates is probably insane, but I have to admit, I have some sympathy for him."

Martin sighed tiredly. "I think we know better than most how inhuman the Avians can seem, and I won't make excuses. But what Yates is trying to do is biological warfare, Casey. It may even be genocide. He needs to be stopped."

"One thing puzzles me though. Yates seems to hold a particular grudge against Leon, and maybe even you as well. Is that just coincidence?"

Martin, at last, rose from where he'd been crouched at Casey's feet. "No. Leon chaired the original judging panel. And as for me, that's easy." Martin smiled wryly, looking down. "I have you."

Chapter Twenty-Seven

"BUT YOU *CAN'T* have contracted it, Alissa!" Martin was virtually shouting at her through the quarantine barrier. "It's not possible."

For her own part, Alissa was remarkably calm as she continued her work, now on the other side of the barrier. "Clearly it is, Martin. Perhaps the gestation period was longer than we thought? Perhaps it was transmitted before we established the perimeter? Perhaps..."

"*Perhaps*," Martin shouted, pacing furiously. "Perhaps if I'd been smarter, I would have worked out what was going on earlier, and none of you would have been exposed in the first place."

Casey stepped up quietly and tried to put a hand on Martin's arm but was violently pushed away.

"No! I don't need..." His head whipped around, eyes blazing. "Christ! Is Jared all right, or have I killed him too?"

A shocked hush fell on the room as Casey stepped in front of Martin, inches away from his fac., "Stop," he said firmly. "Just...stop. This *isn't* your fault, Martin. None of this is your fault. We'll fix this, and everyone will be fine."

Something in Casey's gentle words reached Martin, and he looked down into Casey's confident eyes before stepping into his embrace and breathing hard. "Look at him, Casey," he whimpered brokenly. "Look at my brother and tell me he'll be all right."

Casey had to admit there was truth in Martin's words. Leon lay unconscious on a bed within the sterile area. Hooked up to tubes and machines, the usually larger-than-life QC looked small and impossibly frail. Casey watched the two nurses in full hazmat suits tend to him, cleaning the festering areas on the exposed wings and monitoring readings. Occasionally, Alissa would glance over and then return to her feverish work, her own dun-coloured wings just beginning to show the telltale abscesses of the rotting plague.

Casey's mouth firmed, his lips thinning in determination. "We'll *fix* it."

THE DOORBELL AT Martin's flat rang just as they were taking a break from research, settling down into their daily routine, pushing and testing the boundaries of Casey's control of Martin's wings.

After a softly murmured conversation through the wood, the door opened to reveal a tired Jared Carrington.

"Well, you look like shit, mate." Casey's voice was artificially light as the man strode through the door.

The dark rings beneath Jared's eyes were a testament to sleepless nights, crushing grief, and endless worry. His shoulders looked stiff and sore from tension, and his hair looked lank from days of running worried hands through it.

"Thanks," he replied.

"I would have just asked how you are." Martin handed Jared his own mug and put the kettle back on.

"I think Casey summed it up pretty well." Jared mechanically sipped the black coffee. "Are you going to ask why I'm here and not at Leon's bedside?"

"No." Martin glanced around and finally sat on a chair by the table. "There's little you could do for him. Despite what nurses try to tell us, there's absolutely no evidence that people in induced comas can hear you. In any case, they wouldn't let you into the quarantine area."

"Martin…" Casey hissed.

"He's right, Casey." Jared stared at his hands, idly picking at dry skin. "I'm useless to him."

"I suspect he'd beg to differ," Martin interjected softly. "By the way, of course you can sleep on the couch."

Jared's eyes flicked up. "What?"

Casey and Jared exchanged a confused glance.

Martin rolled his eyes. "It's obvious. I wouldn't want to be in my apartment alone if Casey was in quarantine. It's entirely rational to want to hang out with people you trust, and with whom you can discuss the situation."

Jared smiled wryly and conceded. "He's right, of course. The couch will be fine. At least this way, we'll all get news at the same time." He looked longingly at the soft leather cushions. "Is it all right if I summon my wings? They need a stretch."

Martin shrugged, turned back to the kitchen as the kettle whistled, and filled a new cup before returning and sitting cross-legged on the floor.

"I'm not sure this is the time, Martin." Casey looked down at him.

"Jared will be asleep on that couch within fifteen minutes, and we need to continue working on my wings." He nodded pointedly at the floor in front of him. "Sit."

"Don't let me stop you." Jared settled on the couch, flexing the huge russet wings before folding them neatly against his spine. "I'll just amuse myself."

Knowing when he was beaten, Casey sat, shuffling forward until their knees touched.

"Okay," Casey heaved a deep breath and looked up at Martin. "Ready?"

Martin nodded, and as Casey closed his eyes, the wings shimmered into place. It was becoming easier for them both. Martin was beginning to feel the tell-tale signs of Casey's influence and, at times, even resist his bonded's control of them.

"So, that's getting easier," Casey began calmly, "and faster. Let's try cycling through the change."

Martin nodded serenely, hands gently clasped on his crossed thighs.

Casey mentally began to draw Martin's wings on the paper but frowned. The lines seemed to resist his scribing as if the pen he was using had run out of ink. He tried again, internally watching the line stutter and stop again.

"Push, Casey," Martin whispered. "I'm resisting it."

Casey pushed, imagining the pen pressing harder, scoring the lines on the page. Still, the drawing wouldn't appear. Sweat broke out on Casey's forehead and Martin's as they battled against each other, testing their bounds. There was a shiver at the edges of Martin's feathers before they again solidified.

"*Push!*" Martin said again.

"I *am* pushing," Casey muttered. "They won't..." Casey grunted and tilted his head, concentrating. His eyes closed and mouth tight.

"I can feel you pulling at them, but I'm holding you off," Martin hissed through gritted teeth. "Keep trying, I want to see—"

"Oh!" Casey huffed out an explosive breath, and the tugging at Martin's subconscious lifted suddenly, leaving the Avian toppling backwards at the sudden release of tension.

He opened his eyes and scowled as he pushed himself up off the floor. "Why did you give up? I wanted to..." The startled look on Casey's face, white and shocked, brought him up short. "Casey?"

"Bloody hell, Casey." The voice came from behind Martin. Jared's voice, equally surprised. "Did you just—"

"Yeah, I think I..." Casey pushed himself up from the floor, turning slowly to gain confirmation from the two Avians.

There on Casey's back, where Martin's inked wings usually resided, were instead the image of a set of ginger-and-brown hawk wings, shot through with gold and copper.

"WELL, THAT'S JUST not right," Martin whispered.

"What the *hell* are Jared's wings doing on my back?" Casey was standing in the cramped bathroom, glancing over his own shoulder to see them reflected in the mirror.

"Yes, what the hell are my wings doing on your *bonded* partner's back, Martin?"

Jared was standing tiredly in the doorway as Martin turned Casey back and forth with gentle hands, testing the marks with his fingertips in disbelief.

"Well, it appears that, although Casey's ability may have originated from our bonding, it's not limited to my wings." Martin ran a fingertip along a crisp ginger line as goose bumps rose on his back.

"Can you stop poking at them?" Casey muttered. "I feel like a lab rat."

Martin stepped back and tapped a thoughtful finger on his full lower lip. "I suspect Casey's ability reached out to the nearest available wings. Given I was resisting and you were on the verge of sleep." He reached to touch the tattoo again before Casey shrugged away. "Like lightning taking the most direct path."

"Yes, it's fascinating." Jared rolled his shoulders. "Can I have 'em back?"

"What? Yes, I'd think so. Simply a matter of him giving them back, much the same as he does it with mine." He looked at Casey. "Go on."

"I feel like a performing monkey," he huffed. "All right, hang on." Casey dropped his chin to his chest and settled his breathing. "Feels weird."

"Could you manage better than *weird?*" Martin was staring at Casey's back, then across at Carrington as if he expected the feathers to physically traverse the distance.

"Like—shit, I don't know—not like *you.*" Casey frowned. "With your wings, it's like they *fit me.* Jared's are all wrong."

Martin sighed patiently. "Wrong, *in what way?*"

Casey grimaced. "It's like one of those fancy restaurants where they make food look savoury, but it's sweet when you put it into your mouth. It's still food, but it's creepy."

"Keep trying, Casey. I can feel them coming back." Jared shrugged his shoulders. "And my wings are not *creepy.*"

"Got it!" Casey smiled suddenly, and the air in the bathroom shimmered again, Jared's wings back in their rightful place. The markings on Casey's back faded, leaving the space vacant for Martin's iridescent raven lines again.

The relief on Martin's face was quickly hidden as he brusquely shuffled Jared out of the room. "I think that's enough for tonight. Jared, get some sleep, and we'll talk in the morning."

Jared glanced between the two of them. Casey was leaning heavily on the bathroom sink, the strain of the undertaking etched on his face; Martin was almost quivering with the need to take his partner somewhere quiet and reaffirm their bond.

"Take it easy on him," Jared whispered. "This was tough for both of you."

Martin's eyes widened and followed Jared's gaze to where Casey had taken a seat on the side of the bath, looking a little green.

"I..." Some of the frantic energy left him as he took in the slumped shoulders of his lover. "Thank you."

Jared leant closer. "Just think about what *he* needs, okay?"

Martin nodded tersely and pushed Jared quietly toward the lounge. Casey was all that mattered now. Everything else could wait for the morning.

"DON'T DO THAT again." Martin whispered the words into Casey's neck as he slipped into bed beside him. "I hated it."

"I didn't *do* it the first time," Casey mumbled. "It sort of just...happened. It's not like I know what I'm doing."

"I don't want it to *happen* again," Martin growled.

Casey chuckled softly. "Are you jealous?" Casey laid a lazy hand on Martin's cheek. "Are you jealous that I had another man's wings on my back?"

"No!" Martin's brow furrowed in consternation. "Of course not."

"You are." Casey's exhausted eyes sparkled. "You've come over all dominant and possessive. You're jealous."

"I'm not." Martin slid sideways, settling over his lover's hip and slotting a leg between Casey's. "I just…"

"It's all right. You've always been a bit protective of your *things*. I see how you look at people who touch your stuff."

"You're not a *thing*, Casey."

"That not what I mean." Casey buried his hands into Martin's hair as his lover mouthed and licked at his skin. "I mean I don't mind being something you treasure. Something you consider valuable. Something you"—Casey arched gently as Martin's hands roamed slowly over his body—"couldn't bear to lose."

"All of that, Casey. All of that and more." Martin nosed at Casey's nipple before sucking it firmly. "Friend, colleague, partner, lover…bonded."

"Yours," Casey whispered.

"Yours," Martin murmured back. "I'm utterly yours." Martin's voice caught on the words, and he turned his head to rest it on Casey's chest. "Are you tired?"

"Yes," Casey murmured before expanding. "Knackered, but I need you too."

"You lie back and let me do all the work." Martin grinned and began working his way down the bed, kissing and licking Casey's skin as he went.

"It'll make a nice change," Casey rumbled fondly, "and compensate for all the shopping I do."

From the other end of the bed, Martin muttered, "Cheeky," before settling at Casey's crotch and drawing a deep breath. "I love how you smell. Have I mentioned that?"

"No," Casey drawled, relaxed and yet aroused.

Martin licked a broad stripe from root to tip. "And I love the way you taste. I must have mentioned that, surely?"

"No...no, I don't think so," Casey grunted, his hips bucking a little.

"And those little sounds you make, needy, demanding, and yet somehow apologetic for wanting. I love those too." Martin pointed his tongue and made a slow, teasing, circuitous route around the head of Casey's cock as Casey whined.

"But most of all, Casey Wicker. I love that when I take you in my mouth—" Martin licked at the head, firming his grip around the base so he could control Casey's thrusts. "I love that you shout my name, heedless of who might hear. I love that you cease to care who knows that you're in my bed, in my mouth, in my body. That you're mine, and I'm yours."

With those final words, Martin closed his mouth and engulfed Casey entirely, sinking down his length until the head nudged the back of his soft palate. True to his word, Casey *did* shout Martin's name then, along with some cruder invectives. At the sound of his name, hoarse with passion, Martin hummed in delight and drew back, only to plunge down again, taking Casey's flesh into his own again and again.

"Oh...God, Martin...I...yes, oh, God, yes," Casey whimpered and groaned helplessly as his lover used his talented tongue to stimulate and press, cradling and stroking as the wetness and warmth enveloped him.

Mimicking Casey's motion, Martin took up the rhythm against Casey's leg, thrusting against him in unison, providing his own erotic tempo. Casey groaned at the feeling, tilting his leg and rubbing against Martin even as he lost the ability to put words together.

Together, they sought completion. Martin, true to his word, did most of the work, leaving Casey to bask and wallow in the care and attention lavished on him. With his fingers buried in Martin's curls, cradling his head, he managed to tap out a warning accompanied by an urgent grunt, and Martin's mouth stilled briefly, savouring the way Casey thickened further against his tongue before pulsing into his eager mouth. At a hum of satisfaction, Casey gasped and shuddered again, and then a third time before Martin licked him clean and eased him from his lips.

"Casey?" Martin eased up the length of Casey's body, curling tight against him where he lay sated and lax.

"Mmmmmm?" Casey murmured, still easing back to reality.

"I'm sorry I was jealous," Martin whispered hesitantly.

"I'm not." Casey flexed his hip against Martin's groin. "Do you want me to...?" Casey tried to grind against him again.

A large hand settled on his thigh and stilled the movement. "I'm fine for now. Sleep."

Casey slept.

MARTIN'S MOBILE BUZZED on the bedside table. After disentangling himself from the complex Gordian knot of Martin's arms, legs, and wings, Casey scrabbled for the device before it surrendered and went to voice mail.

"Casey Wicker," he murmured, trying to sound like he'd been awake for hours instead of sprawled face down in a post-sex haze of sated exhaustion.

Alissa's gentle voice whispered through the earpiece, "I'm trying to reach Jared. Is he there with you?"

"Yeah, he's on the couch. You want me to get him?" Casey was already halfway out of bed, expecting the worst. His tone had Martin already reacting and climbing out the other side as Casey hit the speaker button to free up his hands to pull on yesterday's clothes.

She stumbled over her reply. "It's not urgent, well, yes, it is. But, I think it would help if Jared were here. If all of you…"

Martin snatched the phone from where Casey had thrown it on the bed. "Alissa, just tell us what's happened."

"Martin…" There was a catch in her voice as she said his name.

Casey and Martin shared a look of despair at the fragility the single word carried.

"We'll be right there. Hold on, Sparrow, hang on. We're on our way." Martin bolted from the room, already calling Jared's name. Casey ducked into the bathroom knowing the clock was ticking and the other two men would be beating down the door within five minutes.

LESS THAN AN hour later, Martin used his spare key, and the three of them slipped in through the kitchen door, making their way back to the makeshift ward Alissa had established.

What they saw broke Casey's heart. Alissa was sitting dejectedly on the floor by her desk within the containment area, her head pillowed on her arms where they lay on her raised knees. Beyond her, the hospital bed containing Martin's brother provided a stark reminder of the battle they were facing. The incessant beep of the machines a constant indication of Leon's crumbling health.

The equipment in the room had expanded since they'd been there the previous day. Centrifuges, a gas chromatograph, and other bulky equipment had been set up and were all running tirelessly.

As Jared circled the plastic sheeting to take up residence in the chair pulled up next to the unconscious man on the other side, Martin knelt as near to Alissa as he could.

"Sparrow," he murmured gently, drawing her out of her exhausted torpor. Her head rose slowly to look at him through the barrier.

"Hello, Raven," she leant back against the wall at her back, head slumping on her shoulders. "I'm sorry I called you. I just...I can't face this alone anymore."

"And you don't have to. We won't leave you again." Martin mirrored her position, back against the wall, knees pulled up.

Casey, at a loss as to how to contribute, left the four of them alone while he went hunting for makeshift bedding and supplies. In the midst of so many unknowns, one thing was clear. Leon's house had now become their base of operations, and Agent Wicker was tackling it like a warzone.

"SO, CASEY'S IMMUNE, and so am I?" Martin checked the results again as Alissa nodded. "How does that work?"

"It must be your bond. That's the only reason I can think of. I'd thought at first that it was purely the fact that Casey's human, and that the virus only attacks Avian DNA, but he's somehow transmitted the immunity to you as well. I've synthesized this from Casey's blood."

Casey looked at the tiny phial over Martin's shoulder as he scrolled through page after page of test results. "At least that means we can treat you. Have you used it yet, Alissa?"

"I've tried. It seems to be a double-edged sword. The pathogen hides when we put our wings away, so we can't treat it unless they're visible. But when they're visible, the virus replicates so fast that the cure can't get a hold."

Casey nodded thoughtfully. "I'm no expert in immunobiology, but it sounds more like a vaccine than a cure."

"Test it on me." Jared's voice came from the opposite end of the room, firm and decisive.

"Jared—" Casey warned.

"No, I'm serious. Test it on me. I'm uninfected, although God knows how. I'm sick of being stuck here, unable to do anything more than making cups of tea. Test it on me or so help me, I'm going in there with them anyway." He pointed to Leon and Alissa.

Martin's eyes narrowed. "I've seen that look before. He doesn't use it often. I'd believe him."

"But Jared—" Alissa entreated.

Jared pressed a hand against the plastic sheeting. "I need to get in there, Alissa. We're running out of time, and I need—" Jared's voice broke. "Damnit, I have to be with him, please."

Alissa nodded in surrender and turned away to start preparing a syringe to be transferred through the quarantine airlock, leaving Jared to slump back into his chair next to Leon's bed, still separated by the plastic enclosure.

Casey moved to Martin's side and tugged at him until he rose from the floor and followed him to a quiet corner, pulling him close to whisper seriously. "Listen, I'm going to ask you to let me do something, and you're not going to like it."

"I agree. It's the only solution," Martin whispered back.

Casey couldn't suppress a sad smile. "You're already twenty steps ahead of me, aren't you?"

"Less than ten. You're practically on my heels this time." Martin chuckled softly. "But you're right. I hate the idea."

"But you'll let me do it?" Casey raised a hand to cup Martin's cheek, seeing the discomfort behind the bravado in his lover's eyes.

"If there was any other way—" Martin glanced over his shoulder at his brother, barely hanging on. "The thought of risking you—"

"I'm immune, Martin," Casey tried to sound reassuring.

"There are too many unknowns." Martin's breathing picked up, and he murmured suddenly, "No, I've changed my mind. I don't want—"

"Martin." Casey encircled Martin's waist with his arms, pulling him into a hug. "Shhh, calm down. It'll be okay. You've seen the reports. The science is sound." Casey gentled his lover with touch and logic, the two things most likely to soothe the nervous man.

Martin buried his face in the crook of Casey's neck, panting as he tried to swallow down the anxiety. "Casey..."

"I know." Casey ran fingers through silky curls. "I know."

For long minutes, Martin stood, holding Casey as logic warred with emotion and Martin shivered with tension in every muscle. Then, with a final, cleansing breath, Martin seemed to surrender to the inevitable, and his shoulders drooped.

"All right," he mumbled against Casey's shirt collar. "Just one thing."

Casey drew back to look down into Martin's face. "Hmm?"

"If this kills you, you need to come back." Martin gave a weak smile that didn't reach his eyes. "I'm not going to be the one explaining this to your mum."

"WHEN WILL WE know if the vaccine is effective?" Jared sat slumped on a plush Chesterfield in the corner of the study, Alissa watching him uneasily from the other side of the plastic divider and Casey bent over him, taking his pulse.

"Twenty-four hours. We're a bit worried at how hard the dose has hit you, so we need your system to bounce back a bit before we do a scratch test. Get some sleep." Casey tucked the blanket around the Inspector's body and turned out the light.

Walking back to the enclosure, Alissa, Casey, and Martin leant in close. "He's okay; that's the good news. The fever's spiked and dropped away, and his pulse is solid as a rock. We should know by morning."

Alissa cast a glance toward Leon's neatly made hospital bed and nodded. "Leon's stable for now. I have him in an induced coma, and that seems to have slowed the progress."

"What about you?" Martin asked quietly. "How are you?"

Alissa shrugged. "As good as can be expected. I'm exhausted, but as long as I don't summon my wings, I should slow the disease as much as possible."

Martin and Casey shared a glance laden with meaning, and Casey nodded decisively before Martin continued, "We think we may have an idea."

TWENTY MINUTES LATER, the three of them had a plan. If Jared's vaccine is effective, then all three men would enter the quarantine zone in the morning. Martin and Alissa would both summon their wings, leaving Casey's back theoretically available for Casey to pull Alissa's wings to him. Although Leon's condition was more serious, and in Casey's opinion, more urgent, Alissa and Martin both agreed that the risk to Casey should be minimized until they understood the consequences. With Alissa's wings in Casey's safekeeping, they'd vaccinate Alissa, allowing the immunity to halt the progress of the disease. Although they all agreed that scientifically, they were making it up as they went along, it seemed to make sense.

As the clock struck midnight, they settled in to grab what little sleep they could before they faced the battle at dawn.

Chapter Twenty-Eight

"MARTIN." CASEY'S VOICE seemed to come from miles away, and yet when he opened his eyes, Casey was mere inches from him on the couch, whispering down to him.

"Mmmm?" he breathed back quizzically.

"You were tossing in your sleep, mumbling something about gas. You said I should wake you when you do things like that."

"Gas," he murmured thoughtfully, levering himself up on his elbows. "Are you sure it was gas?"

"Pretty sure. You said gas, and council, and swan, and I think you said 'Mbox' although by that stage you were mumbling pretty badly."

Martin blinked and rubbed at his eyes as he sat up. The room was still dark, and Jared's snores were deep and even from the armchair several feet away. "Gas...gas..." His brow furrowed. "And what the hell does Mbox mean?"

"Don't ask me. My dreams are usually flying or falling or puppies with an unlikely number of legs."

Martin flopped back down onto his back with a sigh. "I have the feeling everything we've done recently is connected—the pastor, the Crown jewels, even the bomb. It's just—" He reached out as if grasping things. "—just there, Casey, and I can't quite..."

"Maybe it'll make more sense in the morning. Go back to slee—"

"Mbox," Martin exclaimed. "Not Mbox, Casey. M...BOX. The box the priest had, the ones with the wafers. I had an initial carved on it. My subconscious saw it, knew it was important."

"Let me guess. It was an M?"

Martin struggled out from beneath the sheets and began pacing the room. "The Crown jewels, a bomb, wafers that force wings into existence, a disease that destroys them. But still, there's something. Talk to me, Casey. Help me sift through the details."

Casey ran a hand through his hair while he wrapped the blanket around himself. "All right, slow down and keep your voice down. Alissa and Jared need their sleep."

"Come on, Casey. I've nearly got this." Martin was pulling pieces of paper out, scribbling details on them.

"You think the M is Matthew Yates, the Avian that went mad after the failed bonding, right?"

"Right...yes...more."

"And that he's targeting Leon with the disease because of his failed bonding."

"Yes, yes, Leon headed the council that sentenced them. More."

"I don't see how that bomb in the Crown jewels is connected. I mean, I can understand why he'd want to kill the royal family but—"

"Oh!" Martin froze midscribble and dropped the pen. "Casey! That's it! That's..." He strode across the room and crashed to his knees in front of Casey, pulling him toward him and kissing him soundly. "*Brilliant*! That's so brilliant, I could kiss you."

"I think you just did—" Casey grinned at him. "—but what did I do?"

"You were right!"

"Nice to know. About what though?"

"Yates doesn't want to *kill* the royal family. He wants to do far worse." Martin had regained his feet and was pacing again.

"What's worse than killing them?"

"He wants to expose them to the world. The bomb was an aerosolized version on the wafers. He wants to summon their wings... and then use the disease to rot them in front of the world."

Casey rose to his feet. "Wait, Martin, just hold on." He put a hand out to still Martin's steps. "That doesn't make sense. We found the bomb."

"Of course, we did, Casey. But that's only half the problem." Martin looked grim. "Because now we know, since the wafers, he can add it to the food instead."

"WHERE'S MARTIN?" ALISSA scanned the vacant space behind Casey as he entered the room.

He took a seat at the tiny table where Jared was tucking into eggs and toast. "He had an epiphany last night. He's gone to save the world," he said, grabbing a piece of toast from the pile.

Alissa's smile quirked at the side. "I'm surprised he lasted so long, to be honest. How are you, Jared?"

"I feel good," he replied and then looked to Casey as he poked the digital thermometer in Jared's ear. "How am I?"

"Yeah, he's good. Vitals normal, appetite..." He looked at the Inspector as he lifted another forkful toward his lips. "Normal."

"Are we waiting for Martin to return?" Alissa peeled back the plastic cover on a prepared meal and put it in the microwave, then shut the door on it. "Leon's stable, but I don't know for how long."

"No, he said to go ahead without him." He dropped his cutlery on the empty plate, and together, he and Jared moved toward the quarantine entrance. "Ready?"

"BREATHE, CASEY." ALISSA was holding his biceps as Casey gasped and struggled. "Hold him, Jared, or he'll hurt himself."

"It's burning, Alissa... God, how could you stand it?" Casey writhed as the image of Alissa's wings on his back flared red and angry, scabs and suppurating sores breaking the skin amongst the dun-brown lines etched on his back.

She cupped his cheek with her hand and tried to hold him close, careful not to touch the infected skin of his back. "It's your immunity fighting the disease. It means you're winning, Casey. Just hold onto me."

"Martin," he cried. "I want Martin. Why isn't he here?"

"That's the bond calling, Casey. I'm sorry he isn't here. I've called him. He's on his way back. I promise." Jared sat astride Casey's thighs, stopping his legs from thrashing against the pain.

Casey nodded tightly, tears pooling in his wide eyes. "Yeah." He sucked in a long breath. "I know...fuck...I know."

Now that Casey had ceased struggling and was managing to breathe through the pain, Alissa asked, "How bad is it, on a scale of one to ten?"

Through gritted teeth, Casey muttered, "Eight. It's easing off a bit now, but it's bad."

Alissa checked his blood pressure again and gave a worried shake of her head. "Your numbers weren't good, Casey. Even with painkillers, the reaction was severe." She looked up at Jared. "I'm not sure…"

Jared sighed. "I know…don't say it." He looked over his shoulder at where his partner lay, still and sedated and being kept alive by machines.

As Alissa lifted the syringe containing the vaccine and pressed it to her own arm, she pursed her lips and shook her head. "Let's just see how this goes, and then we can make a decision."

Chapter Twenty-Nine

"MARTIN..." HIS NAME came through the fog of pain in his head, and he opened his eyes to the too-bright light. The singsong tone did nothing to alter the dread he felt rising at the voice, remembered from so long ago.

"There you are," the disembodied voice continued. "I was worried that we'd hit you just a little too hard."

Yates. It wasn't a surprise, although waking to find his hands tied was unexpected. He'd spent most of the night working with Avian contacts throughout London to track the rogue Avian down. The last he remembered was a sharp noise close behind him—*too close*, pain, and then darkness.

With a grunt, Martin rolled onto his side, using his shackled hands to lever himself into a sitting position, only to fall back as the room spun.

"Oh, not too quick. You might be a bit dizzy," the voice chided. "A blow to the head can rattle things a little, I find."

"Where—" Martin rasped.

"Martin, it doesn't matter *where* you are." Yates spoke as if berating a small child. "It matters *why* you're here."

With a grimace, Martin righted himself again, leaning against the wall to steady himself. "All right, *why* am I here?"

"Because you were looking for me, so I thought I'd help. Wasn't that sweet of me? Helping you, giving you what you want?"

Martin lifted his bound hands to shield his eyes from the spotlight pointing at him, trying to scan his surroundings as his vision cleared.

He was in a dull grey room, exposed pipes lined the walls, and a thick metal door stood, triple locked. There were no windows and a small camera nestled high up, near the ceiling.

"Feeling better? Good. We'll have a little chat, see if we can reach some sort of agreement, and then...well, we'll take it from there." There was the electronic noise as the microphone clicked off, followed by a series of louder clunks as the locks on the door were disengaged.

The door opened, improving the light marginally as it silhouetted Matthew Yates, motionless on the threshold. He took three confident strides in, shadowed by a man with a chair, who placed it on the floor directly in front of Martin and left without a word.

Yates stepped around the chair and sat gracefully in it before gesturing the man away with a wave. He stared down at where Martin lay prone against the wall.

He shook his head and tutted. "Look at you. That's a nasty gash on your head. Really should get that looked at. All that blood." He waved a hand in Martin's general direction. "Head wounds can make a terrible mess, can't they?"

Martin reached up with his bound hands to touch tentatively and found his hair matted against his skull. He blinked hard and considered for the first time whether his concussion was more severe than he'd first deduced. *Casey would know. I wish he were here.*

"Yes." Yates nodded in mock sympathy at his unspoken but obvious sentiment. "Yes, I'm sure you do, but"—his eyes hardened suddenly—"he's *not* here, Martin. You're alone, just like they left *me* alone."

Ahh, there it is, the heart of this entire problem. Revenge. "You want to expose the Avians."

"I want to *destroy* the Avians "Yates spat "like they destroyed what Sebastian and I could have had."

Martin heaved a deep breath, feeling better for the sudden rush of oxygen he glared back. "You know I can't let you."

Yates laughed and leant forward. "You're really not in a position to stop me, Martin, or have you not noticed the fact that you're restrained in a cellar?"

"Nevertheless," Martin replied evenly, "I *will* find a way to stop you."

"Ahh, the endless Bishop confidence. I'd forgotten." Yates rose from the chair to pace the room. "We don't have to be adversaries in this, Martin, you and I. We have so much in common."

Martin remained silent, allowing him to continue.

"You *must* see it, that we're the same in this," Yates queried, a vague note of pleading in his voice.

Martin shook his head.

Yates turned swiftly to stare down at him. "We *are*! What happened to Sebastian—that could have been Casey. You *know* that! And this—" Yates tore his jacket off and threw it into a darkened corner. "*This*...could have been you."

Pressing through the gaps in the back of Yates's shirt were the stumps of his ruined wings, the broken ends of bones white and smooth in the dim light. There was no trace of skin or feathers on what little remained of the huge lustrous wings that had once been the envy of every Avian of Martin's generation.

Martin gulped down bile, unable to stop the gut-deep reaction to the carnage at Yates's back and stared, unable to look away from the horror.

"They *took* it all, Martin. They took him from me. They didn't *need* to, but they *could*, so they *did*." He stepped forward, within Martin's reach but unafraid. "Tell me, what would *you* have done if they'd taken Casey from you?"

Martin swallowed and finally looked away, shaking his head harshly at the possibility.

"Don't tell me it would have been different, I've *seen* you with him." Yates leant closer, his hot breath stirring the matted curls. "I *know*."

With realization came the anger, and Martin turned back to stare up at his jailer, eyes hard. "All right, you're right," he conceded. "I'd have been as set on revenge as you are, but not like this. This doesn't *solve* anything."

The smile that had bloomed at Martin's confession disappeared, as quickly at his insight. "I don't *want* to solve anything," he retorted bitterly.

Martin smirked. "But you *do*, don't you? You said it yourself, you're like me, you're a problem solver. That's what you do...you *fix* things. Just like I do."

Yates returned to his chair. "This can't be fixed. This can only be destroyed," he said with finality.

"If you say so..." Martin fell silent.

"What?" Yates spat.

Martin continued to sit quietly.

"*What!*" Yates shouted, the noise echoing in the small room.

"Give future Avians a choice we didn't have," Martin murmured.

Yates's eyes narrowed, and he leant forward, indicating Martin should continue.

"The work you're doing with the drugs, the ones to summon, the ones to destroy. Only you could have altered the chemistry of medicines over a thousand years old. I admit, I'm impressed." Martin paused to allow Yates's ego to bask in the praise. "I doubt you'd have much trouble to adjust them again to...prevent the wings coming back."

He let those words settle in the silence of the room, watching his face as he considered the implications.

"Imagine for a moment, if future Avians had the choice. Choose their human lover or..." He left the sentence hanging.

"Or their wings? Interesting." Yates leant back in the chair and considered. "What's to stop me simply using it on every Avian, removing all their wings?"

Martin's mouth curled up at the corner. "Nothing, but then, what threat would you retain over them?"

Yates smiled. It wasn't pleasant. "You really are like me, you know?"

Martin sneered back and murmured, "I know." He paused for a moment. "One last thing."

Yates's eyes narrowed. "I'm listening."

"Leon. If I manage to find a way to save his life, you're finished with his retribution. He's not to be harmed further."

"And what do I get for this concession?" Yates asked sceptically.

"I won't hunt you down, and I'll see to it that neither does the council."

"Brave words for a man locked in a cellar."

Martin shrugged. "You're going to let me go, obviously. This was never about killing me. This was about finding someone to validate your revenge." He shrugged again. "Fine, I validate it. I even agree with it to some degree. The council needs to be...educated. I can't do it, but you can. So, you'll cut these bonds, you'll leave, and in an hour, so will I. I'll tell them you escaped when you knocked me out." He touched a finger to his head gingerly. "Which isn't entirely untrue."

"But why should I let you go?"

"Because one day, you're going to need someone on the inside. You may not like it any more than I do, but it's going to be me. There's nobody else. And so, you need to let me go."

Silence fell between the two men for long minutes until Matthew quietly drew a knife from a sheath at his waist and slipped it into the cable tie binding Martin's wrists and drew it sharply upward. He then turned and walked out of the room without looking back.

MARTIN STUMBLED, BLOODIED and exhausted, through the door of Leon's study, and sought out Casey within the quarantine area, releasing a pent-up breath when he located him. The nagging dread that had been his constant companion while they'd been parted slipped away, and sensing his proximity, the smile that spread across Casey's face as he turned to make eye contact was matched by his own.

Martin straightened his shoulders and did his best to mask his concern with detachment. "Managed to survive the plague, then?"

Casey grinned, seeing the false bravado for what it was. "Better than you, it seems. Look at you, Martin. You look like you've been bathing at an abattoir." Looking more closely, he saw the glazed look in Martin's eyes. "Hang on a second. That's actually your blood."

"Mostly," Martin murmured, swaying slightly. "I've been taught a rather pertinent lesson as to why I should always take you with me."

Casey looked to Alissa in sudden urgency. "Can I get out of here? I need to take a look at him, and I'd quite like to do it privately."

At Alissa's nod, Casey was through the airlock before another word was said, enveloping Martin in his arms as the battered agent sighed and sagged against him.

"Christ, you're a mess." Casey deftly felt around the edges of the gash on his head, careful not to start the bleeding again. "I need to get this sorted out. You might even need stitches."

"Is he all right?" Alissa was pressed against the other side of the plastic and Jared had looked up from his regular place at Leon's side.

"He will be," Casey replied, guiding Martin to sit on a chair. "I'm going to take him upstairs for a shower and put him to bed. Will you two be all right for a couple of hours?"

With Martin's arm draped over his shoulder, the two men made their way out of the room and deeper into Leon's private domain. For all his bluster, it was clear to Casey that Martin had expended the last of his energy getting back to them and the stairs seemed an almost insurmountable obstacle as he dragged one foot after another up them.

"How's Alissa?" Martin mumbled.

"Don't worry about Alissa." Casey settled Martin on the end of Leon's bed while he bustled around the en suite, gathering towels and turning on the taps. "Just keep talking to me. I'm worried about a concussion. Did you blackout at all, vomiting?" Casey ran through a litany of diagnostic indicators as Martin slumped over onto his side and curled on the blankets, mumbling responses as he lifted his feet off the floor.

"No, not yet. I need to get you clean and stitch you up. Then, maybe you can sleep, under observation." Casey hoisted Martin back to a sitting position and manhandled his coat off before starting on the buttons of his shirt.

"The coat might be beyond salvaging," Martin offered muzzily. "Pity, I liked that one. It has some beautiful detailing on the—"

"Forget your damned coat," Casey snapped before lowering his voice at Martin's wince. "Sorry, just... oh, for God's sake." Casey fell to his knees in front of Martin and gathered him into his arms, clinging desperately as Martin leant heavily against him. "Stop getting hurt, all right? My heart can't take it."

Martin nodded and then moaned at the movement. "I'll try. I promise."

"C'mon, let's get you cleaned up." After helping him to his feet, Casey made short work of Martin's trousers before leading him into the warm air of the bathroom, propping him against the shower door while he shed his own clothes. As he turned around to search flannels and a razor, Martin gasped and laid a hand on his shoulder.

"Casey?" he said.

"Hmm?" Casey turned back swiftly.

"Your back's clear. I expected..." He ran a finger down the golden skin.

"Alissa's wings? Yeah, I gave them back a couple of hours ago. Looks like we were right," he said dismissively, bullying him into the shower stall.

Even exhausted, Martin's eyes narrowed suspiciously. "There's something you're not telling me, Casey? You're evasive."

Casey glanced away, considering his options before replying. "It wasn't...pleasant. But it was worth it. We have a shot at saving Leon now, but let's get you sorted out first."

Martin blinked, wondering if he should push for more. However, exhaustion won out, and he moved back as

Casey directed the spray carefully onto his shoulders, avoiding his hair.

As the steam rose with the temperature, the two men reacquainted themselves with each other's skin. Casey made every effort to remain impartial, cleaning the blood and grime away with gentle, clinical hands, in spite of Martin's lingering touches and heavy-lidded gaze. When Martin's hand strayed down and ran an inquisitive finger along Casey's cock, his partner chuckled deeply.

"Stop it. You're a walking trauma-zone, Martin. That isn't helping." Casey nudged his hand away, trailing a layer of soap bubbles with the movement.

"It's helping me," Martin rumbled back. "I feel infinitely better already." His hand strayed again, his own penis twitching hopefully as if to support the argument.

"You're a menace," Casey muttered, dodging to the side, a half-hearted objection in his tone. "You need sleep, not sex."

"Beg to differ." Martin lowered his head to suck at Casey's neck, tonguing at the red spot that resulted. "I think I need both."

"Well, you're not getting...*nnggff*." Casey's words abandoned him as Martin's fingers encircled his cock and gave a leisurely stroke, and he reflexively bucked into his hand. "This is not happening, Martin!"

"You know you want it too," Martin slurred against his ear. "It's been...days."

Casey felt his resolve crumbling as Martin moved forward, and his cock, slick with soap, pushed determinedly against Casey's hip.

Giving in and circling his arm to pull Martin tight against him, he groaned. "That's nice, that's...God, the way you always want me..."

"Always," Martin rumbled, his voice echoing in the small space. "Always, Casey. There's never a moment when I don't want you by my side, with me, in me, on me. Always," he chanted as he rutted against him.

"Mmmm, me too." Casey slipped a hand up to curve around the nape of Martin's neck, drawing his head down for a long, languorous kiss, their tongues tangling together.

As they moved in the enclosed space, clasped together, Martin gave a tight hiss and pulled back as the water struck the gash in his head.

"Right." Casey shook off the buzzing arousal and nodded decisively at the interrupted mood. "That settles it. Out."

Martin whined and reached for Casey again, careful to keep his head away from the spray.

"No," Casey replied. "Out. I'll patch you up, and then… then, we'll see about some extracurricular activities."

Knowing when he was beaten, Martin eased out of the cubicle, ensuring he brushed against as much of Casey's naked skin as possible on the way and delighting in the frustrated groan he received in response.

Casey made short work of Martin's wound, clipping the surrounding hair short and using a mixture of butterfly tapes and stitches.

"Okay, wings out," Casey said expectantly.

"Why?" Martin's brow furrowed.

"Because you'll sleep better, and because, with all this swapping back and forth, I want to make sure it still works." Casey placed his hands on his hips as Martin's frown disappeared. "Besides," Casey added thoughtfully running a hand up Martin's flank, "I want them. Turn around."

Martin sniggered and turned his back to Casey, who ran his hands along the pristine, pale skin of Martin's back, then leaned to kiss his way up the prominent bumps of his vertebrae. "You're getting thin."

Martin's head tipped back. "I've been busy."

"I'll take better care of you," Casey murmured.

"You always do."

"Ready?" Casey asked in a hushed tone, slipping his hands down to settle on bony hips as he pictured Martin's beautiful wings, currently in their rightful place etched in dark lines on his own back.

Martin nodded and spread his feet slightly as the faintest brush of Casey's mind skipped over his consciousness.

With a gentle outward, Casey poured his love for both the man and his wings outward, picturing them as a complete unit, the way he'd first seen Martin in the dimness of their bedroom. How the rush of lust had enveloped him, pouring over and through him in waves, buffeting him with awe and majesty. He watched as the silky, black wings shuddered into being along either side of Martin's spine, shining in the soft light of the morning, white secondary just peeking between the jet-black plumages.

Reaching out, he ran a finger under the feathers and along the skin as Martin shivered and the feathers lifted fractionally, ruffling at the touch.

Martin sighed, and his wings dropped slightly, relaxed at his back as Casey moved forward to rest his cheek against the smooth layer, breathing in the sweet freshness of the freshly summoned wings.

"There they are," Casey whispered lovingly.

Martin pivoted in his arms and turned to face him. "You know, I think you're becoming even more fond of them than I am."

Casey moved in close, pressing along the full length of Martin's torso and tilted his head up. "Perhaps it's a draw. They're part of you, part of your magic, and part of the miracle of you being with me. I'd love you just as much without them, but I'll admit, whenever I see them, I remember that these were the tipping point. The point at which we stopped being you and me, and became us."

"Casey, that's possibly the most sickeningly sentimental words you've ever uttered."

Casey chuckled and only tightened his arms around Martin's waist. "Then how about this instead?" Casey leant up onto the balls of his feet and stretched to Martin's ear. "Fuck me," he whispered.

IN THE END, and to Martin's great annoyance, when he awoke curled around Casey, although the mind was willing, it appeared that neither of their exhausted bodies had been up to the challenge, and at some point, the gentle, tender foreplay had tapered off as they fell asleep in each other's arms.

Chapter Thirty

"ARE YOU SURE you want to do this, Casey? Nobody would think any less of you," Alissa said as she quietly sat with Casey inside the quarantine zone.

"With the alternative being letting Leon die, I'm doing this."

"I know you don't remember much from fixing my wings, but, Casey, you were in trouble. There's only so much pain your system can cope with. I'm worried, Casey. What does Martin think?"

He glanced across the room, where Martin was seated beside Jared at his brother's bedside. "He supports my decision. I may have neglected to tell him some of the more serious side effects, and I don't want you to tell him."

"You don't think he deserves to know?"

"And have him need to make a choice between Leon and me? No, thanks, I don't think he needs that."

"You know he'd choose you, right?"

Casey looked over, and obviously feeling his eyes on him, Martin looked up and smiled at him. "Yeah. Yeah, I know. But he shouldn't have to."

"I DON'T UNDERSTAND why Casey needs to be in a hospital bed." The concern was evident in Martin's face as he started to suspect Casey had hidden some details from him. Alissa cast a desperate look at Casey who sat in a disposable hospital gown, unlaced at the back.

"It's just in case, okay? I told you that fixing Alissa's wings was a bit tricky. Well, we want to be prepared this time."

Martin looked more doubtful as he took Casey's hand in his own. "I know you're lying, but this is your decision. I won't second-guess you. Just...don't die on me. They'd have to find a new agent to work with me, and I doubt anyone deserves that."

"Your sense of humour hasn't improved, you know."

"Then that's something else you need to teach me. I'll add it to the list." Martin leant to brush his lips to Casey's knuckles before looking up into his eyes. "Promise me you'll stick around."

Casey's eyes shone. "I promise." Turning to Alissa, he cleared his throat roughly. "Can we do this, please?"

Alissa wiped a hand across her eyes and nodded, lips tight. Stepping in close, she gestured to Jared to come and support Casey's shoulders.

"Thank you for this, Casey." Jared gripped tight on his shoulder. "You ready?"

"Yeah. Okay, let's do this."

Casey looked over to where Leon lay unconscious, reached out and imagined the man's dusty grey wings, picturing the white secondaries sprinkled through them. He didn't imagine them as they'd been in the past days, ruined and bloody, but as he'd seen them in Scotland as he and his brother wheeled overhead, playing dogfight and laughing in the crisp Highland air.

It was harder than with Alissa and Jared. When he'd captured their wings, they'd been awake, and that seemed to help with the transfer. He could sense Leon's wings at the end of a long tunnel, and it felt like he could just about reach them with the tips of his fingers but couldn't get a proper grip.

With a huff of frustration, he mentally reached again, straining toward the ailing Avian, giving himself over to the transition and throwing himself down the tunnel toward his goal, trusting in Martin to pull him back when it was all over.

With a horrified gasp, Martin watched as deep ragged fissures opened across Casey's back, the skin gaped open, and as the blood pooled and flowed, Martin watched as the ribs that had become sickeningly visible within the wounds were covered by red.

Casey emitted a sudden, weak moan and lapsed into unconsciousness, his eyes rolling up in his head.

"Casey? Casey!" Alissa stepped forward, bullying Martin out of the way as Jared gently turned Casey onto his side and lowered him onto the bed. "Damn it, Casey!"

"What's happening? Alissa, what's going on?" Martin tried to get back to Casey's side until she shouldered him back again.

"Let me work, Martin. Jared, get the oxygen mask quickly. Damn it." She slapped him gently on his cheek. "Casey, come on, Casey, stay with us."

"Alissa—"

"Shut up, Martin, I'm trying to save his life," she hissed at him. "I don't have time for your hysterics."

Martin staggered backwards to collapse into the uncomfortable office chair at Alissa's desk, watching wide-eyed and pale as Jared and Alissa worked on his lover. He'd expected it to be bad. His link with Casey the previous day had given him some indication of the suffering involved, but this, this was beyond belief, and by the urgency with which Jared and Alissa were working, they hadn't expected this either.

"Casey?" Jared's voice was now fierce. "Come on, mate, you can do this. You're a member of Her Majesty's Secret Service, step up and fight."

"I'm losing his pulse, Jared. Keep bagging him."

At a weak moan, Martin's attention flicked to Leon's bed as his brother stirred.

"Martin, come here and take over!" Alissa again. "Jared, go to Leon, see how he's doing. Martin, look at me." She held his eyes for a brief instant. "You need to keep him breathing. If we can keep him alive while his system fights the infection, then I think we can get him back to us."

He looked at her without even an attempt to conceal his anger. "You think? You *think!*"

"Just do it, Martin. Have your dramatic reaction later when we have time. Jared, how's he doing?"

"He's awake," Jared replied wonderingly. "His pulse is steady."

"Hit him with the vaccine."

"Done."

Martin glanced over, while still keeping up the rhythmic puffs on the oxygen bag. Jared gently smoothed hair away from Leon's sweaty brow. With a grunt, he helped Leon roll onto his side so he could watch what was happening on Casey's bed.

A weak moan from Casey brought Martin's attention back. "Casey? Hang on, Casey. You can do this."

"He's losing a lot of blood. Martin, the fridge; go and get a bag of B positive."

"I want to stay —"

"*B positive, Martin!*"

Martin was out and back again without another challenge, handing the bag to Alissa who hung it and attached it to the intravenous line she'd inserted in the brief time he'd been away from the bed.

"Damn it, I can't get him stable." She checked his numbers again as Martin sat staring at Casey's back. It was still a mess of mutilated flesh and sickly yellow. There were small signs of healing, some of the deeper tissue pulling together to cover bones, but blood was still flowing freely down past his waist.

There was a hushed conversation from the other bed, and Martin heard Jared say sharply, "No, not yet."

"I have to, Jared," came Leon's weary voice.

"They're not healed yet. Let Alissa do her job. Give it a few more minutes."

"Now," Leon rasped. "I need to take them back now. The vaccine will stop any further degradation. I can't let him die, Jared. I can't do that to him."

"But, your wings?"

"Are not as important as Casey's life." The voice was little more than a whisper. "Martin, push your wings to Casey. Drive mine out."

"No!"

"Little brother, for once, do as you're told." Leon's eyes flickered closed. "He's saved my life. Let me save him for you."

Martin looked at Leon, then to Jared who gave him a stuttering nod. With a final look at Alissa, who was still bent over Casey, desperately working to keep him alive, Martin closed his eyes and reached through his link to Casey.

Casey seemed a long way away. The vibrant, colourful connection between them, usually sparking with life, was cold and dark, and Martin stood in the darkness and mentally called to him. With increasing hopelessness, he reached for Casey's spirit over and over again without a response. Finally, when he was almost out of hope, there was a sparkle on the horizon. Dim and aching, it winked, alone in the darkness, and Martin rushed toward it, gathering it close to him and holding the feeble spark in his hands, breathing warm air on it, teasing it to brilliance.

In the waking world, Casey moaned again and arched against the pain in his back, wrenching the skin again and forcing new blood to flow.

"Hurry, Martin," Alissa whispered.

The spark grew and bloomed, taking on the bright, earthy colours that Martin associated with Casey's solid, dependable mood. On the edges, he could see the tainted sickly colour of Leon's infection, threatening to subdue and kill the vulnerable light. With exquisite care, Martin nudged at the light, pushing past the taint to tug his healthy wings toward the light, flooding it with power and strength.

With a snap, the wings seemed to clip into place, and the light in Martin's mind flared to brilliance, nearly blinding him as it pulsed and roared back to surround and encompass them.

With a rushing gasp, Casey's eyes snapped open as the skin pulled together and knitted unevenly, the dark lines of Martin's wings painting his skin, forming a latticework over the newly forming scars. A similar gasp came from the other bed as Leon's wings, tattered but covered with pink, featherless skin reappeared at his shoulders.

"Martin." Casey's voice was rough, dry and exhausted. Seeing him conscious and alert, Alissa left his side to go to Leon.

"You're an idiot," Martin murmured fondly. "I nearly couldn't find you."

"Knew you would, eventually."

"Always." He leant to press their foreheads together. "But no more, all right? I don't care if it's the Queen of England. No more."

Casey nodded tiredly and simply let himself be held in Martin's strong arms. "No more."

Meanwhile, Alissa was looking at Leon's wings as Jared cradled his head against his chest. "Do they hurt?"

"Not at all. They're a little numb." Leon leant in as Jared ran his fingers through his hair.

She checked the new, pink skin and the scattering of remaining feathers. "The skin looks healthy, but they're not...normal, Leon. I'm sorry."

"It doesn't matter," he murmured.

"You'll never fly again, Leon," Jared whispered.

"It's. Not. Important. How's Casey?"

"He'll be all right." Martin met his eye across the small space of the room. "Thank you."

Leon looked up with a weak smile. "Well, that makes it worth it. An expression of gratitude from my little brother, it's a special day, indeed."

With a snort, he smiled back. "Don't think I'll make a habit of it."

"I wouldn't dream of it." He closed his eyes and rested against Jared's chest, wrapped in strong arms.

"Is he okay?" Casey asked at the tense look in Martin's eyes, now his brother wasn't watching.

"As well as can be expected."

"How're his wings?"

"Ruined, but infection-free. You did well, Casey."

"Not well enough."

"Leon told me to get you out of there. You did enough."

Casey nodded, leaning into Martin's slim form. "Martin?"

"Hmmm?"

"I'm exhausted."

"Let's get you to bed, then." Bending, Martin slipped his arms under Casey's knees and shoulders, straightened, and with seeming effortlessness, lifted Casey into his arms.

With a nod to the three remaining Avians in the room, Martin pushed through the quarantine airlock and made his way up the stairs with his precious cargo.

henceforth be recorded in our history as Casey Wicker—nest-mate, only the second human to ever hold that title and the benefits inherent therein."

As the words left his mouth, more Avians began to stand. "You shall additionally be granted roost privilege, which your bond-mate Martin can explain at a later time. Lastly, Casey—" And with the use of his first name, the formality dropped from Leon's tone, and he stepped slowly down the stairs toward the centre of the room.

Leon turned a slow circle, addressing the crowd. "Agent Wicker is not yet aware of the standing of the Bishop family in Avian society, and the gravity of what I'm about to say. However, the repercussions will become apparent to him in time."

"Casey." Leon turned to him and lifted Casey's left hand, holding it up to clearly show the room the simple gold band encircling his ring finger. "Let it be known to all here that I recognize you, and gladly, as the mate and husband of my brother, Martin Bishop. And I welcome you as my brother before all assembled."

A glance to his right showed Martin, tears in his eyes and a hand to his mouth as Alissa and Jared began the applause, quickly picked up by everyone around them. As Casey turned back toward Leon, he could see over his shoulder that slowly, and with great ceremony, the three members of royalty stood and, as a unit, nodded to him.

The cheering built and with a rustling like autumn leaves, the assembled Avians began to beat their wings, the sound joining the applause in celebration.

Casey Wicker was home.

About the Author

Jules Dee doesn't understand what she has done to deserve her magnificent life. She is surrounded and supported by her husband and her friends. Her cats appreciate that her habit of writing creates long hours of lap-time, which they are happy to consume and repay her with purrs.

When she isn't writing, she spends her days running the Technology Service Desk for a Local Council in Metropolitan Melbourne and fixing things that are broken.

Email: author@julesdee.com

Facebook: www.facebook.com/jules.dee.author

Twitter: @authorjules

Website: www.julesdee.com

Also Available from NineStar Press

Connect with NineStar Press

Website: NineStarPress.com

Facebook: NineStarPress

Facebook Reader Group: NineStarNiche

Twitter: @ninestarpress

Tumblr: NineStarPress